What is already Known

What is already Known

An Anthology

Edited by Seán Virgo

Thistledown Press Ltd.

© Thistledown Press Ltd., 1995
All rights reserved

Canadian Cataloguing in Publication Data

Main entry under title:

What is already known

Consists of selections from works published by Thistledown Press.
Includes an index of contributors and a chronology of titles published by
Thistledown Press.

ISBN 1-895449-53-7

1. Canadian poetry (English) - 20th century.*
2. Short stories, Canadian (English).*
3. Canadian fiction (English) - 20th century.* I. Virgo, Seán, 1940-
II. Thistledown Press Ltd.

PS8251.W438 1995   C810.8'0054   C95-920218-8
PR9194.9.W438 1995

Book design by A.M. Forrie
Title by Patrick Lane
Cover art by Lorne Beug
Set in 10 pt New Baskerville
by Thistledown Press

Printed in Canada by
Hignell Printing
Winnipeg, Manitoba

Thistledown Press Ltd.
633 Main Street
Saskatoon, Saskatchewan
S7H 0J8

This book was published with the assistance of a special project grant from the
Saskatchewan Arts Board.
Thistledown Press gratefully acknowledges the continued support of
The Canada Council and the Saskatchewan Arts Board.

Saskatchewan
Arts Board

CONTENTS

PREFACE 15

INTRODUCTION *Seán Virgo* 17

Ω

CHORUS *Helen Hawley* 23

[WE DID NOT LEAVE THE GARDEN] *Patrick Lane* 25
FARMING *Leona Gom* 26
LION'S TOOTH *Bert Almon* 27
WILD LIFE *William Klebeck* 27
THE DEVIL'S BREATH, SASKATCHEWAN, 1988 *Marilyn Cay* 28
THE ONION PICKERS *Don Summerhayes* 28
CHINOOK *Peter Christensen* 30
CHINOOK *Kim Maltman* 31
A SUITE OF SINGLE SYMMETRIES *Charles Noble* 32
THE DISPOSAL OF HAZARDOUS WASTES *Monty Reid* 35
CLOUD *Kim Maltman* 36
WHEN LIGHT TRANSFORMS FLESH *Robert Hilles* 37

Ω

[THE NATURAL MAN] *Patrick Lane* 39
WINDSONG *Glen Sorestad* 40
HOLY THURSDAY *Mel Dagg* 41
ALIEN LOVE *Catherine Buckaway* 53
OCTOMI MEETS THE WILD ROSE BERRIES *Andrew Suknaski* 53
TALISMAN. BROWNING, MONTANA *Bert Almon* 55
FALL *Sara Berkeley* 55

Ω

[REMEMBER THE HEART] *Patrick Lane* 57
INTERIOR WITH DOG *Anne Campbell* 58
THE PARADISE GARDEN *Nancy Senior* 58
LILITH *Sherry Johnson* 59
THE SPIRIT LURKS AGAINST THE WALL *John V. Hicks* 60
THE EMANCIPATION OF FORM *Eva Tihanyi* 60
HUNTER STRANDED ON AN ICE FLOE *Andrew Suknaski* 63
AN IMAGE OF CHRIST ASCENDING INTO THE HEAVENS *Doug Beardsley* 65
SNOW FALL: UNDER THE STUDY LAMP *Brenda Niskala* 65
NERUDA IN THE KITCHEN *Bruce Hunter* 66
INFLUENCES *Tom Wayman* 67
ONE HILL AND TWO ROCKING-HORSES *Tillen Bruce* 69
IT'S YOUR MOVE *John Lent* 73

Ω

[ALL THAT IS LEFT] *Patrick Lane* 75
I WILL NOT BE THE GRANDMOTHER *Brenda Niskala* 76
SEVENTY *Lorna Crozier* 76
SPRING FLOWERS *Rhona McAdam* 77
A GENTLE LOOK *Robert Hilles* 78
PROLOGUE: SHELTER *John Lent* 80
A STUDY OF US TOGETHER *Sara Berkeley* 87
HOME MOVIE NIGHTS *Sara Berkeley* 88
THE DUCK'S NEST *William Klebeck* 89
TWO FISH, ONE MORNING *Glen Sorestad* 90
BURNING MY FATHER'S CLOTHES *Andrew Wreggitt* 92
OUR CAREER IN LOVE *Robert Hilles* 94
ALASKA HIGHWAY, 1965 *Andrew Wreggitt* 94
IT'S A HARD COW *Terry Jordan* 97

Ω

[WOMEN WALK TO THE SEA] *Patrick Lane* 111
METAMORPHOSIS *Leona Gom* 112
WATER RITES *Mary Bazylevich* 114
THE ARRIVAL *Paulette Dubé* 121
PROJECTION: A LUMP IN THE BREAST *Sherry Johnson* 122
DULCE (THIS DULCE) *ET DECORUM J. Livingstone Clark* 123
WAYMAN IN THE WORKPLACE: TEACHER'S AIDE *Tom Wayman* 123
TEENAGERS *Dennis Cooley* 125
OLD MEN AND ICE CREAM *Brian Brett* 126

END OF THE STRING *William Klebeck* 126
SOLAR PASSAGE *Bert Almon* 127
A WHITE BOUQUET OF EARTH *Sherry Johnson* 128
CUT *R.P. MacIntyre* 129

Ω

[THE MOLE'S CRY AS HE SLEEPS] *Patrick Lane* 139
DAS ENGELEIN KOMMT *Gertrude Story* 140
WHAT THE DEAD DREAM *Bruce Hunter* 147
JEWISH CEMETERY AT LIPTON *Lorna Crozier* 148
SUICIDES *Leona Gom* 149
IN THE CEMETERY *Don Summerhayes* 149
EDICT #4, COWS *Jay Ruzesky* 150
THE TOWN IS STILL AS THE WIND *Peter Christensen* 150
TANGANYIKA *Brian Brett* 151
[HE WAS LIKE A FOX] *Gertrude Story* 156
GUILLOTINE *Eva Tihanyi* 157
THE HANGING *Florence McNeil* 158
UNCLE *Sara Berkeley* 160
CANCER *Leona Gom* 161
PICKING UP MOM *Peter Ormshaw* 161
WEST INTO NIGHT *Glen Sorestad* 163
THE FATAL ERROR *Ernest Hekkanen* 164
GLORY TRAIN *George Whipple* 171

Ω

[LOVE AGAIN] *Patrick Lane* 173
THE ORIGINAL PAIN OVER AND OVER AGAIN *Brian Brett* 174
NIGHT MUSIC *Eva Tihanyi* 174
INTIMACY *Allan Barr* 175
NOT YOUR VOICE *Garry Radison* 176
LAST NIGHT *Chris Collins* 176
PASSAGE *Rhona McAdam* 177
A GOD CAN DO IT *Doug Beardsley* 177
TRAVELLING COMPANIONS *Tom Wayman* 178
TELLING FORTUNES *Gary Hyland* 179
ME & MEN & WHISKEY *Kate Sutherland* 181

ON THE HISTORICAL NATURE OF COVETING *Sherry Johnson* 186
THE HONEYMOON *Shelley A. Leedahl* 188
A CONVERSATION *Robert Hilles* 192
INFINITE BEASTS *Rhona McAdam* 193

Ω

[THE THROTTLE OF PIGEONS IN WINTER] *Patrick Lane* 195
ANIMAL LOVE *Rhona McAdam* 196
HER STORY *Monty Reid* 196
RAVEN WIND *Jim Green* 198
TAKING WING *Glen Sorestad* 199
ANIMAL KINGDOM *Rhona McAdam* 200
POEM WRITTEN ON WHITE PAPER *Allan Barr* 200
STRONG OF LIFE *Peter Christensen* 201
TURTLES *John V. Hicks* 201
THE FAMILIAR ANIMAL *Bert Almon* 202
ANNUNCIATION *John V. Hicks* 203
LIKE GOLD TO AIRY THINNESS BEAT *Lesley Choyce* 204
SNAILS HAVE MOVED INTO MY BATHTUB *Brenda Niskala* 212
MIGRAINE *Rhona McAdam* 213
PENSEROSO *John V. Hicks* 213

Ω

[PLEASURE. SUCCESS. ORDER] *Patrick Lane* 215
THE EXQUISITE BEAST *Gary Hyland* 216
THE MAZE GAME *Cecelia Frey* 217
CITY EVENING *Helen Hawley* 221
THE WARNER BROS./SHAKESPEARE HOUR *Bert Almon* 221
COMING HOME *Anne Campbell* 222
THE SKY'S GONE OUT *Sara Berkeley* 223
FULL LUNAR ECLIPSE *Sherry Johnson* 232
LOOK MISTER *Greg Button* 232
STEALING GEORGE *M.A.C. Farrant* 233
WAKE-UP *Chris Collins* 240
THE POET AND FRIENDS (2) *J. Livingstone Clark* 240
THE CAT CAME BACK *Dave Margoshes* 241
DIAPHANEITY, THE VISIBLE ORIGINS *J. Livingstone Clark* 247
ARTIST IN THE STREET *Bruce Hunter* 248
AFTER THE STORY BROKE *Sara Berkeley* 249

Ω

ZAI JIAN *Ken Mitchell* 252
NIGHTS IN THE YUNGAS *Stephen Henighan* 254
RUTH *Peter Ormshaw* 258

Ω

WORDS CONTAIN SLEEP *Robert Hilles* 261
THESE ARE THE HOUSES *Ken Cathers* 262
SUMMER MORNING *H.C. Dillow* 263
CROW IN THE RAIN *Greg Button* 263
DRAWING BY A SCHIZOPHRENIC *Brian Brett* 264
YOU ARE AMAZED *Garry Radison* 265
DREAM *Ken Cathers* 265
THE PARABOLIC PLAIN *J. Livingstone Clark* 267
THE TULPA *Eileen Kernaghan* 268
FISH MAGIC *Allan Barr* 277
THE MASS IS OVER *Sara Berkeley* 278
A HYMN TO GOD THE FATHER *George Whipple* 278
DROUGHT *Ken Cathers* 279

Ω

COMPLINE *John V. Hicks* 280
[THERE ARE NO LAST LINES] *Patrick Lane* 281

Ω

NOTES ON CONTRIBUTORS 283

CONTRIBUTORS 287

PUBLISHING CHRONOLOGY 289

ACKNOWLEDGEMENTS

BERT ALMON. "Lion's Tooth", "The Familiar Animal" from *Blue Sunrise*, 1980; "The Warner Bros./Shakespeare Hour" from *Deep North*, 1984; "Talisman. Browning, Montana", "Solar Passage" from *Calling Texas*, 1989. Reprinted by author's permission.

ALLAN BARR. "Intimacy", "Poem Written on White Paper" "Fish Magic" from *The Chambered Nautilus*, 1992. Reprinted by author's permission.

MARY BAZYLEVICH. "Water Rites" from *The Winter of the Leechman*, 1995. Reprinted by author's permission.

DOUG BEARDSLEY. "An Image of Christ Ascending into the Heavens" from *A Dancing Star*, 1988; "A God Can Do It" from *Inside Passage*, 1993. Reprinted by author's permission.

SARA BERKELEY. "The Mass is Over", "A Study of Us Together", "Home Movie Nights" from *Home Movie Nights*, Saskatoon: Thistledown Press; Dublin: Raven Arts Press, 1989; "The Sky's Gone Out" from *The Swimmer in the Deep Blue Dream*, Saskatoon: Thistledown Press; Dublin: Raven Arts Press, 1992. "Uncle", "Fall", "After the story broke" from *Facts about Water*, Saskatoon: Thistledown Press; Dublin: New Island Books; Newcastle-upon-Tyne: Bloodaxe Books, 1994. Reprinted by author's permission.

BRIAN BRETT. "Old Men and Ice Cream", "The Original Pain Over and Over Again", "Drawing By a Schizophrenic" from *Evolution in Every Direction*, 1987; "Tanganyika" from *Tanganyika*, 1991. Reprinted by author's permission.

TILLEN BRUCE. "One Hill and Two Rocking-Horses" from *Horse Sense*, 1995. Reprinted by author's permission.

CATHERINE BUCKAWAY. "Alien Love" from *Riding into Morning*, 1989. Reprinted by author's permission.

GREG BUTTON. "crow in the rain", "look mister" from *Inside of Midnight*, 1993. Reprinted by author's permission.

ANNE CAMPBELL. "Coming Home" from *Red Earth, Yellow Stone*, 1989; "Interior With Dog" from *Angel Wings All Over*, 1994. Reprinted by author's permission.

KEN CATHERS. "Dream", "These are the Houses", "Drought" from *Sanctuary*, 1991. Reprinted by author's permission.

MARILYN CAY. "The Devil's Breath, Saskatchewan, 1988" from *Farm*, 1993. Reprinted by author's permission.

LESLEY CHOYCE. "Like Gold to Airy Thinness Beat" from *The Second Season of Jonas MacPherson*, 1989. Reprinted by author's permission.

PETER CHRISTENSEN. "Chinook", "The Town is Still as the Wind" from *Rig Talk*, 1981; "Strong of Life" from *To Die Ascending*, 1988. Reprinted by author's permission.

J. LIVINGSTONE CLARK. "The Poet and Friends (2)", "Diaphaneity, the Visible Origins", "The Parabolic Plain", "*Dulce* (this dulse) *et Decorum*" from *Breakfast of the Magi*, 1994. Reprinted by author's permission.

ACKNOWLEDGEMENTS

CHRIS COLLINS. "Wake-up", "Last Night" from *Earthworks*, 1990. Reprinted by author's permission.

DENNIS COOLEY. "teenagers" from *Dedications*, 1988. Reprinted by author's permission.

LORNA CROZIER. "Seventy", "Jewish Cemetery at Lipton" from *Inside is the Sky*, 1976. Reprinted by author's permission.

MEL DAGG. "Holy Thursday" from *The Women on the Bridge*, 1992. Reprinted by author's permission.

H.C. DILLOW. "Summer Morning" from *Orts and Scantlings*, 1984. Reprinted by author's permission.

PAULETTE DUBÉ. "the arrival" from *The House Weighs Heavy*, 1992. Reprinted by author's permission.

M.A.C. FARRANT. "Stealing George" from *Sick Pigeon*, 1991. Reprinted by author's permission.

CECELIA FREY. "The Maze Game" from *The Love Song of Romeo Paquette*, 1990. Reprinted by author's permission.

LEONA GOM. "Metamorphosis", "Cancer" from *Land of the Peace*, 1980; "Suicides", "Farming" from *Northbound: Poems Selected and New*, 1984. Reprinted by author's permission and with the permission of Sono Nis Press, Vancouver.

JIM GREEN. "Raven Wind" from *Beyond Here*, 1983. Reprinted by author's permission.

HELEN HAWLEY. "Chorus", "City Evening" from *Gathering Fire*, 1977. Reprinted by author's permission.

ERNEST HEKKANEN. "The Fatal Error" from *Medieval Hour in the Author's Mind*, 1987. Reprinted by author's permission.

STEPHEN HENIGHAN. "Nights in the Yungas" from *Nights in the Yungas*, 1992. Reprinted by author's permission.

JOHN V. HICKS. "The Spirit Lurks Against the Wall", "Compline" from *Winter Your Sleep*, 1980; "Turtles" from *Sticks and Strings: Selected and New Poems*, 1988; "Annunciation", "Penseroso" from *Month's Mind*, 1992. Reprinted by author's permission.

ROBERT HILLES. "When Light Transforms Flesh", "A Gentle Look", "Words Contain Sleep", "A Conversation", "Our Career in Love" from *Outlasting the Landscape*, 1989. Reprinted by author's permission.

BRUCE HUNTER. "Artist in the Street" from *Benchmark*, 1982; "What the Dead Dream", "Neruda in the Kitchen" from *The Beekeeper's Daughter*, 1986; Reprinted by author's permission.

GARY HYLAND. "The Exquisite Beast", "Telling Fortunes" from *After Atlantis*, 1991. Reprinted by author's permission.

SHERRY JOHNSON. "Lilith", "Projection: A Lump in the Breast", "Full Lunar Eclipse", "On the Historical Nature of Coveting", "A White Bouquet of Earth" from *Pale Grace*, 1995. Reprinted by author's permission.

TERRY JORDAN. "It's a Hard Cow" from *It's a Hard Cow*, 1993. Reprinted by author's permission.

EILEEN KERNAGHAN. "The Tulpa" from *Dance of the Snow Dragon*, 1995. Reprinted by author's permission.

WILLIAM KLEBECK. "The Duck's Nest", "Wild Life", "End of the String" from *Where the Rain Ends*, 1990. Reprinted by author's permission.

PATRICK LANE. "[Remember the heart]", "[The mole's cry as he sleeps]", "[The throttle of pigeons in winter]", "[We did not leave the garden]", "[Love again]", "[Women walk to the sea]", "[The natural man]", "[There are no last lines]", "[All that is left]", "[Pleasure. Success. Order]" from *A Linen Crow, A Caftan Magpie*, 1984. Reprinted by author's permission.

SHELLEY A. LEEDAHL. "The Honeymoon" from *Sky Kickers*, 1994. Reprinted by author's permission.

JOHN LENT. "It's Your Move" from *Frieze*, 1984; "Prologue: Shelter" from *The Face in the Garden*, 1990. Reprinted by author's permission.

ROD MacINTYRE. "Cut" from *The Blue Camaro*, 1994. Reprinted by author's permission.

KIM MALTMAN. "Cloud", "Chinook" from *Branch Lines*, 1982. Reprinted by author's permission.

DAVE MARGOSHES. "The Cat Came Back" from *Nine Lives*, 1991. Reprinted by author's permission.

RHONA McADAM. "Animal Love", "Infinite Beasts" from *Hour of the Pearl*, 1987; "Migraine", "Animal Kingdom", "Spring Flowers" from *Creating the Country*, 1989; "Passage" from *Old Habits*, 1993. Reprinted by author's permission.

FLORENCE McNEIL. "The Hanging" from *Barkerville*, 1984. Reprinted by author's permission.

KEN MITCHELL. "Zai Jian" from *Through the Nan Da Gate: A China Journey*, 1986. Reprinted by author's permission.

BRENDA NISKALA. "I will not be the grandmother", "snails have moved into my bathtub", "snow fall: under the study lamp" from *Ambergris Moon*, 1983. Reprinted by author's permission.

CHARLES NOBLE. "A Suite of Single Symmetries" from *Let's Hear It For Them*, 1990. Reprinted by author's permission.

PETER ORMSHAW. "Picking Up Mom", "Ruth" from *The Purity of Arms*, 1993. Reprinted by author's permission.

GARRY RADISON. "Not Your Voice", "You are Amazed" from *White Noise*, 1982. Revised July 1995. Reprinted by author's permission.

MONTY REID. "The Disposal Of Hazardous Wastes", "Her Story" from *The Life of Ryley*, 1981. Reprinted by author's permission.

JAY RUZESKY. "Edict #4: Cows" from *Am I Glad to See You*, 1992. Reprinted by author's permission.

NANCY SENIOR. "The Paradise Garden" from *The Mushroom Jar*, 1980. Reprinted by author's permission.

GLEN SORESTAD. "Windsong" from *Wind Songs*, 1975; "West into Night", "Two Fish, One Morning", "Taking Wing" from *West into Night*, 1991. Reprinted by author's permission.

GERTRUDE STORY. "[He was like a fox]" from *The Book of Thirteen*, 1981; "*Das Engelein Kommt*" from *Black Swan*, 1986. Reprinted by author's permission.

ANDREW SUKNASKI. "Octomi Meets the Wild Rose Berries" from *Octomi*, 1976; "Hunter Stranded On an Ice Floe" from *East of Myloona*, 1979. Reprinted by author's permission.

DON SUMMERHAYES. "The Onion Pickers", "In the Cemetery" from *Heavy Horse Judging*, 1987. Reprinted by author's permission.

KATE SUTHERLAND. "me & men & whisky" from *Summer Reading*, 1995. Reprinted by author's permission.

EVA TIHANYI. "Night Music", "The Emancipation of Form", "Guillotine" from *Prophecies Near the Speed of Light*, 1984. Reprinted by author's permission.

TOM WAYMAN. "Influences", "Travelling Companions", "Wayman in the Workforce: Teacher's Aide" from *The Nobel Prize Acceptance Speech*, 1981. Reprinted by author's permission and with the permission of Harbour Publishing, Madeira Park, British Columbia.

GEORGE WHIPPLE. "A Hymn to God the Father", "Glory Train" from *Passing Through Eden*, 1991. Reprinted by author's permission.

ANDREW WREGGITT. "Alaska Highway, 1965", "Burning My Father's Clothes" from *Making Movies*, 1989. Reprinted by author's permission.

PREFACE

What Is Already Known exists because of the co-operation between Thistledown Press and its writers and editors over twenty years. It is a testament to the ongoing commitment of Canadians who support the arts and to the various granting agencies who act as benefactors for such support, particularly the Saskatchewan Arts Board and The Canada Council.

Throughout the last twenty years Thistledown Press has grown in self-assurance as it has developed the strength and imagination to resist easy definition as solely a literary press. *What Is Already Known* illustrates this range. Drawn from a list of 180 titles and more than 100 writers, the diversity and accomplished work in this collection present not only a record of literature produced in a particular time and place, but also an indispensable chronicle of the Canadian literature movement.

Thistledown is part of a complex and amazing national literary infrastructure that includes the network of small presses, journals, magazines, and readings that ensure that Canadian writing remains a distinctive form of English literature. This anthology serves to remind Canadians that our own culture is alive with literature, that at the end of the twentieth century we do have a clear and fundamental ability to recognize who we are.

INTRODUCTION

Reading is (can be, should be, might be, must be) an act of desire and generosity.

The desire is to become more than yourself: to inhabit other places, times and people, and to be changed by the experience. The generosity lies in opening yourself, with complete attention, to someone else's words and understanding. So the true act of reading a poem or fiction is an act of love — a duel and dance between two imaginations, a dissolving of boundaries.

The kinship that a reader may feel for a writer is immeasurable.

I believe that change is at the heart of this experience, as it is at the heart of writing itself. The essence of *Haiku* is change, not stillness; Wallace Stevens' *Supreme Fiction* "must change"; Huck Finn lights out in the end because "I been there before"; *The Double Hook* draws light in through the darkness. And the reader in turn is altered, taken heart and mind into another world from which he or she returns, infected.

The serious writer starts out as a famished reader.

It is an alchemical process, and its crucible is the book.

In Canada, during the last quarter century, another generous desire — that of "small press" publishers — has kept the serious book alive.

This anthology is distilled from, and celebrates, twenty years of publishing by a small "regional" press.

Reading, and raiding, through those twenty years and close to 200 books has been a daunting but wonderfully rich experience for me. Time and again I was taken out of myself and the task at hand, and compelled to sit quietly or go walking down the field, with a voice not my own resonating in my mind. It has been surprisingly like reading the collected poems or stories of an individual writer who has kept the faith through the years, developing a voice and a vision, often unnoticed beneath the trivial surface of our times. I'm describing endurance, in both senses. And the evolution of our culture.

The role of the Thistledown Press "family", as a conduit and way-station for Canadian writing and writers, has become legendary over the years. It is folklorical in every way! But it is the role of the editors, as midwives to so many young writers, and sustainers of several ongoing careers, which underpins this anthology.

They have given editing itself — the first, fierce and generous reading a book ever gets — chief priority. They have searched out the authentic voices of the region and allowed them a chance to be heard throughout Canada. Almost as importantly they have, over time, brought in compatible voices from other parts, overseas even, to extend the horizons. And the books themselves — as artefacts — have been treated with proper respect: design has developed, through experiment and through collaboration with visual artists. There are some beauties.

That testament endures.

I suppose this anthology is a kind of chinese box, a play within a play. It is my taste and judgement applied to Thistledown's taste and judgement. As a writer myself, I have no wish to describe or analyse work which is, almost by definition, eloquent and mysterious, but some brief statement about my tastes, how I arrived at *this* selection, is probably called for — whether you choose to read it as an *apologia* or a manifesto!

My choice of poetry and fiction takes for granted the generosity, and the alchemy, I described before. There is, in my judgement, nothing lazy or static on these pages. And I assume a reader who is alert, passionate and eager to be surprised.

There will always be something strange about the best writing. I don't mean "weird" (though weird, in the true sense of nape-prickling apprehension, it may sometimes be); I mean unfamiliar, yet believable.

I think there are three "shocks of recognition", to extend Edmund Wilson's phrase. The first simply confirms what the reader already believes or remembers. "What oft was thought . . . " etc. or "Same thing," as John Prine would say, "same thing happened to me." The second (which is where the magic begins) makes the familiar take on new life, because it is shown afresh, as if seen or experienced for the first time. The third (which for me is the real transformation) is when you do encounter something for the first time, but realize at once that it is authentic and true. It is like being an explorer who comes face to face with an unknown animal. The creature cannot be related to any familiar species — the limbs, or the skull, or the fur, or the gait are not *right* — yet it is there, breathing, has been living all these years a parallel life to yours, and is now looking back at you with mirroring eyes. Excitement or terror, then beauty, then a world made new.

Poetry and fiction are not sub-species of journalism, memoir or rhetoric. They are the creation of life. "Self-expression," to quote John McGahern, "is no expression at all." There are very few anecdotal pieces in this book; there are none, I hope, which depend for their effect on a neat, self-serving (*"There — aren't I smart (or sensitive)!"*) ending. You will find almost nothing that contains the word "I" in the first few lines.

And no examples of cheap indignation or sentimentality, the life-shrivelling curses of our time.

We have absolutely nothing to teach François Villon, for instance, about injustice, misery, disease, famine, war, alienation, the loss of faith or the world's end. He has absolutely everything to teach us, 500 years down the road, about energy, gaiety and courage, about the zest in the woeful human condition, about the exhilarating precision and music of language.

Walking home after a dinner with the poet René Char, during which the Frenchman had said, "A poem has no memory. I am asked to go forward," Martin Heidegger told his companion, "What Char said is accurate. That is the difference between thought and poetry. Poetry moves forward, while thought is essentially memory, even if poetry remains its viaticum." I think this is true of the best fiction too — it does not depend on our memories for its truths.

But then it *becomes* our memory.

For me, the three aesthetic touchstones of our century are Arthur Rimbaud's *I is another*; James Joyce's author, *refined out of existence, paring his fingernails,* while his characters get on, fully dramatized, with their lives; and Bertholt Brecht's insistence that if your mind is not engaged, as a reader/spectator, then the engagement of your emotions is mere escapism.

The most credible map I know of the human psyche is Jacques Lacan's *Borromean Knot*. The Knot consists of three rings — so interlocked that if any one is removed, the others fall apart. The rings embrace the Symbolic, the Imaginary, and the Real.

Poems and fictions, like people, all shuffle these rings in different proportions. But if any one ring is missing, the writing has failed. (In a perfect piece of work, I suppose, the rings would be indistinguishable, but whether any art except music can or should deal in perfection I very much doubt.)

The Knot works for me as a measure of writing because it's so flexible, generous and non-reductive. Better still, while it's easy to visualize and play with, it is quite impossible to construct, and I think even Maurits Escher could not draw one. Like a poem itself, there is a riddle at its heart.

Of course, I have not applied any abstract, inflexible system to the work I had to choose from — I have trusted my tastes (as one must, more or less) and responded, besides, to a number of poems and fictions which might seem to defy my principles. Because information about the human heart — the true object of our desire — can leap out from the least likely testaments; and because it is the voice, in the end, which makes writing live.

The final truth, overriding all other judgements, is that only good *writing* — the original cadence, the disciplined form, the respect for our wonderfilled, hybrid, precise and suggestive language, its exquisite crudeness — makes writing *good*. The final truth, and the enduring one. "Posterity," as Flaubert delighted to say, "has a weakness for Style."

I have chosen only two pieces from Thistledown's extensive young adult list. The best young adult fiction (so much more engagé and neurotic than the romances of yesteryear) plays a saving role in our culture, but it rarely succeeds in the company of "adult" writing (which is, of course, for all ages). I don't think any writing that speaks to a specific audience could work in this context. But I've included R.P. MacIntyre's "Cut", because the voice, and the story, are no more restricted to a teenage audience than *The Catcher In The Rye* or *Oranges Are Not The Only Fruit* are; and though Eileen Kernaghan's *Dance of the Snow Dragon* is written in the conventional, stylized language of High

Fantasy, its mythic and dramatic inventiveness lifts it out of that genre's limitations.

The decision to weave, rather than to assemble, this anthology — to run over from page to page, to avoid discrete clumps under authors' names, to ignore chronology — has allowed a collaboration to unfold between all these writers. Different minds, different voices reinforce and ignite one another, disclosing ironies and contexts that were not there before.

They remind me, too, that while inventive writing may be a game of hazard, it is not a competitive sport.

In the end, I can become a reader again. And I find a briskness, a cheerful energy in the tone and inventiveness on these pages which I can only call light-hearted. Even the sense of loss — of death, failure, resignation, disappointment — which threads this selection is the reverse of morbidity or depression. It is, rather, a distinctive insistence on feeling at home in the world — of paying attention, even in mourning, to the ancestors, the animals, the land, the buildings, the lovers, the cities, which explain and reflect us.

Above all, there is energy here. And that, as one of our patron saints tells us, "is eternal delight."

Seán Virgo,
Saskatoon, July 1995

If you have need of this weapon, Little Brother,
then take it.

It is made from the tongues of prairie roses
and the tongues of those who did not keep silent.
Ten thousand run-offs will not rust it.
Though it is frail as a man's breath
hanging on frost, it is strong
with the strength of the northwest winds.
The battles are not ended so soon.
The black earth opened to swallow the grasses,
and the antelope, and the hunters of the antelope;
the winter-to-summer sky
no longer blurred with wings
and the buffalo and poundmakers
shook the land with their bones,
and that year's run-off was red in the dying sun.
(A year is not such a long time:
it can stretch over many solstices,
then be reduced to a sigh
when it is over and cannot be changed.)

Next the land fell into the sea,
and the relics of some who had turned up the sod,
gray, warped wood and twisted iron,
hope of harvest,
crumbled to dust.
But there are still battles to be fought.
People waiting, bitter or patient,
each one is an army;
hunters of antelope, hunters of harvests,
hunters of more than consumption.
The new year is young like a meadowlark's eggs,
and there are those who will not be silent.

— *Helen Hawley*

Ω

We did not leave the garden. We were left.
Bewildered. Forsaken.

And you, sweet enemy.
How you left us to die and die.

The snake has only one skin. Take it off.
When she eats you she does not ask your name.

Keep your apples and roses.
East of Eden, the only desert is the mind. Thinking.

— Patrick Lane

FARMING

Something women learned,
from digging in the dirt,
the wet soil curdling
in their hands,
the first revulsion
of beetles and worms
becoming a slow citizenship
of earth impacted
into their pores.

Something they learned,
    before the gardens fell
    from their fingers
    into imported rows,
from the underworld of weeds:
those like the thistle
who put up a thorny front
but whose roots barely resisted.
those anchored deep
like the dandelion
who surrendered their green maturity
at the last minute
for the root tips
clenched around rock.
and the grass,
the great plurality of grass,
its lateral roots
peeling the earth up
in long strips
of connective tissue
which continued forever,

a network of cells,
the skin of the whole planet.

Something women learned,
digging among roots:
    kinds of survival,
      the possibility
      of living here.

— *Leona Gom*

LION'S TOOTH

Call me a weed, but flower, leaf and root will sustain you:
tear me out and I'll come again, begging a little room.
Fragility is my strength: a single breath
spreads me on the winds of the world.

— *Bert Almon*

WILD LIFE

the slough's straight ahead but far enough away so I
can watch this gopher running alongside the front
wheel of the tractor stopping running off again then
swooped up by a hawk that comes out of nowhere
surprising even me and the gopher's struggling jerking
around grasped in the small of the back by one claw as
I slip back the hydraulic lever to lift the cultivator the
gopher's snapping at the hawk's other claw and now I
have to look from the wild life to straighten out but
once I've fixed my line I glance back to see the hawk
hovering above the slough its feet below the surface of
the water for a few moments before it takes off the
gopher dangling

— *William Klebeck*

THE DEVIL'S BREATH, SASKATCHEWAN, 1988

all day
the wind tries to convince me
I don't belong on this earth
it is trying to blow my memories away
along with the topsoil of our land
the wind is the devil's breath
wanting me to forget long manes of grass
and muskegs and sloughs, and mist
rising in the evenings
the wind blows dust in my eyes
and when I open them
I see tall poplars
broken along the empty creek
black spruce smaller than they were
pulling into themselves
trying to survive
the wind wants me to think
it will be like this forever

— *Marilyn Cay*

THE ONION PICKERS

My eyes water at the sight:
twenty broadhipped
kerchiefed madonnas
under the sun
of the onion fields
lolling like hussies
on the edge of the city.

They are silly as girls
and bawdy with heat

and the reek and weight
of the ribald globes
they dandle over
and over all day
in their tough hands.

Lord, how they love it —
these rowdy grandmothers
and mustachio-ed aunts
all lumps from the neck down —
away from their men!
They collapse on their sides
giddy with laughter.

One whistles at me, waving
a wicked inviting
curved knife, cupping
her hand up and up
and burlesquing
her practised lewd chop
of onion from stalk.

I think of them crowding
the innocent bus,
shedding more boldness
at each stop, but not
silent, their tongues still
purple as onions,
dresses still bulging
with smuggled beauties.

— *Don Summerhayes*

CHINOOK

Cypress trees stampede wind
across the Porcupine Hills
over the wheat dunes
                toward Brocket

Along the Old Man River
Patrick Plaineagle feeds horses
watches the fox
steal chickens

The chinook cleans the cold
takes the stallion
      to the river ice
breaks the glass vein

Sends high water
      rolling stones
out of the Rockies
The runoff   cuts the earth
moves cottonwoods
brings the mountains down

Stallion

stands

cock sways   in the wind
rolls his lip
        over the smell of a mare in

heat tramples the foothills

— Peter Christensen

CHINOOK

It's early when you leave the house, impossibly cold, two sundogs to the east glittering through the hoar frost on a few huddled trees. Even the snow is spiked with frost, so bright in the low sun it makes you want to sneeze. It's cold, even for January, so your chin's tucked down, as far as it will go, into the folds of a scarf, and it's a while before you notice the blue arch forming in the west. Everyone who's out walking then is tensed up against the cold too, but like you they're all watching the arch, watching as it gets closer. It takes a while until it's overhead, but even with the frost and the air still calm you sense the warmth coming. Everybody starts to smile as the wind picks up and pretty soon it's wild. The temperature rises 80 degrees in an hour, snowbanks collapse before your eyes. In the streets everybody's put on their best smile and the wind is banging bits of things about, harder and harder, flapping the hair and clothes together, but the smiles just keep getting bigger until pretty soon they're so big you're almost afraid the wind will blow them right off the faces and whirl them up in a huge gust, higher and higher above the buildings, and the thought makes you laugh, and then you look around and everybody else is laughing too, and tugging away at the smiles which by now are all hopelessly tangled together, bobbing crazily way up in the sky like

                                                tiny

                                                      paper

                                                                kites!

— *Kim Maltman*

A SUITE OF SINGLE SYMMETRIES

i. *He Laughed in His Face*

The first man to see the first man
came on a plush leather horse
that breathed fire into the snow.
The first man was fed up in the snow
right to the eyes so the lids wouldn't close.
His arms had folded long ago unto themselves.
The first man struck the first man
as funny.
The horse galloped around and around
the stake in the snow.
The first man grabbed the tail
and the circus dragged on
into the night of its death.
The first man on the one horse open
was splitting
and didn't want to have to slay
the first man over the snow
and be laughing all the way.

ii. *Leviathanless Canadarm a Plug for Escaping Canadians Limp on the Ground. Curved Stick in the Memory.*

A huge yellow turtle
huddled across the western sky.
The Grey Cup skipped
over the chocolate snow dunes,
the prairie hooted at the hedge.
A Canada goose hung outside the picture window,
his head tied in the all year round Christmas lights wire.
The boy said, "look at the part of a 'V'".
The farmer posed,
"what would you like for Christmas son?"
"A boomerang that can do my homework,"
the boy zeroed-in with much to-do.

iii. *Having a Premature Retro Fit*

    Christmas for baby brother
    was like baptism in the already rain.
    A dry, one-way culture would soon
    drive him.   To.
    He would smash a golf ball
    into a tree; it would fire back
    in December just when he had forgotten
    get him in the Christmas spirit.
    Yet we are born outside the family tree
    so why not cut it off
    a fixed date
    from the rotor roots
    let our backward selfish gifts be
    a spark in heaven
    over our heads a guided mistletoe,
    the impossible w*eig*ht of our
    reflexive, imm*an*ent birth.

iv. *Phantom of the Operation*

    Down the dark basement of the shop
    was a little lamp on a work bench.
    A watch back was open with a succession
    of larger and larger wrenches
    coming from a tiny gear.
    On the big steel handle of the last wrench
    a man pulled just hard enough
    for his teeth to show but he seemed
    not to move he went so slow.
    Outside a man sprinted across the yard
    reached out a long wooden wrench
    and batted into a feedlot five bales
    that had begun dropping off the stack.
    He pivoted, pounded towards the chicken coop
    where a weather vane turned and nudged a hen
    who took three careful hop-steps
    and gracefully booted an egg off the roof peak.
    As the man came near he adjusted the wrench

and then took the plummeting orb
on the run into the gentle jaws.
When a stranger asked him,
"Who's the boss around here?"
he answered, "Well there's just me
and m'brother. Pop teetered into the *well*
when we was just tots."

v. *Space Burgher. Reproducing the Way to His Heart.*
Empty Blindness. Wurst à la Kant.

Wearing a new shirt into
a plush men's wear shop
cool walnut panelling
back from the clean cement
the soft leather shiny shoes
pivot on. Addressing the thin
men hung on the rack. Like
a field marshal. Finding
a fortune cookie in the dark
platonic pocket.

Outside a sports stadium
high white wall
lots of lawn in the afternoon
sun, lazy and hurting with some
energy. Play with the buffalo
for a while.

Going with your belly
ballooned out of your navel
in the back of the half-ton
bouncing to dinner
with the spare tire
over the fields eating dust.

— *Charles Noble*

THE DISPOSAL OF HAZARDOUS WASTES

The cultivator unfolds the earth: old
letters. We read them again and again.
The shovels turn the worms up and they lie
like veins on the surface, stunned by light.
Dirt runs through them like blood.
When they move the birds get them,
pluck them in their beaks like string.

Here in the yard a nest of mouths
they stitch together. They stand
on the lip of twigs and dangle the worms.
Drop them, preen, and are gone.
They feed all day. The next they
follow the sprayer across the second
quarter, its booms spread out
for balance: tightrope
of earth.

The air takes the spray apart
and even though there is no wind
we can smell it. It hangs
in the yard like the must
of old papers bound with twine
and stacked in the basement.
What is it we write
to ourselves?

The day after, we found the gawky
bodies on the lawn. Plucked out,
veins blue with pesticide, transparent
skin. We picked them up and
threw them in the ditch. A cat
will probably find them. And as we
walked from the house to wherever
we could hear the birds, their songs
tumble over and over
out of the air.

— *Monty Reid*

CLOUD

The cloud comes in low
a single blotch of white
in the blue sky.
Hawks circle
over the grain fields,
each a tiny shadow. You
are standing still
the rifle cradled in your arms.
Your eyes glint in the gold light.
At your side, the others
urging Shoot! Shoot!
at the slightest movement.
You are alone and not alone here,
have become a kind of alien existence.
You fire randomly and hand the rifle off.
The shadow passes.
For an instant
you are at the center,
feel a heart pulse
and cannot tell
whose
or why

— *Kim Maltman*

WHEN LIGHT TRANSFORMS FLESH
(BOW RIVER, CALGARY)

A river passes here every day. Its water seeks the soft shores at night, drinking the earth like a child drinks Kool-aid. The river has dreams too as it passes downtown making the high-rises into liquid. Lovers have walked its shore until their bodies have seized water and air. In the streets, others have forgotten the river. Drinking different water treated against a civilization of microbes. Still the river passes neglected and feared. The rocks below twisting in a mad dance. The air so cold beneath the surface it freezes in small pockets. Death is the responsibility of water. This river serving as a chilled entrance. You may wonder why there are few trees along its massive shore. You may find yourself wanting to walk across it at its shallowest point. A river passes here each day and nothing is impossible. Let the lovers show you what the water means.

— *Robert Hilles*

Ω

The natural man.
Fish a little. Hunt a little. Blow your head off.

You are naked when I find you.
There is grace in coyote's kill. He eats as well as he can.

As Buson said: *Pretty clever, eh?*
There is a bank on both sides of the river. Paddle fast!

Or take silence.
Ah, slow, slow. The alphabet began with the moon.

— Patrick Lane

WINDSONG

The tiger lilies still explode
in wild dashes of orange
forcing up through the tangle
of golden rods and brown-eyed susans,
crowded into their last stand
between grainfields and roadsteads
in the land of disappearing fences.
The wind scurries in and over
each fiery lily burst with its secrets,
with its promises and its lies.

Big Bear heard the wind at Fort Pitt;
it told him not to sign the treaty.
His horse stood patient and listened.

> *the grandmother's men can not know*
> *what the wind says they do not know*
> *the cry of the wind as the last buffalo*
> *sank to its knees on the bloody grass*
> *they can not hear the wind voices*
> *whispering over the flaming lilies*
> *whispering of the people's final hunt*
>
> *all they hear is the shrieking*
> *of the iron horse on the steel*
> *the rattling sound of silver coins*
> *with the grandmother's head on them*
> *the white man's talk of land and ploughs*

Only his people hear the wind voices
murmuring their warnings through poplars.
Big Bear heard the voices and listened,
listened with the lilies on a hill
above the twisting South Saskatchewan
where there was no barbed wire
and there were no more buffalo.

— Glen Sorestad

HOLY THURSDAY
FROG LAKE, APRIL 2, 1885

"What time is it?"

Theresa Gowanlock is calling from the top of the stairs to a woman who shares her first name, Theresa, Theresa Delaney — an incredible coincidence considering they are the only two white women in the settlement.

"About 4:30," says the Delaney woman. "Judging by the light."

The two women stand in Theresa Delaney's kitchen in the first grey light before the dawn of Thursday, April 2, 1885.

"I hope I'm not disturbing you," apologizes Theresa Gowanlock. "But with all the guns going off and the dancing, I couldn't sleep. And just now I heard voices."

"Imasees and John Pritchard came to tell my husband the Métis have stolen our horses."

The night before last Pritchard had delivered a letter to Theresa Gowanlock and her husband from Agent Quinn advising them that the Métis had defeated Crozier at Duck Lake, and that they should leave their house at the mill and come to the settlement at once. Odd, she thinks, and says, "I wonder about that half-breed interpreter, John Pritchard. He knocks on our door with a letter from Quinn and then he comes to your house carrying messages from Big Bear's son. Who does he work for?"

"Why he works for himself," Theresa Delaney says, "like any interpreter. He may be the only man in the settlement who knows what's going on.

"Still, I don't think we really have anything to worry about. Our Indians have no grievances and no complaints to make," she insists. "They are happy in their home in the wilderness and I consider it a great shame for evil-minded people to instill into their excitable heads the false idea that they are persecuted by the government.

"When I say our Indians, I mean those under my husband's control. I look upon the Indian children as my children and my husband looks upon the men as being under his care. They regard him as their father." She pauses, watching her houseguest take in her words.

Theresa Gowanlock turns over in her mind the phrase first used by the McLeans, now by this woman: "Our Indians."

A staccato of rapid rifle fire scatters her thoughts, a sound she will never get used to, the random unfocussed violence of these sudden bursts of gunfire. A tense expectation fills the air. She hears it in the talk of the men and the demented out-of-control gunfire. She says, "And isn't there the slightest shadow of a doubt in your mind that not the Métis, but the Indians themselves might have taken our horses?"

"Always. Always, my dear. But even if it were true, it would never do to let them think, for even a moment, that we doubt their word."

"It's not that I'm braver than you," continues the Delaney woman. "I'm not. I just won't let them see. Once they see you are afraid, they take advantage. They come in here, right into my own kitchen and sit down and help themselves as if you'd made it all just for them. They are the worst possible freebooters."

There is a soft knock on the back door, barely discernible, as if someone knew that people were downstairs in the kitchen to answer it at this early hour. Theresa Delaney stands in the open doorway while a man talks to her in Cree, but Theresa Gowanlock's view of him is blocked by the Delaney woman's back. She watches the Delaney woman close the door, admiring her confidence but unsure of her judgement.

"That was Big Bear's son," says Theresa Delaney. "He feels sorry the horses have been taken. He and his men are entirely to blame. They danced all night and then fell asleep and it was then that the Métis took the horses. But we shouldn't worry because he, Imasees, King Bird, will personally start looking for the horses as soon as it is light." She says this in a rote monotone, remembering the words, translating them now for the Gowanlock woman.

King Bird. What a beautiful but odd and incongruous name for someone as implacable and stolid as Big Bear's son. No wonder most people call him by his Cree name, Imasees. "And do you believe him? What did you say?"

"Of course, I believe him. I told him it's almost light so he'd best get on with it."

But Theresa Gowanlock is not so easily reassured. Since she and her husband left their home at the mill and came to the settlement two days ago, the men have been in a continuous small informal meeting and whenever she gets within hearing they quickly change the subject, lapse into amenities about the weather, or worse, into silence; her husband huddled with the others in this, the latest phase of his betrayal. It is a bad sign, she thinks, when men and women do not share confidences. Already Quinn, Delaney, and her husband are discussing the stolen horses.

The Delaney woman leans across the table and in a low confidential voice says, "I have my own private opinions upon the causes of this latest unrest but do not deem it well or proper to express them. There are others besides the half-breeds and Big Bear and his men connected with this affair. There are many objects to be gained by such means and there is a wheel within a wheel in the North-West troubles.

"But never mind all that. Your hands are shaking! We'll take a brandy with our tea. It's the least we can do while we wait for this disturbance to end."

The Delaney woman stands on a chair and reaches onto a high shelf for a brandy bottle.

"That's a beautiful cupboard."

"Why thank you. Williscraft, the old man working at your husband's mill, made it for me. He has such a way with wood."

"Yes," Theresa Gowanlock hears herself say.

But of course, she knew that, recognized his work, for she has one very similar in her own kitchen, and admiring Theresa Delaney's only makes her realize how much she misses her new home and causes her quite suddenly to confront a terrible truth: she will never see it again, nor the treasured pieces of herself with which she so carefully filled it: the furniture from her mother and father's farm in Ontario, the china and family heirlooms that define who she is. Now there is no past and she has no identity; now there is only the tenuous present of a few articles of clothing she carries on her back.

"It will end, you know," Theresa Delaney is saying. "It always does. It's nothing really. You should have been here last summer. All of Battleford barricaded inside the fort for a week while the Indians faced off against the police and not a thing came of it, except in the end one of them went to jail. This is the same sort of thing. You'll see. Say when."

The Delaney woman pours brandy into Theresa Gowanlock's teacup and waits for her to say "when", but she is thinking of her house and doesn't, so finally the Delaney woman takes a small portion for herself, then stands on the chair to return the bottle to the cupboard. "Best not to leave the bottle on the table," she says. "Or for that matter, anything else you might want for yourself."

"My own house would be nice," says Theresa Gowanlock, standing, when the first wave of brandy hits her. She clutches the corner of the table as if it were the only tangible thing left in the world to hang onto. "We're not like you," she insists, hovering over the Delaney woman who sits silent and amazed. "They are not *our* Indians. We, that is, my husband and I, do not work for the Department of Indian Affairs and we are not tied to these people in any way. No, we came out here on a business venture. How I ever let that man make me believe for even one minute that this was the land of opportunity I will never know.

"*Battleford!* That's all he could talk of. Battleford was supposed to be the capital of the North-West. Battleford was on the railway line. Then, overnight they change the route, Regina's the capital, and Battleford? Instead of the railroad, Battleford gets *your* Indians."

She feels better now that she has vented some of the tension but bad that the Delaney woman has borne the brunt of it. "I have no right. Not after the kindness you've shown me. I'm sorry."

"Don't be sorry, Theresa. There is no need. Not between you and me. Since you came in December I've begun to feel at home here for the first time. My life is no longer a lonely life. Now, more than ever, there are just the two of us. Don't think for a moment these men have the slightest control over things here, because they don't. They as much as admitted so yesterday."

Theresa Gowanlock thinks about her husband's error in judgement in predicting the economics of Battleford and their future. She thinks about her husband and the other men meeting in the Delaney house for two days, grappling with the reality of where they really are. And young Bill Cameron, just back from Big Bear's camp, claims the Indians behave as if they'd never known him; even Quinn, an old hand with the Sioux from the States who works for the Department here, said, "I know these Indians well enough to insist we should all leave the settlement immediately."

Inspector Dickens and his men have already left.

"You are on your own now, I'm afraid." Dickens attempted to impart this with some sobriety as the official notice of the departure of the police, but Theresa Gowanlock detected the demented glee in his announcement, as if for him, things were never right unless they had gone as horribly and irrevocably wrong as his own life. "Keep to your dwellings! It's not safe to be abroad!"

And if this is so, why, against the advice of both Quinn and Dickens, have her husband and the others decided to stay on? Stubborn pride. The need to assert that all is well and that the men are in control, when in fact even she can see that neither is true.

The horses have been stolen. Not that it matters; where would they go with horses? Yet without them their isolation is final, complete; they are cut off from the rest of the world. Big Bear's son has been looking for them. Just thirty minutes have elapsed since he reassured the Delaney woman he would find them and surely he has, for now he has returned.

From her chair where she sits at the kitchen table, she can see Imasees standing at the foot of the stairs looking up at them with his arms crossed, as if waiting for someone or something to descend. Half-way up stand Quinn and Delaney and further up, the fringed leggings of an Indian at the top of the stairs. And then without warning or notice she is suddenly watching, one by one, the wooden stock and blue metal of a Winchester rifle, three revolvers, another rifle, not a Winchester, but her husband's old single-shot Snider, the guns passing down from man to man to Imasees who stands at the bottom of the stairs collecting them.

"Exactly what is going on here?" Theresa Delaney asks her husband.

"Imasees and his men are short of firearms and they need ours to defend us from the Métis."

"For God's sake, man," interrupts Quinn, "let's drop the pretence, at least among ourselves. This thing could turn to soup fast. We are prisoners. They have our guns and they have our horses."

Outside somewhere a door is being smashed in — Dill's store or the police barracks. The looting has begun. She wonders what will be left of her house at the mill. They have given themselves over freely and in good faith to the Indians. They are no longer in control of their own lives. And not once did anyone ask her opinion. At what moment did the men decide, against the advice of the police, of Quinn, against all good sense, to stay on in the settlement?

Perhaps it was Father Fafard arguing that they should stay as a demonstration of faith. Or Theresa Delaney's husband thinking it would be a shame to abandon the government provisions. Hadn't Big Bear given John Delaney a peace pipe and told him he was beloved by all the band?

And at what point did the men realize the truth and decide to keep it from her? It doesn't matter now.

Outside, as each hammer blow of the axe smashes into the splintered door of Dill's store, something inside her is breaking: trust, suspension of disbelief, the veneer of her gullibility, wanting to believe Imasees and his men are protecting them from the Métis, all her hopes and aspirations, shattering one by one, blow by blow. She is on her knees now, stripped of all self-deception, naked in the knowledge she can no longer shut out, quietly crying to herself.

Absorbed in their own talk, the men are silenced by her soft sobbing, the sight of her huddled form cradled in the arms of Theresa Delaney.

She tries to stifle her crying and focus on faces blurred by tears: Big Bear, an anxious worried old man stripped of all power and control over his men; the broad implacable face of his son, Imasees; Wandering Spirit, Little Poplar. They are all here, some twenty Indians watching her, the white woman, the first to break.

One of them leans over to talk to her husband. Now her husband is trying to calm her, but she won't listen. He is saying, "They want you to know that you should not be afraid. They will not harm you."

But it is all lies. The men have already resumed talking. Her husband will deal with her now. Except she won't let him. She is being difficult. There, he says it, this man holding her by the wrists, shaking her, her husband, "Don't be difficult, Theresa."

She doesn't care. She will not be deceived any longer, not by him, not by any of them.

But she must regain control of herself or she will never know what is happening. If she just sits here quietly and watches, she can see Wandering Spirit talking to Quinn, demanding something. Big Bear's war chief shakes his fist at Quinn, poor Quinn, who tried to warn them. Now it is all coming down on him. She listens, trying to make out the words.

"Who is at the head of the whites in this country?" Wandering Spirit demands. "Is it the government, or the Hudson's Bay Company, or who?"

Quinn can only answer with a harsh forced laugh. How little they know of us, she thinks, suddenly realizing the significance of Wandering Spirit's question and of Quinn's bitter laugh.

The toll of the church bell echoes through the small settlement and across Frog Lake — Holy Thursday. This morning it will be John Pritchard's boy, his hands wrapped around the rope, ringing in early morning mass. The day, she realizes, as the church bell clashes with the yells of the Crees pillaging Dill's store, has hardly begun and anything might happen.

"I think you should all go to church and pray," says Wandering Spirit. "But first," he adds as an afterthought, "my men will kill an ox."

"Why yes!" John Delaney jumps up. "That can be arranged."

But Wandering Spirit is merely informing him what his men intend to do, not asking his permission. Delaney no longer has any power or control here. Does anyone, she wonders. It comes to her now why Wandering Spirit's question to Quinn disturbs her. The Indians do not have a plan. They are making this up as they go along, and for her, this is even more frightening.

"Go to the church," Wandering Spirit demands, moving through the house.

"We'd better go with the others," her husband says, as if they have any choice in the matter.

She tightly grasps her husband's hand and begins walking slowly up the hill toward the church, the Delaneys, Quinn, the other whites, and the Indians behind them.

The smell of burning wood fills the air. Dill's store is in flames and the Indians dart in and out of the smoke and move hurriedly between buildings. Amidst the smoke and raucous cries, the steady, strangely out-of-place ringing of the church bell, she moves up the hill, as in a trance.

Wandering Spirit circles the group on horseback and just as they reach the top of the hill catches sight of Cameron. "Why don't you go to church with your friends?" he shouts, waving his arm toward the others.

She wonders what will happen if Cameron decides to disobey this thinly veiled order, but the young Hudson's Bay clerk quickly joins the procession.

Theresa Gowanlock and her husband move between two armed Indians standing guard on either side of the church door. As they step inside, young Father Marchand, down from Onion Lake to assist in the service, is about to close the door but is stopped by Father Fafard. "Let the doors remain open so those who wish may enter."

Fafard turns and walks down the aisle, toward the altar, his back to the congregation, so that she and everyone else in the church except Fafard himself see Wandering Spirit's silent moccasined feet stalk down the aisle behind the priest who, stooping forward now to don his white vestments, steps to the altar and turns to see, here, in the centre of his church, the upturned, streaked-with-black-war-paint face of Wandering Spirit, his Winchester butt-ended and pointing heavenward, Wandering Spirit kneeling before him, his rifle in his hand.

The small church seethes with the energies of these two men, this conflict between a priest and his congregation of Woods Cree on one side, and on the other, a war chief and his Plains Cree warriors. Standing at the back of the church Theresa Gowanlock hovers on the periphery, on the brink of this clash of opposites that threatens to consume them all.

And at the centre, Father Fafard begins the invocation in Cree, then falters, as the Plains Cree outside whoop and holler and move through the open door strutting and weaving into the church.

"I forbid you to do any harm," Father Fafard tells them. "Go away quietly to your camps and do not disturb the happiness and peace of the community."

Wandering Spirit rises and faces his own men. "Go!" he shouts.

As the Plains Cree shuffle out of the church, they glance back at their leader who waves his rifle at the whites huddled in the rear of the church. "Go to his place," he says, his rifle pointing at John Delaney.

When Theresa Gowanlock and the others come out of the church they are surrounded by armed Indians waiting to escort them back to the Delaneys'. They are almost fifty feet down the hillside when Little Bear, glancing back from his horse, sees Father Fafard silhouetted against the church door, about to close it. He wheels his horse and gallops back to the church. The priest has almost closed the door when Little Bear leaps from his horse, forces the door open and pumps his fist into Father Fafard's eye.

"Hurry and catch up with the others," orders Little Bear.

Hands pressed to his face, the priest staggers forward, a small robed figure stumbling blindly down the hill toward her. This is the end, Theresa Gowanlock thinks, the end of everything.

The Delaney house has become a central gathering place to which the Indians are directing all the whites in the settlement, for what purpose and to what end she cannot imagine or is afraid to think.

Wandering Spirit keeps trying to get information from Quinn. Who is their leader? The Queen? The government? The Hudson's Bay? Who is it? It strikes her again how little knowledge these people have of the world she comes from.

Cameron is ordered to the Bay store to provide the Indians with whatever they request. Father Fafard's eye is already swollen shut. Chief in name only, Big Bear alternately offers reassurance and warning.

"I am afraid," he blurts to John Delaney, "afraid some of my young men will shoot the whites." Then quickly adds, "But don't worry. You will be safe."

No one is in control. Wandering Spirit gives orders, but Imasees is always present. Silent, since the deception of the horses.

For surely it was deception. She senses his hand in things, though in what way she cannot tell.

Perhaps it is the continued pretence that these Cree warriors are protecting them from the half-breeds, an extension of the story of the stolen horses with which Imasees began the morning, that makes her think this. Imasees, standing at the bottom of the stairs collecting the guns. Their guns.

Wandering Spirit wants everyone to go to the Indian camp, but Quinn is arguing with him.

"We will all go to our camp now, so that we can be together and defend you better from the half-breeds."

This is all a lie. But to what end, she wonders.

Quite unexpectedly her husband comes to her. "You had best put your shawl around you for it is very cold," he says, as if they are going for a walk together, but then adds, "Perhaps we will not be gone long."

But he doesn't really know and what he says makes very little sense, though now that she thinks about it, no more and no less than anything else he has ever said.

She has been walking for some time now, her back to the ruin of black smoke billowing from the church and the gunfire in the distance behind her. She is no longer startled by the shots as when they woke her this morning, for there has been intermittent gunfire ever since. This just serves to illustrate, she thinks, listening to the latest burst of shots from somewhere behind her, how you adapt to circumstances, even when the circumstances are out of control.

The trail to the Indian camp breaks out of the poplars into a field that hints of spring in the sight ahead: George Dill and his dog, running alongside each other, a small spaniel jumping playfully at his master's leg. Dill thrusts his head back and pumps his arms wildly, running full out now, the dog bounding and snapping excitedly at his leg, the dog believing this all a game, and perhaps it is, for all around Dill lead zips and thunks softly into the spongy wet spring ground and he is almost there, almost to the cover of the bushes beyond the edge of the field when a bullet spins him around and sends him toppling backward into the poplars.

Two men run past her.

"Don't shoot!" one of them screams as his hat flies from his head and she sees by the shock of his white hair that it is Charles Williscraft, the old carpenter, helpless and bare-headed, running for his life, "Oh, don't shoot!"

She turns in the direction of the firing to see a rider aim down on her husband.

"I am shot," he says, and staggers away from her, then turns and stumbles back, clutching his chest with both hands.

His legs crumple as she catches him under his arms, his weight pulling her down.

"I am so sorry," he says.

"Hold still," she soothes, cradling him in her arms.

Slumping forward, his chin on his chest, he watches her unbutton his blood-soaked shirt to a chest wound percolating air and blood, and it is the last thing he sees, his life slipping away, so warm, as it seeps across the back of her hand touching the wound, the small splintered fragments of bone between her fingers.

Leaning over him, she sets his head on the ground and, unable to look at his eyes, glances up for the first time since the shooting and sees no one standing in the field. No one. Just the dog at the edge of the field, tail wagging, head poked into the bushes where Dill fell. If she gets up she too will surely be shot. She is afraid to move. There is nothing she can do but lie here beside a dead man and let the cold ground seep into her.

The dog whimpers and sniffs at Dill's body and lets out a long low whine that builds to a howl, then turns and lopes across the field to discover the others. Each time it finds a body, it turns in a frenzy on its hind legs, yelping incessantly.

She flinches as a Cree wheels on his horse, takes aim, and with a single shot silences the dog. Clenched tightly against the body of her dead husband, she watches through squinted, almost-closed eyes as the riders move toward her. Crisscrossing the field they weave in and out among the corpses, so close the hooves shake the ground.

A rider reins in, his horse hovering right over her. Its nostrils nuzzle under her arm, its breath brushes down her back. She must lie perfectly still, but can't, soaked through to her skin, trembling so with fear and cold. At the first touch of hands on her back she scrambles to her feet, moving away in terror from an astonished Cree who stands and stares after her.

She trips and stumbles over Father Marchand's leg. A young Indian boy tears dead grass from the ground and, wadding it into a ball, daubs at the gash in the priest's throat. The priest struggles to get his breath, choking on his own blood.

"Tesqua! Tesqua!" At the edge of the field an old man waves his arms and shouts in Cree, "Stop! Stop!" But Big Bear has no control here. Events have taken on a volition and momentum of their own. Ignoring their chief, the men move in on her, tightening their circle till it seems she will be trampled. From the height of their horses, they loom over her, bodies painted yellow, porcupine quills jutting from black hair daubed with clay, feathers dangling from braids, faces streaked and dotted with black paint stare down at her. Terrified, she backs away, desperately thrusting her hands in front of her as if to somehow push herself entirely from this field of slaughter, careful where she steps, looking over her shoulder to avoid tripping over another body . . .

"Theresa! Theresa!"

It is the Delaney woman, fifty feet away, kneeling between her dead husband and the black-robed body of Father Fafard. "Over here, Theresa!" she calls, standing up. They run to each other and in the comfort of their embrace shield themselves from the mounted Indians who surround them. Stopped by the women, the warriors lean out over their horses and watch them hold each other. They speak quietly in Cree while their idle horses stamp the melting snow and bend to snatch the grass uncovered by their hooves, in this the first moment of calm after the killings. Then a rider breaks from the circle, and shouting, waves his rifle across the creek to the Indian camp.

"Close your eyes and keep moving, Theresa," whispers the Delaney woman, still holding her, then breaking their embrace. "Be brave, for the water will be cold as ice."

Theresa Gowanlock holds her skirts high above water up to her knees, so cold the current cuts into her legs, numbing them until she can't move. She stands stock still in the middle of the creek, the cold current rushing against her legs. It comes to her now, as if she hears through the shock of the murders, his last words, spoken to her minutes ago, now, for the first time: he was sorry. He has left her alone in the world with his name, left her alone in this, and all he could say was he was sorry.

Someone is calling her name.

But Theresa Gowanlock cannot move out of the creek. There is nowhere to go. On one side, a field filled with corpses; on the other side, the Indian camp. No, she will simply stand here in the middle of the creek where it is safe.

A broken branch from an overhanging poplar floats by. She turns to watch it diminish downstream, a distant speck that bobs on the water, then disappears altogether. She has become that small branch, a broken twig connected to nothing, caught in the eddies of a powerful current.

Someone is calling her name.

Stunned, she stands in the frigid water, the current pulling at her legs, refusing to move, realizing in the first minutes after the killings, what has happened. The shock recedes enough for her to regain a vague awareness, someone calling her.

"Tess! Tess!" the Delaney woman calls from the far shore. "Whatever are you doing out there?"

Beyond the creek, wisps of blue smoke drift upward between the lodgepoles of the Indian camp.

Theresa Gowanlock slowly moves forward through the water toward the women she first saw on the bridge at Battleford.

— *Mel Dagg*

ALIEN LOVE

Although Macleod has forbidden it
the call of flesh is strong   a primal need;
sexual abstinence wars with my hot blood.
I sneak from camp and find her
amid the scent of wood-smoke —
the mint of stone fire-rings,
this woman of the wilderness.
All autumn falls on me,
for she is beautiful —
her hair — a midnight sheen
her eyes — the blackness of ebony.
Beneath her brown touch the aching
glory of my need finds blessed release;
I pour my seed into this alien flesh.
Afterwards, our passion spent,
we feast on nuts and berries
that hold the sweetness of a summer past.
Then patient as no other lover can be
she watches me as I return to camp.

— *Catherine Buckaway*

OCTOMI MEETS THE WILD ROSE BERRIES
(AFTER THE STORIES OF LIZZIE OGLE)

the next morning octomi rose
from some stones and sage brush
his belly was still grumbling with great hunger
he hadn't eaten for three whole days
and the journey grew slower
as he approached wild rose bushes in a coulee
octomi's eyes brightened
at the sight of bright red berries
their fragrance made him dizzy
and when he arrived
one of them smiled and spoke softly

"cheyah . . . tokeeylah?"
(old brother
where are you going?)

"meesohn . . . okchee oughmow"
(just wandering around
young brother)
almost fainting from his hunger
octomi asked if the berries were good to eat

the sweet berry cooed " . . .oh yes
there is nothing sweeter than us
but if you eat us
your big brown berries between your legs
will grow very itchy
and may even bleed . . . "

octomi said he didn't care
he was *so* hungry
and so he walked and walked through the bushes
enjoying the lovely berries
finally
he even got down on his knees
to savour the sweet fallen ones
their fragrance was so fine and intoxicating
the whole earth seemed to shudder
beneath him
finally he thought
"i've had quite enough now
i better stop before i hurt too much"
he was beginning to feel a bit sore
and itchy
so off he went
humming his favourite song

"toyah towampee
ishtah nahshapee"
(if you open your eyes
you will have red eyes)

— *Andrew Suknaski*

TALISMAN. BROWNING, MONTANA

The first museum we found was the wrong one,
a zoo of stuffed animals, predator and prey
lying down together for once. On the outskirts
we discovered the Museum of the Plains Indian,
low brick as distinctive as school or hospital.

Inside we saw the buckskins and headdresses
of chiefs neatly fitted on faceless dummies.
"Are they stuffed too?" a child asked. Nothing
so cruel. There were glass beads behind glass,
a picture of a buffalo hunt painted on buffalo hide,

and the amulet, a circle of smooth brown stone
figuring the sun, bearing an etched crescent
for the moon, bride of light, and a single point
as the morning star, their child. A warrior's magic,
with no curator's sign to explain his defeat.

The stone didn't burn through the glass, I didn't
carry it off in my white soul as borrowed power.
We just walked out under the big sky of Montana,
where I will never watch the moon and morning star
cross the face of the sun we see by and never see.

— *Bert Almon*

FALL
(U.C. Berkeley 1989)

We sit over Indian bones
and over the silent, sitting up, buried ones.
Bob Hass laughs about Dickinson
and tells us it is
okay to be slow,
and confusion
is all part of what is meant to be.

I finger the silence

that follows a poem's end.
It is the sound
of having been there, the hard despair
that follows pain getting words
and after rain you can hear the drops
staying in the trees.

Sometimes the day tumbles early
but coming up from the Mining Circle
the grass yearns down to the figure of a girl
in bronze, green as rain, and such bewilderment
is part of what is meant to be.

— *Sara Berkeley*

Ω

Remember the heart. Fog on the still river. First frost.
Passion. Flowers. The love of cities in old windows.

The painting is a dead eye. A window goes nowhere.
This one is alive. This one has a chance to live. This one.

Look in or out. Beauty is starved and love is afraid.
Dead children. The night in mothers. Remembered delight.

The heart is an argument with darkness. Moon sliver.
Dead eye. The room rings. I do not answer it again.

— Patrick Lane

INTERIOR WITH DOG
(A PAINTING AT THE AGO, BY HENRIK DE BURGH)

A girl about nine looks out from a picture, points
to a spaniel. It stands on its hind legs; this is a trick.
Behind her a fool in a queer cornered cap looks out; a
woman moves from a hall towards light
coming from the back of the picture. Outside moving
toward the same light there is a corridor:
trees, a man ready to ride a great white horse.
He talks to an old woman, barely seen, perhaps it is a man. It was
the angle of the large black and white tiles on the floor
that drew me to this picture.

— *Anne Campbell*

THE PARADISE GARDEN

Outside the white wall
beyond the birds
singing on the battlements
solitary atoms may wander

But here in the garden
irises grow
beside lilies of the valley

A lady holding a lute
smiles at a baby
plucking the strings

In the middle of the garden
the blue-robed queen sits
reading a book

A monkey peeks out
from behind the robe
of a pensive angel

who dreams of escaping
from this close happiness

— *Nancy Senior*

LILITH

I

Yet another garden painting.
Yes, there are three in this one too.
Adam, a woman, and
another woman.
They all wear the same expression,
that of a thirteen-year-old-boy
in a brothel: scared and excited.
The name of the painting is
"The Eighth Day".

II

On the ninth day Adam rested.
This next painting shows us
what Eve and Lilith are doing
deep in the forest, while Adam is
pretending to sleep.
There are so many entangled limbs
that it is hard to tell where
one body ends and the other
quivers like a goldfish.
There were many touches and kisses.
Lilith showed Eve everything,
and it was good, O it was a good afternoon . . .
       (If you look carefully,
       you can see Adam's eyes
       glowing red in the darkest corner
       of the picture)

III

This last painting is the most
interesting.

Lilith lies on the ground at Eve's feet.
They are naked, grace notes
where grace is badly needed.

Adam stands off to the side, naming things
in the newly tanned skin of a doe.
Snake he names *snake*.
Until now we had forgotten him,
a minor character.
He has swallowed his tail,
the ring on Lilith's left hand.
She is smiling.
>(To know nothing but flesh.
>This is the way that Lilith lives.
>The only one who never took the bite,
>she's the only one now
>who looks like she knows something
>important.)

— *Sherry Johnson*

THE SPIRIT LURKS AGAINST THE WALL

We paint the walls in spots so that
visitors will not see the leopards
when they come and go or recline
in meditation or the tail twitchings
of their whiskered dreams. Fanned
by gentleness of olive branches
they enjoy rapture of repose; touched
by the straying tendril of vine
the black eyes flick wide, serpents
striking at the threat of space, coals
subsiding to placidity in acceptance
of the feathered caress. No,
you will not see them. Yes,
they are there, to be lined against
this stone and that, ear against crevice,
tail tip where the split leaf throws
its shadow — but no matter; they are not
for the curious to descry. The spirit
enfolds them, softens their outlines.
The spirit lurks against the wall.

—*John V. Hicks*

THE EMANCIPATION OF FORM

Still Life With Table and Chairs

One table, a chair on either side;
a series of lines: horizontal, vertical

But secretly within
this domestic geometry of furniture
the chairs are becoming horses,
the table's face a calm pool
toward which the horses bend to drink

The mind is a silent accomplice
to what the eye paints

Portrait of a Dancer

Barefoot woman in gypsy skirt,
poised to dance

Beneath her long bright hair
the lines of her face
rearrange themselves,
laughter and anguish
defying one perception

Beside her, a fragmented guitar —
curve, string, grain of wood;
and in the clear surrounding space
a single note rainbows into chord

When she moves
arm, leg, floor are freed,
the eye divided,
every shape let loose

Landscape

It appears so still
but already there are changes

The light expands and contracts

The pond, bubbling with rain,
flattens
into the white porcelain sheen
of frozen snow

A sparrow may
or may not
alight on the pine branch

Out of this possibility
the eye invents its vision,
creates its own form

— Eva Tihanyi

HUNTER STRANDED ON AN ICE FLOE

"When I was small, my father used to carry me on his back when he went inland to hunt caribou. He went out hunting one day, at the floe edge, with a younger boy, and my mother, my little brother, and I were left alone. We were out visiting, I think, when someone came to tell us that they had found the sled and the dogs but there was no sign of my father or his companion."
— PAINGUN KANAJUK from WE DON'T LIVE IN SNOW HOUSES NOW

1

in the kurelek painting
the ESKIMO hunter is seated on a triangular ice floe
his knees flexed
to contain the body warmth
and support folded arms on which to pillow
ancestral dreams
or the final dream of a dolphin
who returned as a whale
to carry him home

leant on something hidden behind the hunter
the harpoon rests
at an angle

kurelek explains
   "such a terrifying experience might happen
   when a hunter takes one
   too many chances
   pursuing a seal from floe to floe.
   to let himself fall
   into intensely cold water
   would mean certain death.
   there is nothing to be done
   but drift
   and wait."

hunter stranded on an ice floe
resembling so much
the ESKIMO sculpture i often admired
in the hudson's bay store that summer
back in the mountains
how i often fawned over it as an excuse to be there
till the beautiful sales woman
fell for me
as if i were a sea worth exploring

the sculpture
a triangular ice floe cut
from whale bone
a cross section revealing the marrow
small holes surrounding a larger one
aglu
'the breathing hole'
where the small ivory hunter with his harpoon
always knelt waiting
for a seal to rise
maybe a hunter like the very one kurelek painted
a hunter slowly drifting beyond the icy edge of home
unheeding the warnings of his father's ghost
that drifted the same way

that young woman drifted on like all the others
to the sea of what i hope
will be more merciful men
i have grown more wary of the heart the hunter
learning to settle for less
my one last dream
to return from where i am
as a whale
if there is anything left
to return to

— *Andrew Suknaski*

AN IMAGE OF CHRIST ASCENDING INTO THE HEAVENS

is silliness at best but we are still
moved; as at a hero's death in wartime
where we feel the tragedy, the rise and
fall of so great a man; aspiration
reduced to some sweat, a trickle of blood;
yet it is the fall we feel, the sense
that he was, most often, one of us when
he slept, ate a meal, drank a little
wine, or thought of a recent love he'd met
beneath the rubble in some captured town;
but this was a mythological birth,
a wedding between the winter
solstice and the rebirth of Spring,
yet we are asked to believe it happened,
once, that he ascended into the heavens,
sucked from the earth by a huge red mouth, his
feet waving goodbye in the worm-dancing
sky, while the apostles stand in a snail's
shell and point their crooked fingers upward
in astonishment, thinking what they will
do with this in future Springs, dreaming
of eggs and rabbits, and wondering who
will ever believe such a spectacle.

— *Doug Beardsley*

SNOWFALL: UNDER THE STUDY LAMP

fragile webbed coffee cup
ready to break
red red the snow   white glaze
white pages   powderlike
crumbling before me
fire flakes are falling

dragons are breathing
on red-shot eyes
there is nothing to see
snow has covered this dirty city
I wait for the empty colour of night
for its dark throat
to consume the light

— *Brenda Niskala*

NERUDA IN THE KITCHEN

Your low-backed dress,
black-seamed stockings.
Your red hair.
No saint, you'd have preferred priesthood;
nuns always hidden away somewhere
and angels are dull.

That serene head staring towards me,
my eyes prisms of water
in which each ringlet of hair
becomes a strand in a wig of snakes,
each with the head of a man.
Nothing evil there,
simply all the possibilities of belief.

Even when you stand still
things begin to happen.
In your kitchen, reading Neruda,
a mango in the other hand,
as if you'd forgotten which would be dinner.
The South Americans, you say, Marquez,
the others, not fantastical but Catholic,
straight from the *Lives of the Saints*.

Your blue gown flutters
as if risen from the ocean floor,
over your shoulder a shawl of beach.

In the room where poetry is made,
the words spread like peacocks
under the jacaranda trees.
Lizards slip from your fingers
into pools of low blue flames.

The mango still in the other hand,
you close the book
and as you split the green skin,
twelve parrots scramble for the window,
bolts of red and blue,
and you spill backwards into the night sky,
wave-rippled after them.
And me, I'm gripping an empty window-frame,
stunned but believing.

Santa Maria, saints are everywhere.

— *Bruce Hunter*

INFLUENCES

I sit down at my desk
— and it turns into Pablo Neruda!
His stout face stares thoughtfully
up from between my pencils.
I say to him: *Please. I want to get on with it.*
On with being Wayman, with my own work.
Vanish. Vamos! And he goes.

But just then my chair feels uncomfortable.
I jump up and look. Neruda again.
Pablo, I tell him. *Please, I insist.*
Leave me alone. I've got to do it.
Back to your Chile. Get south.
Sud! Sud! Leave Vancouver to me.

And he goes. I draw out my papers,
my scribbles. Scratching my beard.
I pore over a fine adjustment,

searching for the perfectly appropriate sound.
Then I notice the curtain
leaning over my shoulder.
"I'd do it this way," it says, pointing.
"Change this word here."

Neruda, I say, getting real mad.
Flake off. Go bother Bly.
Teach all the poets of California.
While I'm talking to him like this
he changes from being my curtains
to a pen. And I see his eyes twinkle
as they fall on my typewriter.

Then, I get cagey.
I'll be back in a minute, I tell him
and leave, carefully shutting him
inside the room.
Out on my porch, in the cold air
I see the North Shore mountains behind the City.
I'm alone now, shivering.
There is no sound over the back yards
but traffic
and a faint Chilean chuckle.

— *Tom Wayman*

ONE HILL AND TWO ROCKING-HORSES
(FROM *HORSE SENSE*)

In St. Martin there is a hill, a large hill that sits at one end of the village. One day a geologist came through St. Martin, got off the bus, ate lunch at Camille Valéry's Homestyle Cooking café, told Camille the hill was left a hundred centuries before in the wake of an enormous glacier and got back on the bus. What Camille did not tell the geologist was that the hill was not a hill, but an argument the village had lived with since it was born on the prairies.

After that no more geologists came through St. Martin, but one day years later, after the story of the geologist was set as firmly in everyone's mind as the hill that rose over the village, some things happened to change all of that.

* * *

On what some in the village of St. Martin remember as the coldest day of the year, a bone-cracker at minus forty, Ambroise Valéry was in the St. Martin Hardware store to buy a spare part for the mechanical Santa Claus in the window of Camille Valéry's café. Ambroise had made it years ago and now, like himself, it was old and unreliable. Instead of lifting a brightly decorated package out of its sack, it would raise it up only a little way, stop, and then return the present to the sack at the same time its jaw opened with a smile. Camille, who had lost his sense of humour when his wife died, wanted Ambroise to come and fix the monster in his window before it broke the hearts of all the children in St. Martin.

Ambroise, who did everything as though he was looking for the answer to life itself, followed his imagination up one aisle and down the next. Whatever he did not recognize he picked up and turned over in his hand, felt its weight, speculated on its purpose and returned it to the shelf or the box it had been in. A habit that had led him in his lifetime to create not only the mechanical Santa Claus but an electric ironing board that short-circuited the entire house when it was first turned on, a water cannon that was supposed to speed garden irrigation during dry spells, but instead drained the well dry in almost one gulp, and his most humiliating disaster, an airplane that had shaken itself to pieces in a field in front of the whole village when he started its gigantic engine.

That morning however, Ambroise had promised himself he would keep his mind on Camille's dilemma and not retreat into his basement workshop with the seeds of a new idea. And then, under the gaze of Gaspard St. Martin who watched from his office balcony, Ambroise saw what was probably the one, single rocking-horse in the village. A gentle creature of the imagination he had never before noticed, Ambroise thought as he pulled it out from a dusty bottom shelf. It would make the perfect gift for little Lucien for Christmas.

Under the lights of the hardware store he saw how horribly misshapen it was. The saddle had been molded into the poor animal's back, the bit of the bridle buried in its mouth. Even the springs that would keep the horse in motion had been fastened into the animal's sides. Worse still was the expression on the rocking-horse's face. It was fierce with hate and watched the world through two glowing red eyes.

Shocked, the old man retreated back up the aisle to the door. He patted his pockets in a search for the glove he had removed to make friends with the beast, looked at Gaspard St. Martin who continued to glare down at him, then turned and stepped back into the cold.

Such a thing, he thought, after he reached the sidewalk from the icy steps, only the devil would dare ride. And with the village, the only place Ambroise had ever known, laid out all around him on the bare and frozen prairie, he started back home, to the hill, with an idea.

As he crossed the street and started up the opposite sidewalk to avoid Marcel Valéry, who was cursed with bad luck worse even than his father Albert had been, Ambroise was met by his brother, Francois, when the door of the bakery opened in front of him.

"Do you not remember what today is, brother?" Francois asked, holding up the Christmas shopping list.

Francois was always surprising him, but that morning Ambroise was much too excited to care. "Today, Francois, I saw in the hardware store what would be for little Lucien a wonderful present, but you will never guess what it was."

Francois, who cared nothing for Ambroise's enthusiasms, shrugged his shoulders. He would let Ambroise have his say and then together they would go shopping.

"A rocking-horse!" Ambroise said, "The perfect gift for little Lucien!"

"So where is this wondrous animal, brother, or have you lost it already?"

Ambroise ignored the reference to the many caps, hats and toques that Francois had bought him for Christmas which he either misplaced or the wind relieved him of each winter. "It is a wicked and dangerous animal Gaspard St. Martin keeps in his store," Ambroise answered instead, "so I am going home to build one myself."

Ever since they were children it had been Ambroise's imagination that littered the village along with his lost clothing. Ambroise who escaped his household duties to build the three-wheeled bicycles that tossed the rider into the ditch whenever they tried to turn. Ambroise who every Valéry in the village talked about as though he was some kind of gentle genius who asked nothing of the world. And on top of all that, Francois was thought to have no imagination at all. Well, he would show them. They would see.

"Only you," Francois said in frustration as he wagged a mittened finger under his brother's nose, "would spend all your time making one rocking-horse when you could have a dozen if only you had planned. Think brother, of all the other Valéry children like little Lucien you might bring happiness to."

Ambroise, who had suffered the tirades of his brother for years, said nothing as he waited for Francois to go away and leave him with his idea. He imagined, instead, little Lucien on Christmas morning slipping noiselessly down the stairs and discovering as he climbed onto the back of his rocking-horse, that everything he had ever heard about Christmas, how it was a time of magic, was true.

"No!" Francois said, as he took Ambroise by the sleeve of his coat. "If there is any merit in this idea of yours, it is that I understand what we must do with it. Come brother, our day is just beginning," and as he started to lead Ambroise back across the street, Marcel Valéry passed in front of them chasing after his hat. A game the wind played relentlessly in St. Martin with the luckless Marcel.

* * *

As a child it had been Gaspard St. Martin's duty to sweep the floor of the hardware store every morning before school, and he had enjoyed starting his day that way. His mother, Florette, would be at the counter preparing the cash drawer. His father, Gaston, would be upstairs in the office going through lists of inventory. The only sound in the store would be Gaspard's broom as the little boy casually swept first one aisle and then the next and dreamed of his future.

Ambroise Valéry's appearance that morning had robbed Gaspard of those few pleasant moments he spent in the past. There was no one at the counter and there was no one upstairs in the office. He was not a child waiting to go to school, but an old man whose mother had long ago deserted him to live with a Valéry, Ambroise and Francois's father, Giscard.

The little horse was on the floor where Ambroise had left it after he dragged it off the shelf. When Gaspard had seen it advertised in a catalogue, the expression on the animal's face had been violent and he had enjoyed that. It was like finding a friend who thought as little of the world as he did. So he had ordered the creature and found a place to hide it in the store. Until that day the rocking-horse had been seen by no one in St. Martin but himself.

Gaspard dragged it shaking and rattling along the floor between the shelves. He lifted the horse over the long wooden counter, where, for more than fifty years, since the death of his father, Gaspard had conducted his business, and set it on the floor again.

The horse had been everywhere in the store, at the back under the stairs, in the basement, on various shelves, but it had never sat with him behind the counter. Never, Gaspard thought with a laugh, kept him company over the holidays.

— *Tillen Bruce*

IT'S YOUR MOVE

I could stand on a hill and merely by moving my head half an inch the composition of the landscape was totally changed.
– Paul Cezanne

saw the god of spring this morning   smile early
edging into that wallglass separating the figures in
Cezanne's *Card Players*   look at it closely
just above the cork   there!   give it morning light
you'll have this road now   lilting into downtown Vernon
bump across the tracks   pull in here at the Coldstream Cafe
see three reflections of your self   as you wedge into
through the double doors   order a take-out coffee
drop four quarters and a nickle in the slot
hear your cigarettes shuffle to a stop

so far inside this canvas now
feel the light begin
see the smell of spring begin

in the car again   the windows down
coffee steam fogging up that right-hand world
both hands shifting   steering   flicking cigarettes
all automatic   but eyes all morning   child-
like   greedy for everything   for gods
surprises   big   and   thick: a smile

intersects grey and gold   is given   flung
across the rear-view mirror

a new start   spring rain
on dust   on snow

if early were landscape Paul   could see it:
saw it: early: winking

waiting

— *John Lent*

Ω

All that is left. Last names. Morning.
Blood ties. Saturn's breakfast.

He said.
The dead. I don't know why I'm alive.

The body also moves, incomparable, describing peace.
We have forgotten how to be strangers.

Parables smaller than a story.
Keep me awake. Let the blood sing. Last names. Morning.

— Patrick Lane

I WILL NOT BE THE GRANDMOTHER

I will not be the grandmother
who tickles children's feet
tucks feather quilts
around tiny sticky-sweet chins
who winks   lifting the top from the candy dish

my hands tight on green snakes
mouth full of bitter cherry juice
I'll prepare my grandchildren for the fight
with hard words   dry bone arms
I'll love them fiercely

— *Brenda Niskala*

SEVENTY

"You are shrinking," my daughter says
but it is only the trees growing
large in my garden. I can still
rub the apples on the lowest branch
and bend the blossoms to my nose.

"You are blind," she tells me.
Wearing a coned hat I read
under the tree in the hottest sun,
lowering my head and peering
through the bottom of glasses.
I must squint to push the letters
back together. Often I shape
new words on the page.

With megaphone hands
she shouts in my ear,

but I hear even whispers
from swallow wings high in wind
and crickets cool in rock walls
and when I hear the bang of the screen door,
I pull myself to the highest branch
and hide with the green apples
from the sharp snap of her beak.

— *Lorna Crozier*

SPRING FLOWERS

As a child, it was my holy pleasure
to find you flowers, to bring you
pie plate gardens of moss and fern.
Each spring I hunted pussywillows
and brought you a tabby bouquet.

It was your vocabulary, that secret
life springing from rain, you who could spot
the snowdrop, forget-me-not, lily-of-the-valley,
their shadowed domain.

Your gardens are wild and rocky sprawls of colour
hand-spreads of earth, shouldering the blossoms
you brought from what ancient love,
child of the prairies. And you have passed to me
an elusive gift, that hides itself in spring forests
an ocean away, that roots its stubborn life
in a soil you didn't touch till middle age.

You tell me you've lost
your artistic flair, but look at me now
mother, I am beneath the trees
you planted in me, and I spread
my pink hands open each spring.
Listen:

        my mouth is full of your words:
listen:
    listen:
        any moment they will break
their gates and spill their round white leaves
at your feet. Tread carefully:
                I am your season.

— *Rhona McAdam*

A GENTLE LOOK

When I was young my father took me
to see a fallen raven. It breathed faintly
on a blanket of earth. Its dark shape
a cinder in the eye of the sun.
My father knelt down to comfort it
despite the threat of its beak. He spoke,
then, using strange words I hadn't heard
before or since. The world darkened
as the soul of the raven entered
my father's fingers. His eyes drawing
the sunlight in until it was twilight,
and we carried its carcass towards some unknown place.
There has always been the darkness of a raven
between us — its shape calming our
conversations. We are no longer responsible
for the other's life our fear
as calm as the raven's last breath.

Today, in the hospital he gives me a gentle look as he
succumbs to the medication. His knees lift slightly
and I can feel the sweat on his palm.
Fear is something that exists outside.
It waits for alarms
that disturb dreams in the morning.

Far below us in a basement death lives
surrounded by mirrors and the blank songs of
shotguns. I watch the trees sway in some
complicated semaphore. A dog barks down the
street as if to signal the return of evil.

There is serenity around our words, now.
He says we are helpless creatures hunting
ourselves. He knows this from listening at doors.
All of this within a white room.
Doctors coming and going, death something they
can comprehend but not share.

My father sleeps now. His hands
signalling the movement of his dreams —
I return to my children as they fidget
in the car. They point to the window
where they waved up to me —
dark and small like a raven in a cloudless sky.

— *Robert Hilles*

PROLOGUE: SHELTER

In the end Peter imagined that he could see it.

He could laugh. His father, after all, had taught him to laugh. His father was the funniest person he'd ever met. He still believed his father's laugh and he still lived in it, too. No matter what had happened, no matter what he'd finally seen in their lives, a wonderful, absurd laughter rescued them over and over again. It annointed their blunderings with an arching dignity that could not be diminished. Too real for that. Delicious in its own sheer way.

He could cry. Sometimes, in the end, he did. How could he avoid it? When he peered into all of the self-feeding circles that had enclosed their lives, when he imagined himself as a boy facing those circles, when he imagined his parents or his brothers and sisters as children, he could cry for the puzzling, the lonely and terrible miscues that had whispered to each of those children in the dark. It wasn't a matter of things being undone. He knew that was impossible. He didn't want something undone anyway. He wanted to do something now. That was the hard part, the tricky part. So instead of laughing helplessly sometimes, all he could do was cry.

But there were times when he seemed able to hold both impulses in his head at once: when he saw their lives and realized where beauty grew and what nourished it. When he shuffled into an intersection that faded as fast as he'd stumbled into it. In those moments he knew he'd lurched into the truth of what had happened. And the emotion there was pure. It was a wondering, painful ecstasy. That was his life, their lives, and it grew as richly as it decayed. It was as vibrant under the sun as it was still beneath the snow.

He would try to sing to those moments. After he'd rediscovered his father out at that cabin on the lake, he promised himself that he would try to do that. He would let everything else fall away and hold onto this fragile, green fuse.

1.

That was where it began.

The house Peter grew up in was built in 1948, the year he was born. It was called a "Golden Home" because it had been built by the Golden Construction Company as part of the subdivisions which grew in south Edmonton after the war to accommodate the baby boom.

Theirs was the largest of four models that this company built thousands of in an ingenious pattern of concealed repetition. It was two stories high, had four bedrooms, and was sheathed in speckled brown stucco. It sported a dark brown shingled roof and trim, and squatted like an obedient sheepdog on its standard city lot — a sheepdog because it was erratic, constantly moving, wildly flung in its tolerance of the nine of them living in it. Though there are always predictable sentiments which cling to the house you grow up in, for Peter it was specific: the grey room in the basement sustained him, drew him back.

In 1960, while Peter was being a good senior-sixer in cubs, playing Little League ball in the spring, and worrying vaguely about when his life would break out of its suffocating routines, his father was taking the evening news seriously. He saw himself in an endless series of buoyant Fred MacMurray movies and found himself wanting: he was not doing all he could for his family. In a feverish clutch of irrational responses to the hysterias of the time, he became convinced that their salvation would lie in the installation of a nuclear fallout shelter in the basement. Secretly at first, then brazenly as he became more committed, he hired carpenters to attack the dark grey vacuum of the basement — specifically a sixteen foot square to the west of the forced-air furnace.

Peter and his younger brother Richard were outside in the backyard weeding potatoes in the garden, thinking of their time later on down at Scona Pool, when three workmen arrived. It was a very hot Thursday in July; the garden seemed endless. With his shirt sleeves rolled up above his thin elbows, Peter's father talked to these men, spreading out construction plans on the boiling hood of his 1958 Ford stationwagon in the driveway. Peter and Richard tried to overhear the conversation but couldn't catch much except to guess from the odd raised eyebrow and subtle banter among the workmen themselves that they thought Peter's father was a bit of a kook. That was not surprising. His children thought he was a bit of a kook, too. He seemed different from their friends' dads with their workrooms and table-saws and endless photos of fish and deer pinned to the posts in those rooms. But Peter knew his father well enough to know that he was rabid about this project, whatever it was. He had that glint in his eye; he had worked out the details. This would be, Peter found out so much later, his gesture to his children, his gift to protect their futures in the face of the times he'd imagined they'd have to survive. He was also curiously secretive. He gave Peter and Richard money that morning to stay away. This was his territory. They took the money and went swimming.

Within a week, after loads of dirt and clay had been hauled out of the basement on a pulley system rigged through a small window at the side of the house, and after bags of cement had been hoisted down the stairs and piled next to the mixer which had been installed beside the wringer-washer, Peter and Richard stood at the bottom of the stairs surveying the results: three-quarter inch plywood lay where the basement floor had been. The workmen had dug downward and this was the roof of the project. A well-sealed trap door had been cut into the far corner of the plywood square. This door had been hinged with brand new stainless steel hinges, and had been locked by an enormous combination lock. There was nothing else to see. The workmen had completed their job. They never returned.

Though Peter and Richard badgered him — alternating their stategies between working in the garden for him and whining incessantly — he refused to show them what had been completed down there. And though their mother seemed more sympathetic, almost an ally at times, even she conceded to his secret, rolling her eyes upwards over the dishes, muttering vague things about the money he was spending which could have gone somewhere else.

Throughout that fall their father would descend every Saturday morning with fresh plywood and gyprock and gallons of paint. He had tucked an electrical cord through a tiny hole he'd cut in the trap door, and would lock the door behind him by an inside lock. The odd thing about these new activities was that as far as Peter and Richard knew their father had never done any carpentry before. And though they were drawn like moths to the obscure light of this mystery, too, eventually, in the face of his fierce insistance that they leave him alone, they gave up. In the end they could actually forget that anything unusual was going on down there at all. Other people's fathers worked on rumpus rooms or played golf. In time, they simply saw his time down there as a part of his life, a hobby that pleased him, invigorated him, eased the troubles and tensions he must have endured raising seven children on a teacher's salary in those years.

Somewhere in the midst of all that industry, however, the nature of the times themselves must have altered their father's perception of what he was doing. In the States the hyperactive order and anxiety of the Eisenhower years — the vortex for the kind of hysteria that had grabbed their father in the first place — had given way to other phenomena. A new, buoyant sesnse of security and culture and sanity had emerged clinging to the rise of the Kennedy brothers like smoke. And even the national rite of passage which attended their assassinations simply spelled the closure of simple fears and the beginning of more complicated ones. The very notion of a fallout shelter must have seemed mindlessly innocent suddenly. Peter often wondered later how his father must have felt as he accepted that his gift to protect his children's futures was having less and less to do with those futures.

His children were becoming obsessed by The Beatles, Bob Dylan, by the race riots down in the States, by novels such as *Black Like Me* and *Franny and Zooey*. The one thing that Peter remembered later was his father simply seemed more shy about this obsession that he still nourished. But he still nourished it.

If anything, while Peter, Richard and Evelyn became more absorbed by their new interests in music and in criticizing the hilarious innocence of the fifties that had carried them this far, their father became even more consistent in his retreats into the basement. Peter remembered one afternoon in the late sixties when the three of them were downstairs practising for a weekend 'gig' at Giuseppi's Pizza Parlour. They were discussing the sequence of tunes in each of the three sets when their father poked his head in nervously and asked them how it was going. Though he seldom mentioned his children's success with the music, they knew he was fascinated by it and even proud of them. He was unlike their friends' fathers in another way now. He didn't seem to get too excited about his children's new hairdos and strange music. He seemed quite unsurprised and comfortable with it all. In this sense their father appeared more and more as someone who might have been right about something all along, as someone who had survived the fifties in his own way. That afternoon he admitted quietly to the three of them that he was installing a wood-lathe and some wood-working tools in his room. He confessed that he'd discovered a new interest in hardwoods. "You must think I'm crazy, eh?" he whispered as he glanced sideways suddenly, taking in their guitars and their spangled and beaded denim costumes, then disappeared. They weren't sure what to think.

In 1971 Peter moved down to Toronto hoping to become a folk-singing star and a world-class scholar. These were his dreams.

He would return once a year for a speedy visit of hilarious drinking bouts with his brothers and sisters who had stayed in Edmonton. They were very much the scoffers of their pasts then: the social critics of the early seventies confident in their educated and self-indulged privileges and perspectives. Inevitably, Peter would sit with his father over a coffee in the kitchen. They'd crouch over the red arborite table and talk about his teaching. And Peter would always ask him how the work was going downstairs.

"Oh, the usual," his father would say. "Getting things done."

"That's great, dad," Peter would reply in that lofty, incubated superiority he'd grown into as a hand fits the perfect glove.

"Well, I wouldn't call it *great*, Peter," he replied one time, grinning out the window with a slight trace of sarcasm. "But it will do."

Peter was teaching at the University of Lethbridge in 1975 when Richard phoned him one night in February to tell him that their father had died the night before of a heart attack. Peter was just in the middle of separating from his first wife then, and that, plus other ambiguous defeats that had begun to haunt him, had done their work to deflate the strident confidence he had felt in everything he'd done so far. This news made him wonder even more about the confluence, the odd synchronicity of boundless hope and endless regret.

The funeral was more difficult than any of them could have anticipated. They had each of them loved this man. They were each of them, too, bringing an innocence to this grief, an innocence caused by the mystery he had presented to them. He seemed often to be standing a long way off in a landscape they were unsure of but which he believed in and felt safe in. There was this distance in their father and they puzzled over it trying to breach it.

One morning two days after the funeral, Peter's mother and his sister Evelyn were getting ready to go out shopping at Southgate Mall. It was his mother's first venture out of her grief. Peter was sitting on the bench in the kitchen, crouched over the red arborite nursing a coffee and a hangover. Evelyn was leaning against the doorframe to the left of the stove, waiting. Their mother emerged from her bedroom with a yellowed envelope in her hand.

"He wanted you to have this, Peter," she said to the surface of the table. "I don't know what it is. I never asked him."

After they'd left Peter opened the envelope. In it, folded into a blank sheet of paper, was a key.

Peter phoned Richard to come over right away. He asked him to pick up some rye on the way: that they had something to drink to. About half an hour later Richard pulled up in his half-ton and the two of them descended the dark stairs to the basement with the bottle and the key.

It was not what they had imagined. After the first fumbles for light and their uncertain footing on a set of steep stairs, they discovered themselves in their father's shelter. The lights had been recessed cleverly into the ceiling and shed a soft, clear patina throughout. There was nowhere to sit, so they sat on the floor. The walls, ceiling and floor were smooth, like polished steel, and had been painted in several layers of grey enamel. It was like sitting in a soft, shining grey cube. In one corner there was a small workbench, painted grey, which supported a lathe and three hand vises. Beneath this bench, behind a grey cloth, were stacked a variety of hardwoods and a small box of hand tools. There was something amorphous and unfinished secured in the lathe. To the right of this workbench was a smaller one which held an assortment of paint brushes, steel wool, boxes of sandpaper, and tiny tins of paint and varnish. Richard and Peter leaned back into the wall and passed the bottle back and forth between them. Eventually, Peter got up and climbed the stairs to lock the door from the inside. He returned to his spot and they both sat staring. They were mesmerized by what they saw in the middle of the room.

Here their father had built an eight-foot-square dais which was, like everything else, painted grey. Scattered over its surface lay a number of small glistening red shapes. There must have been about twenty-five of them. Each was different and there seemed no patterns in conventional geometry to describe accurately either each form itself nor the intricate relationship of the whole effect.

Peter stood up and approached the dais. He didn't want to disturb any of these objects, but he wanted to get close enough to examine one of them carefully. It was an elliptical oak sphere which had been stained a deep red, then varnished over and over until it shone perfectly with the deep resonance of ebony. He realized that it must have taken months to have worked this piece into its present elusive form.

Before they could abandon the sanctuary they looked everywhere for clues — a letter, some instructions, sketches, a diary — anything to make this abstraction concrete, this mystery material. Naturally, there was nothing to find. They had entered the soul of a dream and ascended from it that afternoon, up into the stark, flat February skies over the garden, reeling from the rye, but more desperately from their foolish will to reconstitute that soul as he had already done.

2.

This is where it begins. Here.

The house we grow up in is ordinary enough, what is called a "Golden Home," one of thousands built in Edmonton after the war to accommodate the baby boom. My brother Richard and I sleep down here in what our father refers to sarcastically as his masterpiece. It's really a testament to his unflagging inexpertise in carpentry. In some ways, though, it is his masterpiece. You have to know his sense of humour in these matters.

It is a stifling summer afternoon. I am eight; Richard is six. We've been weeding potatoes in the garden for two hours now, trying to please him so he will smile and give us the money we need to go swimming down at the Scona Pool. We are tired of these efforts. Instead, we creep down into the basement to play cards in our room, and we stumble onto him.

He is sitting in the corner of our room on a chair under the window. It is difficult to see him. This cool summer darkness is that thick. With the little light flickering in from the window above his head, this is like staring into the cold world beneath the potatoes out in the garden: so many rich variations and intensities of black. We can only make out that part of his head that bobs into the thin light from the window, and a flashing light that veers off the bottle that is swaying back and forth like a pendulum attached to the blue veins in his right hand. He doesn't seem to notice us yet as we pause, hushed, in the doorway. We hold each other back in our surprise. He is humming to himself. Now his head drops to his chest. All of this happens in a few seconds, but it seems endless to us, seems to happen in some infinitely slow play of light and shadow. He raises the bottle to his lips, gulps some of it down, wheezes, chuckles to himself slowly and begins to cry. Now he is laughing. Richard tugs at my tee-shirt for us to leave. Our father glances up at this soft sound. His head is lurching everywhere in this darkness. I see his face as his eyes catch the light. He is looking at us but he is not focusing. "Is it you?" he pleads, his voice suspended between a surety and a sob. "Is it you, then?"

We scuttle silently upwards in a tortuous slow-motion fear of discovery until now, near the top of these blistered grey stairs, we finally run, lurching, gasping for air, scattering into this violent sunlight of the garden.

—*John Lent*

A STUDY OF US TOGETHER
(For Niamh)

This is how I go with her,
You can study us together,
We listen to the water notes
That tremble down the ear's tunnel
We hear
The spring's first impulse to tears
That is checked by the wind's sigh,
We both get washed away
On the wild silk, moonroll of Spring tide
My sister and I.

The same anvil beaten and beaten
Until the shape is white-hot beaten,
You can carry away this fashioned thing
And it is not love
But stuff of the marrow and nerves
And of the blood.
Sometimes we are two notes
A breathspan apart — the breath of a tiny bird
With the hint of a minor tone beneath his heart,
Sometimes one is shorter,

We are sometimes both the same,
    and how easy to citizen
This world of two notes
With the faintly minor beat of wings
And a brave face put on things.

Sometimes we listen
To ghost notes making the memory tremble
And the room is washed through
Washed free of all trouble, and we
Are two small girls again, eating ice-cream,
We could be any age,
Seven, eight, nine.

— *Sara Berkeley*

HOME MOVIE NIGHTS

Ratcheted, in stills,
How thin and brown the smooth-limbed
Brothers, throwing off their casts of sand
(Bury me! I am a dead man!)
Framed in loose rolls of celluloid
And I, smaller even than the buried ones
Up there on our sitting-room wall.
I was once caught under a giant wave
They brought me out alive
(They did not save my life
For I was saved on celluloid)
But through the wave I saw them dive for me
All my life they brought me, pearl-like, from the waves
And now, well used to handling the names
Of men long gone from me and unfamiliar grown
And opening the letters home
I do most of my
Wringing of hands
Alone.

— *Sara Berkeley*

THE DUCK'S NEST

My grandson died yesterday. He was eighteen years old. We'd grown apart these last few years. He was a teenager, didn't have much time for his grandma any more. You can't blame him, really. But, you know, now that I realize I'll never see him again, I can't remember him the way he was a few days ago, when he came to visit me here at the home. No, I remember him like he was a long time ago, when Cliff and I were still on the farm. Eddy must have been five or six then. Seeding was late that year because we had an unusually wet spring. Ducks and geese seemed to be absolutely everywhere. I was planting potatoes in the garden one day, working my way towards the hedge of lilacs we had north of our house, when suddenly a duck flapped out of the tall grass, scaring the daylights out of me. Sure enough, there was a nest hidden in the long grass shaded by the lilacs, with two pale-green eggs inside. Cliff and I kept a close watch over that nest and its growing number of eggs. The next Sunday Milt and Lucy drove out from town with Eddy. He was our only grandson then so you can imagine the attention he got. When I mentioned the nest, his blue eyes lit up like little propane flames and we had to go see it right away. As we neared the lilac hedge, Eddy grew serious, crouching real low, moving forward like a hunter stalking big game. But we had picked a good time. The mother was away and the two of us just stood there looking at the full nest. Pretty soon baby ducks will come out of those eggs, I told him, but he couldn't fathom it. His eyes were wide, disbelieving, and all during lunch that day Eddy talked of nothing but the nest and the eggs. I'm sure that's all Milt and Lucy heard about for the whole next week. I kept an eye on the nest but it didn't help because on Friday I discovered that some crows or magpies had found it, destroyed it, eaten the eggs, and of course then I wished I hadn't told Eddy to come back. The next

Sunday came too soon. Almost before Milt had stopped
the old Ford in the yard, Eddy had the back door open.
Grandma, Grandma, he was yelling, let's go see the
eggs. When I told him there were no eggs left, his face
became sombre, but only for a moment. Baby ducks, he
shouted. No, Eddy, I said, walking over to him, some
magpies ate the eggs. He looked up at me. I wanna see
the nest anyway, he said. There's nothing left, Eddy,
Cliff said. Some magpies ate the eggs. But Eddy was
stubborn. I wanna see it, he kept saying, so finally I
took his hand. It's all right, I guess. I'll take you over if
you want. Eddy nodded his head and the two of us
started off towards the hedge of lilacs. After we stood
for a while looking at the bits of green eggshell and
light down strewn around around where the duck's nest had
been, Eddy turned away. Walking back through the
garden, he looked up at me and said, Grandma, I don't
like magpies. That's the face I'll remember my
grandson by.

— *William Klebeck*

TWO FISH, ONE MORNING

Late October, a cold morning,
we were driving home to the farm
from the city for the weekend:
Why do I remember this now?
Why now, with you gone, the memory
like an empty place at a family dinner?

"Let's stop at the lake and fish,"
you said; I argued for a warm bed.
But you persisted,
you often did, and we stopped there —
the pre-dawn chill, deserted shoreline,
the boats of summer now high and dry,

but for one; and we rowed out on the grey
slight chop as dawn shivered
with autumn frost. Offshore we anchored,
fumbled numb-fingered over tackle,
our backs hunched against the cold breeze.

All of this was thirty years ago:
two brothers, a whim you had that I
acceded to as brothers do. Remember
how the grey sky lightened
and the wind grew, made us huddle
on the floor of that old wooden rowboat,
our clothes unsuited to this wild notion?

We cast our chosen lures and cursed
our numb and gloveless hands
that didn't want to be here at all.
Then the first pike hit your lure so hard
it snapped you upright, almost pitched
you overboard; and you fought the fish
until it pounded on the floor beside us —
twelve pounds of fury, its sleek skin
curiously warm to my stiffened fingers.

Soon I too was fighting one, its sudden
strike setting my cold hands to work
as if fisherman's memory was energy
to fuel numb hands with fire. I too
reeled the large and vicious pike
(it could have been a deadringer for yours)
to the boat and you reached into the chill
water, hauled the fish in by the leader.

And we leaned against the sides,
kindled with excitement and laughter,
and stared at the two largest pike
we'd ever taken from these waters.
We fished no more that morning.

Nor ever again. It was the last time
we fished together, though I have since

dreamed many trips we should have taken,
as our lives pulled us separate ways.

But now, this sudden retrieval, this double
barb of memory: that day, when for a time
we were as one — a single fisherman,
hooked, sinew and bone, to a single fish —
one cold morning in October when
for a time there was no time at all
and we were either nothing or everything,
two brothers crazed with the wisdom of fools.

— *Glen Sorestad*

BURNING MY FATHER'S CLOTHES

Burning my father's clothes
in a metal drum behind the house,
my mother afraid to give them away,
afraid to see them walking by on a stranger
The oily black smoke coils
up through the trees
and out across the snow-covered hills

Here is the coat I remember
from the trip we took
to somewhere
I am lying in the back seat,
my mother asleep in the passenger side
Headlights flashing in his face,
he drives all night like this
in the silence of our sleeping
The world was safe and dark and intimate
His solitude with the white lines,
the flat prairie, the eyes of deer
sparkling in the ditches
and the dull glow of some city

still an hour's drive away
Waking up to see him there I remember
even the smell of this coat, tobacco,
these deep closets of memory

Burning my father's clothes
The only child
standing in the snow and smoke and silence
I pile the shirts and jackets on
and the orange flames strike at them
over and over
The smoke billows up
and everything is given to the sky,
unwilling and stubborn,
ashes settling on the shoulders
of my own coat

The smoke sweeps through the trees
and up into the hills we worked together,
across the fence we built
And there is not a bird in this thicket,
no rabbits, or mice pushing through the new snow
Nothing moves or grows or mourns
for anything lost here
Only the smoke of my father's clothes,
spiralling up,
then falling in the cold air . . .

the face of my mother
anxious
hovering in the window

— *Andrew Wreggitt*

OUR CAREER IN LOVE

My daughter dreamed I was in a large room, and my eyes were turned away from her as though I were embarrassed or frightened of her. She showed me her hands, pale and barely visible in the dim room. I was paralyzed unable to move; my body, made out of papier-mâché, wept in the corner. I spoke in tongues rambling at her, blaming my insanity on something heavy and meaningless. She said she cried then and her tears exploded on contact with her skin. I want to wake up and tell her that everything is OK. I can feel my mouth move but nothing comes out. I cannot lie to my daughter. It is my dream she remembers.

Love makes us bend in strange places our bodies more opaque than usual. The rooms frighten us even though they are just places we leave our bodies in. Our thoughts controlled by the chemistry of some unnameable material. We are watchful of ourselves; our lives the process of thoughts unravelling. Our terror the product of a commitment to feelings. I sleep on the right side of the bed. You bend your legs in the night and call out. I turn to touch you with a hand as small as our place in the world. Soon you will wake from this dream and I will go check on Breanne.

My daughter told me about her dream, without waking. And I listened my own mouth breaking into a smile.

— *Robert Hilles*

ALASKA HIGHWAY, 1965

The call, coming as it did, in the middle
of the night,
a sudden voice outside our tent,
a man's voice that seemed to rise
sharply out of this dream we were sharing,
the slapping of the creek,

       the moon flat through the canvas,
                permeable
Coming as it did, with a nervous
shuffling of boots,
             opening
into the voices of other men murmuring by a campfire,
collecting flashlights, choosing partners

The little girl gone since late afternoon

A woman putting on coffee,
another clutching a small sweater
and looking up into the blackness,
as if the veiled dark could be parted by force
of will,
by the long white bone of her longing
My own mother shutting me into the tent
with the force of her voice   thrown
across the gravel from the campfire
nervous and quick

I heard the calling of men far off in the trees
and the solemn, hushed moving of others
just beyond the canvas,
in the wide-awake dark
Thinking of the little girl in the trees,
closed up like a pine cone,
the moon falling behind the mountain, extinguished,
the two of us caught in the same memory,
its slow unfolding

The call, coming as it did, out of nothing,
disembodied and urgent
when she heard it too,
her name suddenly there beside her

The way we share this even now,
twenty-three years later, grown up
and found
Even in the trees off the highway,

low sky of branches by the Liard River
where that voice still lives in a descending
                                              pattern
                            of sound waves
The small warm spot where the child lay down
and gave up her fear for a moment,
still warm with that presence
Something that is set in motion
and does not stop,
                    the call
coming as it did

How we were picked up and held, both of us,
in those last few black moments
before dawn, by our relieved
and haunted mothers,
as the searchers slept uneasily
in the cold
absence of the moon

— Andrew Wreggitt

IT'S A HARD COW

By day my father mined guano from the bat caves of southern New Mexico. By night he'd sit with my brother Thomas and me near him, telling stories of the old country, of castles and idiot princes, of flawless white horses pulling aged queens through mountain villages on giant-wheeled beds. He'd carve small human figures out of our firewood as he talked, or sing songs of his childhood, softly playing the violin. With those same fine-boned fingers, for six days out of seven, he'd load a wagon with droppings to be hauled out of the subterranean depths to the desert above.

Our house was filled with the rock samples he'd brought home and skeletons of baby bats, picked clean by guano beetles within minutes of losing their hold and falling from their mother's sides to the floor hundreds of feet beneath them. He would come home with yet another set of small bones in his pocket and describe to us the sight of the bats sleeping, glistening with winter dew, sometimes frost, hundreds of thousands of tiny jewels in the mine's half light and how, as they trembled, the moisture that had condensed on their fur fell like a light spring rain on the miners below.

At times I'd walk down after school to meet my father and, when he'd finished work, we'd sit together outside the largest cave and wait for the light to fade. He'd slowly roll a cigarette and smoke it, whispering to me about his day as I sat listening for the bats to waken. The noise of their wings would begin as far-off thunder, seeming to get closer as it got louder, and I'd look to the sky for dark clouds and always be surprised when there were none. Then the sound of their squeaking would rise above everything else, gaining volume, getting more frenzied, and just as I'd feel the push of warm, damp air against my face they'd explode from the cave mouth in a giant spiral and it would be dark for a moment before they scattered in all directions to feed.

Each time I watched, my father's hand would be on my shoulder, calming my excitement and fear. To stop my shaking he would speak in a slow and even voice as though I were not afraid. He'd talk about the bats and make zipping noises between his teeth to describe the sound of their wings as they plummeted from the sky each morning to the caves and their sleep. I would imagine them falling like stones, their bellies heavy with insects, banking at the last possible moment, inches above the desert ground, to their roosts in the cave below. As we walked home I would be safe beside him, quiet with the wonder of it all.

As much as my father's voice filled our home, and my childhood, it was offset by my mother's silence. The house seemed to empty with him as he left in the morning, and her sounds, those coming from the kitchen or the small noises of someone working in another part of the house, could not fill it back up. She spoke to her sons only if necessary, instructions for school, or practical matters. She had never forgiven my father for wanting to leave their home, the warmth of family and friends and, with it, the job he'd been offered teaching at the university there. Sometimes, now, she spoke barely a word to him for days on end, waging a constant, silent battle that seemed to give her strength as he grew more bewildered by it.

They'd boarded a ship for America on a cloudless spring day — he, flushed with the promise of a better teaching position in Albuquerque, and she six months pregnant with me and terrified that this baby might be stillborn like their first. My father had done his best to allay this fear, walking arm in arm with her on deck, marvelling at what sea life could be glimpsed, talking excitedly about his hopes for their new home.

When they'd landed he'd been awed by the clamour and size of New York and had wanted to sightsee, but she had pursed her lips and insisted they buy their train tickets immediately. By nightfall they were travelling again.

That summer, while trying to escape the heat of New Mexico in a whitewashed cabin near the foothills of the Sandia Mountains, they'd had their first child and learned that my father's command of English was not sufficient to land him the position he'd come for. By autumn, we'd moved for a job he'd taken in the guano mines two hundred miles to the south and she'd discovered the full power of her silence, seeing my father beg for forgiveness and finally weep. She just jammed my mouth to her breast in answer and refused to even look his way.

He would not, however, give in and go back to their homeland; he worked hard every day, waiting for another chance to teach, and came home each evening to his family to study his new language.

A few years later, not long after Thomas was born, my father received word that his job at the university had been denied a third and final time. My mother reacted to the news with a renewed bitterness that swamped the household; it affected everyone, and Thomas cried constantly.

My father tried to soften her anger. He rocked Thomas in his arms and sang to them both. He worked longer hours for extra pay and brought home gifts to please his wife. She didn't change.

I remember him coming home from the mine, stealing up behind her and kissing the back of her neck. Without looking up from her sewing she spoke to him for the first time in days.

"Go have a bath Joseph, you smell like shit."

Then one afternoon I heard the sound of sirens over the drone of the schoolteacher's voice but thought nothing of it until Thomas and I walked home and found a neighbour lady waiting for us instead of our mother. The woman was washing dishes when we arrived.

"She's gone to see about your father," she explained. Her hands were red and dripping and she pulled at some loose threads in her dress as she spoke.

The miners had been blasting an access tunnel to a new cave when my father and a few others, shovelling a large valley out of the guano, looked up after one of the explosions as hundreds of years of powdered bat shit, fifty feet deep, shifted and slid down on top of them before most had a chance to draw a breath. Two survived by running and clawing their way close enough to the surface and having luck enough to be found in the panic that followed. One man died from the blade of a shovel as his fellow workers dug furiously to rescue him.

My father was buried for nearly ten minutes, surviving only because he'd fallen in a sitting position. He'd pushed his back against the slide as it moved over him, trapping just enough air in the hollow of his chest and stomach to scream into, defenseless as the beetles feasted on the exposed skin of his face and neck. His arms were pinned in front of him, his head bowed and held motionless. He continued to shriek, horrified by the pain and his helplessness until the insects were biting inside his mouth and he had to crack their bodies between his teeth and spit them out before he sealed his lips against them and passed out.

Two weeks later Thomas and I waited outside the hospital entrance and watched as he stepped out the door with my mother. He looked so thin, his face and hands bruised and scarred enough to startle us.

They'd had to move him to a large, well-lit room in the hospital, leaving the door and windows continuously open. Even then he was frightened, and when he refused to get into the taxi we had waiting, we all walked the few miles home in silence, watching my father's body jerk periodically as though from electric shock. He constantly wiped his mouth and eyes with both hands.

At home, from then on, he slept in the living room with all the lights on. Each night he would wake Thomas and I with his shrieks and I would have to cover my brother's ears and hold him until he stopped trembling and went back to sleep.

During the day my father spent most of his time outside. He would escape the confinement of the house by walking — through the streets of town, out into the desert, his arms almost always in motion, flailing the air around his head. Often he'd stop and for no apparent reason stand as though rooted to the ground, his eyes vacant, his head snapping sideways from the spasms that jolted his body, the Adam's apple on his skinny neck bobbing as he swallowed. He looked like a scarecrow and I heard men call him that.

One evening, though I tried hard to move him, he stood for so long in one place that he startled me when he finally woke up from his trance. He yelled when he realized where he was, frightened that he might be caught in the oncoming darkness, and ran home with me trying to keep up.

Sometimes if the sky was perfectly clear he would stand in our front yard with his head tipped back, his mouth wide open to the heavens like a nestling waiting to be fed. Strangely enough, this was the only time he seemed calm; the agitation in his body would gradually disappear and with one final shudder, like some ancient steam-driven machine, he would be still. If even one small cloud appeared in the sky above him he'd snap his mouth shut and the twitching would start again.

"He'd drown if it'd rain," the woman from next door was telling my mother. "And the way he has the children carrying on. My oldest two don't get a chance to sleep anymore, the noise he makes at night. Isn't there something you can do for him?"

In the days following my father's accident, one by one the neighbours had trickled by the house with cards and small gifts, some genuinely concerned, others merely curious after hearing of his odd behaviour. It was almost like a funeral viewing; large red-faced men sat staring, uncomfortable and silent beside my mother. Frail old women, looking sorrowful in Sunday dresses, craned their necks to see, and when his head jerked they gasped as if the dead had moved.

As time passed and the novelty wore off, we were left more to ourselves. My father gained back some of his strength and started his walks, but it wasn't long before the people in town began to voice their disapproval. Soon, even old friends began to visit less frequently, or not at all, and the first of many neighbours arrived with shuffling feet and apologetic explanations. A man had been sent to make an offer for our house and suggest that we move to a place "less upsetting" to my father. My mother was shocked and it showed the next day.

As I was coming home from school I could see my father standing in the yard again, his face to the sky. Suddenly she was there beside him, struggling, trying to pull him inside. It was the first time I had ever heard her shout. I ran to the house and peeked in past the open door. My father was sitting in the kithen. My mother stood in front of him, shaking him roughly by the shoulders, her face inches from his.

"Damn you Joseph, come back to us. You're ruining our life here with this stupidity of yours. Quit it!"

He stammered a few words, then stopped to brush something imaginary from his eyes. He looked puzzled, as though uncertain whether she had actually spoken. She screamed, balling her fists, and struck him hard on both sides of the head. My father jumped up, utterly confused now, and backed off a few steps, touching one ear where she'd hit him. She gasped, stunned for a second by what she'd done, then raised her hands in the air, above her shoulders, as if to deny that she'd touched him. She stepped back so quickly that one foot twisted out of its shoe and she fell back into a chair behind her and started to sob. My father stood watching for a moment, then reached for her shoulder. As she pushed his hand away she saw me, and was suddenly transformed — her back straight, her dry cheeks denying there had ever been tears. I stared, amazed by what I'd seen, until her face took on such a look of severity that I ran to hide.

It was dark when I returned. Light shone out of every window, making our house look bigger than the others on the street. I crept up and looked in again. My father was sitting in the living room now, staring straight ahead while my mother jotted numbers on a piece of paper at the kitchen table. A man who lived a few doors down the street sat there with her. She looked up as I walked in, but I couldn't read the expression on her face. My father turned his head. He'd been watching Thomas, asleep on the couch. He shifted to make room for me and I slipped in beside him.

Behind us, over the sound of a scraping chair, my mother spoke as the neighbour prepeared to leave. I turned to watch.

"I think five thousand above your last offer would still be fair and then you'll be rid of us. That's really what you want, isn't it?" The man shifted uneasily, not looking at anyone, playing with the brim of his hat.

"Well ma'am, I think they might agree to that. I'll do my best." He looked anxious to leave and nodded his head a number of times goodbye. No one returned his gesture, and as he backed out of the house my mother closed the door.

A week later she had almost everything either packed or sold. I could hear her downstairs, sorting through our things long after I'd gone to bed each night. I assumed she was taking us back to her home in Europe, the ordeal for her finally over. But the truth was she couldn't have faced a life there with my father in such a state. She'd made plans for us to go to Canada to stay with my father's brother. He'd recently separated from his wife and lived with his only son, a boy my age. We could help out on their farm.

"We'll all be better off this way, believe me." She spoke firmly to my father as if to end any further discussion of the subject. He didn't reply.

When he stepped on the train he was already shaking and my hand slipped out of his because of the sweat in his palm. We found seats facing one another and I watched him slump beside my mother muttering about the closeness of the air and the confinement of the railway car.

As the train began to move, and its noises grew louder, his nervousness increased. Because of that I asked to sit with him and my mother and I exchanged places. I could see he was trying to calm himself, but the whites of his eyes began to show at times as if he'd lost control of them. He leaned close, his arm around my shoulders, and began to whisper a story I'd heard many times — one that I'd always loved, but he got it all wrong this time, confusing it with another.

At one point he fell silent for so long that I thought he was asleep. When I tried to move, however, his grip tightened so much that his fingernails dug into my skin. A wheezing sound came from his mouth, his sweat soaked my shirt and I was frightened. I tried with all my strength to pull away but his weight trapped me where I sat. He continued.

"And we came upon the skeletons of giant bears, their rib cages the size of rooms, some still in the strange positions they had died in. The broken bones of other animals were scattered among them." His voice had lost its softness and he moved away from me, closer to the window. His hands gestured wildly as he spoke.

"Bones covered the valley as far as we could see. The birds were long gone, but they had done their job well. A white desert it was, and we found the brutes' caves but we did not go in."

By Albuquerque he lay cowering on the seat, his head on my lap, and I tried not to look afraid as the other passengers stared at us. My mother acted as though she barely noticed, moving only to pinch his nose as she dropped a pill into his mouth, and then once to drag her feet out of the way as my father rolled onto the floor between us questioning why the train wouldn't stop.

Her answer was to stare out the window, turning only to nod when the conductor asked permission to move my father to the baggage car, which was roomier and had open windows. A short while later his hands were pried from the bottom of the seat by two men, and he was carried off screaming and flailing at them.

We sat for hours listening to my father's cries over the noise of the train until Thomas couldn't bear it any longer. "Help him, please!" he sobbed to a family across the aisle.

Only then did my mother move — turning Thomas around, slapping his face sharply as she pulled him back into his seat. He stopped crying, but sat wild-eyed, his breath coming too quickly, and to settle him down she had him breathe into a paper bag she'd brought food in. She looked almost ready to cry herself as she gathered Thomas into her arms, but just then the conductor sat down to talk to her. I heard her whisper an apology and then give instructions to have my father bound and gagged rather than put us off the train.

It was just outside of Denver when she dozed off, and I grabbed Thomas' arm and we ran to the back of the train and found our father lying in a heap on the mailbags, bleeding from the scratches he'd given his face.

I hid the rag they had gagged him with and he was quieter with us there, even sleeping during the day. We'd comfort him when he woke up unsure of where he was. We slept there with him, his shoulders our pillow, waking regularly as spasms shook his body. A few times each day he seemed almost well again and we pretended to search for his violin in our luggage. I knew it had been sold. He laughed and said he couldn't play it anyway, holding out his bound hands to me.

The conductor would stop by with food from my mother or something he'd cadged from the kitchen. With a wink at Thomas and me he'd switch on the lights at night. He apologized and explained why it wasn't possible when Thomas asked him to untie our father. But he sat for hours and told railway stories, pausing dramatically when he expected us to laugh. He shook his head and made clucking sounds with his tongue when we explained about the accident. He assured my mother of our safety and she did not intrude.

The next time we saw her was days later, just across the Saskatchewan border. As the train was slowing she walked calmly into the baggage car and started to fuss with our clothes and smooth our hair. When we had come to a stop we helped our father to his feet and looked out onto a small, windy town whose new cars and painted houses stuck out abruptly from the natural flatness around them.

Uncle Harold was a tall man, much larger than my father and younger looking, harder. He stood on the platform with his big hands moving, smoothing the creases on his weathered neck. It was early morning, already hot, and we shaded our eyes from the sun. His jaw worked and he spit a stream of tobacco juice as we walked toward him. Kurt stood behind a few paces, almost hidden, and his father motioned impatiently for him. They wore matching shirts and jeans, one a miniature version of the other. Harold extended his hand as if by habit, glanced briefly at his brother, and ignored Thomas and me. He was looking at my mother, his eyes travelling up and down her body. When he finally dropped his hand and spoke, he was still watching her.

"Well Joseph, after all these years I finally get to meet your family." What accent he might have had was almost gone. I'd find out later he was proud of this. "But things haven't changed much if I have to spend my time looking after you." My father's hands were still tied and he held them in front of his face. Harold grabbed the rope and jerked it sharply, the way I'd later see him discipline a stubborn horse. He jabbed his finger in the direction of the car and I hated him instantly. He took my mother by the arm and they walked in front, with Kurt ambling after them, hands jammed in the pockets of his jeans. Thomas and I followed, on either side of my father.

When we reached the car we waited while Harold paused and talked to my mother. When he finally unlocked the back door, my father shook his head, still shielding his face. He ducked a bit, like a boxer might. Harold squinted at him, then shrugged and opened the front door for my mother. As he walked back around the rear of the car he stopped. He spoke to no one in particular.

"He's hardly what you'd call a man anymore, is he?" He paused then looked at my father. "You were always soft, Joseph. That's why father sent you to study and me to work. Look at you now, you're no good to anyone. Why didn't you just stick with teaching school?" He spit again and got in the car.

"Kurt, walk these people to the farm if they don't want to ride." He spoke over his shoulder through the open window, gunned the engine, and was gone.

I untied my father's hands and we started to walk. We were well outside of town when Kurt, who until then had been silent, watching my father, mumbled something I didn't hear the first time, so he spoke again.

"It's a hard cow," he said, shaking his head as though resigned to believe what he was saying. Thomas and I looked at each other, puzzled, but we were to find out many times in the coming years what he meant. It was his father's favourite saying. Whenever there was a disagreement, or something unpleasant to be done, if we were sick, or balked at going to school or doing some piece of farm work, Harold would end the conversation with what was always his final word on the subject.

"It's a hard cow to fuck, boys, but we need that calf." Sometimes he'd laugh and walk away but other times he'd shout it and hit us hard enough that his ring cut into the back of our heads. It was Harold's philosophy in life and he was proud of its strength and simplicity. Consequently, Thomas and I tried to stay out of his way. He just didn't like us.

He loved his son, though. He used a different tone of voice when talking to him, softer, not like his orders to us, and I don't think he ever raised a hand to him. Kurt never said much but he once told me that things had been different when his mother had been there. His father was quieter now and a bond had grown between them after the separation. They spent a lot of time together at their house in town, the work on the farm mostly taken care of by our family and hired help. Harold would come by to leave orders or to pass time drinking coffee with my mother.

While she was content to busy herself around the house, my father liked the feeling the prairie gave him and would spend hours in the fields. He'd settled into the life of the farm fairly well and had calmed considerably when one day, as he and I were walking by a shed near the hay meadow at the far end of the yard, we came upon my mother and Harold lying together in the grass. My mother saw us first and started running toward the house, buttoning her dress as she went. Harold stayed where he was, not hurrying as we came toward him. Then, leaning back, hands behind his head, he looked up at us with this smirk on his face. He slowly crossed his legs.

An animal-like whine came from my father. His body heaved violently as he turned, and he fell, but picked himself up again and ran into the shed. I don't know what he went in to get, but he came out with a can of gasoline. He pushed me out of the way with more strength than I'd seen him use in months. His mouth opened and closed mechanically and the veins in his head seemed ready to burst as he stumbled the few yards and poured the whole thing onto Harold's lap. When he lit the match he was shaking so badly I thought it would go out.

I was shouting, "Drop it! Drop it!" to myself, and then out loud, but finally it was his arm that dropped, limply to his side, and he just turned and walked. Neither of them had made a sound until Harold laughed.

I stood beside my father in the house as my mother loaded some things into Harold's car and they drove off. Again, he said nothing. I wanted him to yell, to rage, to pull down a shotgun and shoot out the windows, anything, but all he did was stare out at the prairie, his body jerking from the same small spasms as before.

Hours later I was still there with him, waiting. When he finally turned toward me he was as tired as I'd ever seen him. I knew from the way he looked at me he was asking me to understand. But I didn't. I wanted an explanation and all he could do was shrug his shoulders and shake his head.

That was it. That was his answer, and I just couldn't face it, or the silence, and I walked out on him, back to the meadow. The can was still there in the grass and I stomped it into the earth until I had to cough for air, then stood on it, afraid a snicker might come from it that my head knew could not be there. I heard Harold's laugh again as I caught my breath, and I picked up that flattened piece of tin and threw it as far away from me as I could. When I got back to the house my father hadn't moved.

Over the years it got so that a week couldn't pass without hearing Harold's car come up the lane. Winter was the only exception, when he'd spend time in some warmer climate with my mother. More and more, the other seasons would find him looking over his farm, shouting at his workers or walking his fields, damning the weeds, or the drought, or the rust on his crop. You couldn't get away from his bellowing except when my father was around. Then, in an instant, his face would take on the same smug expression he'd worn the day my father stood over him in the grass.

I believe that sometimes he drove out just to torment my father with that look, and he'd laugh his same laugh when my father turned away. As time passed both Thomas and I began to fear him less as he gave us reason to hate him more, but all we could do was keep each other awake at night cursing him, pretending that a day was possible, sometime in the future, when he would get his due.

Then, one summer evening when we were away, Harold came by the farm. He'd been buying drinks all afternoon for a bunch of strangers half his age, and to keep it all going asked if they wanted some excitement.

He'd picked up Kurt on the way there and he told him to round up the first three horses he could catch. When he had they led them behind their trucks to a pasture in the south where the tableland dropped off into a valley.

They tied about fifty feet of rope around the horses' necks, the other ends to their bumpers, and with shouts and rifle shots and by hazing the horses with their jackets they finally forced them off the edge, laughing at the terrified animals, laying bets which would be the first to scramble back up again.

The mare that my father had helped me buy that spring was having trouble making it up the slope. She kept slipping on a section of gravel, and when they finally used a truck to pull her to the top, the noose was jammed so tightly around her neck she couldn't breathe.

She kicked Kurt, who was sent to free her, and broke four of his ribs. Then, as she lay gasping on the ground, Harold rushed up and killed her with an axe.

When I found her, my father had to hold me down where he'd tackled me beside our old truck. I was trying to get to town to burn Harold's house to the ground.

I had my dream that night for the first time and it's kept coming back to me, getting clearer, somehow making me stronger. They come for Harold out of the morning grey at full gallop, swords rattling aginst their saddles. They've surprised him in bed, he's not been careful, and so he's running naked across the grass. There are six terrible whitewashed horses, paint caked on their flanks, red circles around wild eyes, matching bright red lipstick on their foaming mouths. Their breathing comes fast and hard, visible in the cold. Six women riders, their bodies as white as their mounts, their lips the same red, turf flying over their shoulders as they chase him down. Before he can fall they throw ropes of braided hair over him and as they spur their animals in different directions, he's screaming . . .

This afternoon, Thomas and I waited for Kurt to get home from school. He was in the new car Harold had given him and when the electric garage door opened and he parked, we followed him with a shotgun and a roll of strong wire. Thomas held the gun while I ordered Kurt to take off his clothes and lie face-down on the concrete at the rear of the car. I closed the door.

When I tied his arms and feet together behind him he was already weeping and begging for mercy, so I tried to explain that it was nothing personal, this little bit of fun we were about to have. It was for his father's education. I thought I had it all figured.

I wired his legs to the back bumper, and rigged another wire around his neck to the bottom of the garage door. Then I blindfolded him and stuffed a rag in his mouth. I told him it wouldn't be right for him to see what was going to happen when Harold got home. But before we left I jammed a piece of wood in the garage door track so that, at most, the door would move a couple of inches, just enough for things to get snug enough to make our point. Then we left. I dropped Thomas off at the farm and drove away.

I imagine Harold driving up and watching the door jam, then shouting, mad as hell at yet another hard cow, trying it again and again. Then he's yelling louder and hammering on it, finally puffing to the side door to find what thing had dared cross him. I want him to come after me when he understands. I don't know what I'll do but I know I want it that way.

Now it's me looking out onto the prairie, but from the windows of this truck. The dried up alkaline sloughs I'm passing look like snow patches in the spring. Nothing moves but the sun, adding subtle colour to the salt flats as it sets.

And then I'm not watching anymore. I'm slowing down and finally stopped, not believing, then turning back, panicked and driving crazy, almost sick from shouting at myself — for such stupidity, for even hoping to imagine this might have won us something, for not realizing that the sonofabitch might get mad enough to just jump out of his car and use all that anger of his to wrench open the door with his bare hands.

— *Terry Jordan*

Ω

Women walk to the sea. Prosperous and obedient.
Their sweet indignity. Happy among stones.

Everything is island. Symbol of failure and hope.
Violence, they say, as if the word could ruin them.

Their prayer. A fish strangling on air. A drowned man.
Love or die. Or walk among gulls. The sea greets you.

Among stones. Caress yourself. The only thing is you.
This is the oldest song.

— Patrick Lane

METAMORPHOSIS

something is happening
to this girl.

she stands on one leg
on the third block
of her hopscotch game,
lifts herself forward
to the next double squares,
and, as she jumps,
something changes.

her straight child's body
curls slowly in the air,
the legs that assert themselves
apart on the squares
curve in calf and thigh,
angles become arches;
her arms pumping slowly
to her sides adjust
to a new centre of gravity,
the beginnings of breasts
push at her sweater,
her braids have come undone
and her hair flies loose around her.

behind her
the schoolhouse blurs,
becomes insubstantial
and meaningless,

and the boys in the playground
move toward her,
something sure and sinister
in their languid circling.

slowly she picks up the beanbag.
when she straightens,
her face gathers
the bewildered awareness
of the body's betrayal,
the unfamiliar feel
of the child's toy
in her woman's hand.

— *Leona Gom*

"Natalia! Natalia! Have you been running again? You *know* what can happen if you run too fast. Your heart will jump out of your chest!" My mother's voice is reproachful as she unties the hemp cord holding the boiler lid tight to keep the water from sloshing out onto the hot black soil.

"Nu! It's just what I expected. Half the water is gone. You've been running again. It spilled on the road. It's not proper for a girl your age to run. You're in your thirteenth summer already! You could have broken the wagon wheels."

Another time I might have told her the truth: I wasn't running, not this time, even if my breath came in painful gasps and my limbs trembled. I wasn't running. "Mr. Sander's dog chased me," I lie. Let her think I've been running. Just blame it on the dog. That's safe; my mother hates dogs.

So she dips the water out with two-gallon pails and carries it into the pantry to pour into yet another large enamel vessel. It will stay cool a long time, for its bone-chilling coldness hasn't gone away yet, in spite of being out in the bone-melting heat for nearly half an hour. She mutters her usual complaints about decent Old Country people and the uncivilized habits of the young, no doubt encouraged by new Canadian lack of respect and ignorance of propriety. And what would King George's lovely wife, Elizabeth, named after Elizabeth of Austria, think of my deportment? She clucks like a broody hen who's forgotten where she laid her eggs.

In the cooler darker world inside the house I let the fear out and it invades my cells and the air in my bedroom and the whole world seems to tremble with me. The hammers pounding inside my chest are louder now and there seem to be so many of them, hurting me, taking the air from my lungs. The danger has dissipated in action, but the fear is raging a delayed battle inside me.

There's no one to tell about what happened. You don't tell your mother, who may cause a scene, disturb the serenity the villagers pretend exists here. The news would drift with the wind, permeate the corners of every house. People would know what you'd rather have kept a secret. "She enticed them," people would say. Even the women. Forgetting other years, they'd just adjust the straps of their embroidered white aprons with an air of 'I told you so' and 'Still waters run deep.' You could become a *fallen woman*.

So you just go into the coolness of the clay-and-wattle plastered house built in the old Galician peasant style and sit on your bed in the dimmest place there is and try not to die.

* * *

It's 1944. Nothing is right, even though an important war is happening. The young men have gone away, some across the ocean, and nobody wants to think about how some of them won't be coming back. Mrs. Cherevyk next door has to think about it. She already knows her brother Peter is dead. Peter didn't want to go, but they made him go anyway and overseas, too, because everyone has to fight for freedom. Still, you wish he didn't have to go. You hide in whatever dim place there is when something awful happens. Sometimes you hid inside your own mind. Like you did when Peter died on a beach somewhere, like when today happened. You pretend. If disturbed by anyone while hiding, you pretend to be reading, which your mother thinks is the same as studying. You pretend to be praying, which is virtuous and makes you look peaceful.

But inside, you remember it over and over. How something almost happened to you, something you've heard men in front of the pool hall talk about in vague snickering half-sentences which left you with a taste of decay. You think maybe the real part of you is gone and might never return. Maybe this is all you'll ever be again, this thing whose heart pounds in disorder while you watch all around you, watch for the next time. The danger is out of sight for now, but your body is a live wire quivering with a force you don't know how to neutralize.

* * *

It's a July afternoon when the earth is drying beneath a sea of air pressing hot against the land, shimmering, as I pull the little wagon along the dusty back road. Horse-drawn wagons use this road mostly, and people going on foot. Sometimes a model-T Ford chugs by, the English sheep farmers going to the bank in a bigger town. There are rumours they carry revolvers to protect their money, and take a different road each time to fool the rest of us who are Ukrainians, who might rob them because we're too lazy to work. They've never been robbed yet. Maybe Ukrainians are too lazy to kill for money. I don't know.

But there's nothing on the road today, not even the usual garter snakes making zig-zags in the dust. To the south of the road are two cemeteries side by side and a few large plots of land, each two acres or more, where people live a little removed from the main part of the village.

From this road which is a little higher than the streets of the village, I can see whatever happens there. On a little rise is the Catholic Hall. Once a week a man comes from another town to show movies in the hall, with a P.A. system from which he broadcasts wartime songs, a sort of announcement he's arrived. On movie evenings, I sit on the verge of the road, my bare legs green from the rain-fat grass and clover growing there lush as though there'd never been a drought. I listen to the tinny music which never changes from week to week, and always, without fail, there's Vera Lynn singing "White Cliffs of Dover" from the loudspeaker in the back of the movie-man's pickup truck, her voice a cry for the dead.

On this day there's little to show the village is alive, no movement; it's a painting overlaid with a silvery shimmer of heat waves. A faint chugging starts up somewhere near the main street. It sounds like a stationary engine, the heat waves muffling the sound of its noisy heart.

I step carefully in the dust fine as black face-powder, trying to keep my only pair of shoes clean. But the dust rises in tiny puffs as I walk against the heat. Another sound, humming louder with every second, then becoming a thunking rattle. A farm truck, faded red, shudders lazily along the gravel highway parallel to the line-road but a few hundred yards away. It slides into the distance, pushed along by the cloud of beige dust it has raised, until it and the dust are lost behind trees where the highway and the back road merge into a 'Y'.

The town well is a half-mile up the highway from this fork. I've been going down this road since I was ten, bringing drinking water and cooking water from the tested well. I do this every few days all summer. The road seems short usually, but today the heat makes it endless. Even with a wide-brimmed straw hat shading my head and shoulders, the sun is painful against my body.

The well is in the town pasture where the villagers keep their milk cows from spring until fall. There's a gravel pit near the well. My father sometimes gets a little gravel here for the chickens. Coming near the pasture gate, I see a team of horses in the shallow pit, only their heads visible. I've heard the town council is making cement sidewalks on the main streets to replace the raised wooden boardwalks. I'm sorry the boardwalks will be gone for now there'll be nowhere to sit along the street and watch the farmers coming in to shop late Saturday evenings. The men in the pit must be hauling gravel to make the cement walks.

Carefully, trying not to be seen, I peek over the edge of the pit. Two boys from my school are shovelling gravel into a wagonbox. One is a kid they call Joe Louis at school. His real name is Frederick. But he's called Joe Louis, or just Louis, because of his fierce two-fisted assaults on *anything* smaller than himself. The bigger boys tolerate him as one tolerates an unpleasant but non-fatal disease. He doesn't bother the big kids. The girls call him Fat Fred behind his back, but the drayman's daughter, whose father is darn near the biggest man on earth, says it all the time and Fat Fred just turns purple each time and doesn't say a word.

The other boy is Paul Durnay. Paul displays his genitals in the classroom when the teacher's out or busy at the blackboard. He unbuttons his fly under his desk, whispering 'Look, Jeannie,' or 'See this, Olga?' Nobody looks anymore; everyone knows what 'look at this' means when Paul says it. You'd think he'd catch on and quit, but he still does it.

I wish they weren't there, that it could be someone else in the pit, loading gravel. I think about turning around and going back home very, very quietly, staying on the smooth grassy ground until I'm back on the highway, but I don't dare come home without water. My mother would ask questions I wouldn't know how to answer. Could I say, "There were boys at the gravel pit and I got scared"? I can imagine her answering scornfully, "Nu, and have you never seen a boy before?" How could I tell her about Paul exposing himself in school, about Fat Frederick/Joe Louis pounding me since I first started school? If I did, it would happen more than ever, with the older kids taunting me about tattling again. Besides the water pails in the pantry are almost empty.

The only solution is to be sneaky and clever, to do everything quietly and carefully so they won't hear me from the bottom of the pit. Maybe the noise of shovels scooping gravel, the snorts of the horses, the jangling of the harnesses would drown out the sound of the hand-pump, the splash of water. I take off the boiler lid and set it carefully on the hot surface of the ground near the well. The piece of white cotton covering the mouth of the boiler is dusty now, but I can't shake it clean. The flare of a whiter light could attract their notice.

The pump squeaks a little as I pump for a lifetime. Then at last the water gushes into the pail I've hung over the pump-hook. Maybe I can fill the boiler and be gone before they notice me.

The water lies deep, deep. The old people say this is why the water is pure in spite of being in a pasture. The gravel, they say, strains out all the dirty stuff. All I know, the water is crystal and too cold to drink as it comes out of the spout. The boiler is half-full when I notice the silence.

There's no sound of shovels scraping gravel, no snorts from the horses. I stand very still. Then I hear pebbles rolling down the sides of the pit, the crunch of boots against gravel, a sound louder than the sudden roaring in my ears. A chuckle from below the top edges of the pit.

Before I can think what to do, they're standing on the level ground, looking at me in a way I don't like, whispering together only fifty feet from where I hesitate, trying to remember what to do, trying to remember what I did other times when I was alone and a boy was not.

"Nataliaaa!"

They stand quietly together a long moment, whispering, then step away from each other. They walk toward me with their bodies a little hunched over, and I think of gorillas I once saw in a Henry Aldrich movie. Their arms are sweaty parentheses enclosing whatever statement their half-crouched bodies are making. As they come closer with incredible slowness, I see their eyes gleaming narrow like oil-filmed water you sometimes see lying in wheel-ruts.

"Nataaa-liiia! Naaa-taaaa-lia!"

The voices creep toward me slowly as the movement of a minute-hand.

You can't scream here, in this empty space where no one can hear you, where even the cows have retreated to the coolness under the willows a little way across the bog.

The fingers at the ends of the four gorilla-arms flex and extend, preparing, preparing. The boots take small steps toward you. Closer. And closer.

The books you read tell you about romance, forever-love. They don't say what you should do in times like this. You only know something must happen, that what you do may or may not decide what will happen.

Your brain feels numb. It waits for a message to come, a message it can send to your limbs which feel only the pins-and-needles of panic. At last something comes from the edge of a consciousness which can't be your own; the orders it gives you are too swift, too vicious to have come from your own self.

A weapon! A weapon! The thought flashes into your brain and your eyes are no longer frozen as they search the scorched earth within the range of your vision. It's the first time you've considered the word 'weapon.' Before this, sticks were sticks, and stones were stones. Nothing had ever been a 'weapon.' Now there is a possibility of weapons.

You look for a stick nearby, maybe within reach of your arm, even a piece of broken half-rotted board, or a small branch a cow might have dragged from one of the willow bluffs. There's always some sort of jetsam here at other times. You'll find a nice long stick and hold it tightly in a desperate hand with your arms stretched far, far out from your body as you spin on panic-propelled feet, whirling faster and faster and the force of your body spinning will translate to wide blurred circles of destruction, dark and slivery at the farthest point of your extended forces: $E = MC$ squared. You could never understand the formula but now you know it means you might live at least until your fourteenth birthday.

Or maybe a stone, even one as small as your clenched fist. You could throw it with the force of a fury stored inside you from the time you first learned about the power of evil. The forehead of Joe Louis who is really Fat Frederick stopping the flight of the stone, like the forehead of Goliath stopped the stone from the sling of David. Maybe Paul-with-the-genitals struck instead, either of them lying wounded, bloody, repentant.

It's your own fault, you'll say. *You asked for it.*

But there are no stones, only small pebbles. No sticks either. Nothing to swing with deadly fury, nothing to throw with desperate accuracy.

The pail hangs on the pump-hook, the sun reflecting on its polished steel. If only it were not half-full. If it were empty . . .

It's so simple, something inside you says, as the boots come closer. If the pail were empty, you could swing *it* round and round yourself like a speeding comet circling the sun. The metal edge would find the flesh of an approaching enemy and bite deeply. *Empty the pail!* The command allows no argument.

So you take the pail off the hook and it seems as though someone else is doing it for you. You turn back toward the boiler to pour in the water. A dry prairie voice inside you forbids you from emptying the water on the ground. But your thrifty intentions are lost when you see the danger only six feet away now, only six feet away and moving oh so slowly with exquisite control and all the human look about it gone. Your arms jerk then with a movement your brain did not order.

The bare chests have little wiggly lines where sweat has trickled down the gravel-dusted skin. Particles of sand and food fill the spaces between their teeth. The teeth. Grinning, grinning, but not really at you.

Afterwards, you don't remember for a while how your arms moved in a frightened spasm and how the water arced out with an immensely slow beauty. It's a dream, you think, as you watch from somewhere outside yourself. The way the water moves so slowly, so majestically. A graceful plume of liquid, clear as you imagine a diamond must be, its edges rippled with crystal drops breaking away, falling, falling. The coldness of it so pure, blue as the blue in rainbows born in the hot air around the arc of water as it reaches for its target. The blood in your body has stopped with the slowing of everything around you, and there's time for you to marvel at the wonder of rainbows which come of themselves when you least expect them.

Then your heart starts to beat again and your blood tries to burst its vessels. Everything becomes faster and you see the curve of water has landed. Paul-with-the-genitals stands in an attitude of shock. The water has struck just above his open belt buckle and gushed down behind the front of his unbuttoned fly, into his boots.

I close my eyes. If they kill me for this I intend to die bravely, perhaps like Joan of Arc, with my soul intact.

Gravel stutters under hard boots and I open my eyes, ready to scream and scream and bite and kick, though no one will hear me, though they might not feel the bites through impervious layers of their need, the need to demean.

Joe Louis is running back down the gravel slope and I'm startled for a moment. Maybe, I think, maybe he's gone to get a weapon deadlier than his fists. A shovel maybe. But he calls out to Paul, "Come on! We're already late."

I take a chance and look at Paul. He stands in the pool of water which has taken with it some of the dusty sweat from his skin. He's covered in goose-pimples, wide-eyed, staring first at me, then at the water trickling down his body, oozing from his pants and boots, sinking into the hot gravel.

It's a look I've never seen before, and I'm not sure what it means. It may have something to do with water and how the earth can die without it. He backs away from me as slowly as he and Fat Fred had approached me, but now he's shivering. Somehow I know I won't have to scream.

My arms are too weak to finish filling the copper boiler, yet I feel guilty about its half-emptiness. This is not the frugal, decent way of doing things. My mother will ask questions but I don't care. Perhaps tomorrow I'll come back. Tomorrow when my heart has remembered its proper rhythm. Tomorrow I'll come back and get all the water I want.

— *Mary Bazylevich*

THE ARRIVAL

the house is called the palace
they bring me to a wooden sidewalk
Papa gives me five cents
Maman holds my face for a while
she is peppermint and lavender water

they "will be back soon"
and knock at the door

a man with a toothpick in his face lets me in
the air inside is old
we go down some noisy stairs
the room opens to a table and four chairs
and some windows bare

lady comes to me and cracks a little round bread
her mouth says "eat Skinny"
and i do
while she opens my shoes
plays with my sweater
and has both hands on my sac

if i move my face now i'll cry

— *Paulette Dubé*

PROJECTION: A LUMP IN THE BREAST

I know who you are.
Guilt stone. Rage ruby.

You are sensual and disgusting,
a tongue moving inside my left melon.
O my id-baby, my ego-monkey.

Little love stone.
When they cut you out of me
I will take care of you,
the one part of me that cannot be
diagnosed. Inside your formaldehyde jar
you will hold your place among pigs.

I know your secrets.
Black passion flower.

Little stone. O little bitch.

— *Sherry Johnson*

DULCE *(this dulse)* ET DECORUM

In the luminous Pacific blue we rode
lightly in your brother's sloop
and I didn't mind your shaggy pubic
hair, nor did he. But his prissy
pommy friend, an editor at *Reader's
Digest*, seemed awkward all day.
None of us were naked, exactly,
but what jungles you bequeathed
upon our deck   great hairy bushes
filled with carnivorous blooms.

I liked the danger of your foliage
even more than the sharks in
the broad river mouth. Then back
to Sydney harbour on a stiff twilight
breeze, your rug calling out to
its seadrift kin: rockweed,
dulse and kelp.

— *J. Livingstone Clark*

WAYMAN IN THE WORKFORCE: TEACHER'S AIDE

Through the late snows of March, Wayman ploughs into the parking lot
his car sputtering through the slushy drifts.
Wayman is here to spend hours marking
what the students have scrawled off in seconds between the bells:
endless crinkly sheets of Grade 11 English essays.

Only Wayman takes it seriously. Every apostrophe is always misplaced.
Every sentence runs on like a television set. One student writes
he likes to hang around hippies "because they are so down and out
they make me feel positively good." Another compares
a hamburger sauce of ketchup and mayonnaise, oozing out of a bun
to "the wounds of a dying soldier."

Some afternoons nobody comes. The classes
simply take the day off. Wayman stays at his desk in the library
marking, marking. Every so often
he looks up from his piles of paragraphs
and stares at the empty chairs.

He hears a noise in the quiet. Behind him on the library rug
the Director of English 11 sits, in the full lotus.
He is throwing the I-Ching. "When the students are absent
I have a chance to pursue my hobbies," the Director says brightly.
"Did you know that extending the lines of the Star of David
yields the figure of the Maltese Cross?"

Wayman pushes his nose deeper into his papers.
Outside the first green April buds begin, and inside
Wayman begins to sigh. In the spring
his nuts boil over like an old radiator. Day by day
he watches the skirts in the hallway creep slowly up
the 17-year-old fleshy thighs. Breasts seem to swell
under thinner and thinner cotton blouses.
Wayman checks and re-checks his columns of grades.

And on the last day, in June, all the green trees flower.
Wayman turns in his pencils and walks out
past the clock and the picture of the Queen.
He starts his car and drives out of the schoolyard
into the summer. Headed home through the warm afternoon,
     he realizes
he has been marking time.

—Tom Wayman

TEENAGERS

languid as lizards
as lazy lizards they lie
Dana & Megan gaze
inside folds of sleep
& stare mornings glare
as if looking
for bugs glued by night
3 feet in front of them

have basked skins in moondust
sniffed fur under roofs of their mouths
transformed over night their lady
ships have become gila
monsters snapping turtles salamanders
lamia whose eyes turn
emerald or lime or ruby & glow
in the dark strange night
creatures who when light splashes
on their faces in morning
turn mudeyed
blanch & shrivel
in neckthrust turn bugeyed
& coldblooded on us heavy
as nightmare flick
tongues begin to hiss us
into fearful grasshopper silence

— *Dennis Cooley*

In that dark room, the petrified forest of memory where stony trees wear branches of emerald ice, blue jays sing staccato in a river of sun shafting through the trees. Wander, child, and fear nothing except silence broken by the twitching scrape of branch bark. Never look down; the blinking claws of crayfish have eyes. Never look around.

Behind every shadow of stump and stone lives an old man, his face like a rag, his enormous pockets filled with candy and pain.

— *Brian Brett*

END OF THE STRING

We won't be gone long we say after entering the ice caves near Bragg Creek but Jim Brad and I disappear for two hours crawl following unravelled string through fissures and cracks with only one flashlight and Grandad and Glenis back in the second cavern with no light not even matches waiting in pitch coal where-are-you blackness as we sqeeze and grunt our way up always up the thought of getting out another way or at least the end of the string in our minds and at one point standing leaning against the flat wall of a fissure the other wall a foot in front of our faces and when Jim pans the light up way up it's so high I can't see the top Wanna try it we're slipping and sliding our way over cold knobs of ice that offer no foothold handhold at all and it's getting to be a long way down to the base of the fissure just as we level out into another cavern and find an empty Baby Duck bottle on the floor a used condom and a note *Janet & Michael March 21/78*

— *William Klebeck*

SOLAR PASSAGE

The sun raises sparkles on a concrete porch
where a girl just over the doorstep of puberty
(her nipples like twin buttons under the shirt)
is eating the red heart of a melon slice
down to the green rind, exuberantly spitting
seeds beyond the iron railing into the grass.
Her brown curly hair shakes like heat ripples
as she laughs in flirtation with neighbour boys.

That image sets me down on a wooden porch,
the light stroking a gloss into the gray paint,
where my cousin Linda and I, both eight, sat
in giggling exile as the doctor inside performed
the secret post-partum rituals on my mother.
Our backs were to the door, and through it
my new sister was crying as we sat roasting
our feet and haunches on the splintery wood
and ate tomatoes, the bribe for our absence,
a shaker of salt between us.

                                No one recalls
a taste, but a laughing girl summons back
our furtive chatter about sex and birth
(how babies are conceived by touching tongues)
and I see the red fruit in my hand, the seeds
suspended in time, still floating in fluid cells.

— *Bert Almon*

A WHITE BOUQUET OF EARTH
for Sharon

Where I come from the hills are filled with bleached clay.
It is the purest clay on Earth.

And there once was a time
when I thought I knew
everything. I held up
my white bouquet of earth
to the sky, but that sun
was already dying.

> (I thought I could hear
> the voices of myself speak
> from the mouths of opening wildflowers)

Then the river had been high.
For once I thought it would be
a good year, and then I let out a cry
because everyone I had ever loved
was hurting.

The wildflowers had begun to die.
I sat out in my little boat
anchored with a smooth stone
cut with tears, holding on to my
small truths, what little ones were left.

> (And the perch bit on my worms.
> The wolf willow was silver,
> and held the strange power of the moon)

Only the river moved beneath me.

— *Sherry Johnson*

If you want to have fun these days you got to jump up and down on people's heads or go live in somebody's nose. Like, who needs it? You can't even have sex without worrying about your thing falling off.

And then there's school.

I don't have anything against school. Any idiot knows you got to get your grade twelve. School is like something you got to do sooner or later. Some of my best friends go to school — I just don't understand how they can do it. It's like eating yogurt. You know it's supposed to be good for you — you just wish it had some taste and would stop making you gag. You make one mistake and everyone's jumping down your throat with rulers and chalk and guidance counsellors. They're so damn sure of themselves. They know everything. Somebody should take schools and put some flavour in them, move them to the twenty-first century. Who needs to know about the Crimean War? Or some poem by a dead guy about a cat licking windows? Give me a break.

Anyway, I can't stand it, so I quit. As a result of quitting, I get kicked out of the house.

"We're not going to support a life-style where you just bum around," says Dad. "You got to do something."

Dad is a Doctor. He likes it when you call him that even though he doesn't heal people or fix them up. He teaches at the University — philosophy. This kills me. He lives in a world that he's made in his mind. It's filled with people like Descartes and Kant — these guys who were philosophers. Descartes was the one who said, "I think, therefore I am." Yeah, well, I fart, therefore I am.

Anyway, he wants me to do something with my life. I don't fit in his head.

"Like what?" I ask.

"I don't care. If you can't go to school, then you can get a job. Work. Those are the rules in this house if you want to live here. If you don't, get out."

There's other rules too, like no sex or drugs. It's funny how the rules thing works. I mean there's rules for me, but does he have any? No, he has a rack full of guns and every fall he turns into Mr. *Field and Stream,* the Big White Hunter. He goes after deer mostly and over the winter we eat a lot of venison. We eat it so he can kill it. It's one of the rules he's worked out in his head, to keep company with Descartes and Kant. You get really sick of it after a while. I bet the deer aren't too happy about it either.

So, fine. Those are his rules. I'm not going to argue. I have other places to stay. On the street, with all the other "shitheads, lowlife, and scum". That's what my dad calls them.

What he doesn't know is that they're friends, a kind of a club, like the Elks or Lions, without the fancy hats. We got a motto too — "Watch Out or Die Ugly." Some people come here to do the ugly part. Most come here because there's nowhere else to go.

The first thing you learn is how to protect yourself. There's some really crazy people around who got that way when someone tried to eat them when they were three, or they got so strung out they don't know where they are, or don't have enough brain cells working to know which way is back. That's how come I got a knife. I keep it tucked in my sleeve, along my forearm. I don't use it, but I want people to know I have it. It's like you're saying, "Don't mess with me. I would hurt you."

I got my name for a stupid thing I did once. I'll tell you about it to show what kind of space you can get your head into without even really trying. I was at a party where somebody snagged some cash, so we had lots of booze. It was pretty late and we were talking about what you had to do if you wanted to commit suicide and Roxy was saying she knew someone who cut their wrists across, like where your watch band is. Except I know you can't do it that way. You have to cut up and down along your arm so you really wreck your veins. And to prove it, I cut my wrist, across.

There was lots of blood but dying was not what I did, otherwise, my name would be "Dead," instead of "Cut". Roxy has kept her distance from me ever since.

The truth is, it takes a lot more than a cut to kill someone. That's why when you hear about somebody dying from fifty or sixty stab wounds, it's not that the murderer is trying to be particularly nasty or anything, he's just trying to finish the job he's started. So unless you get really lucky and go for the throat, it usually takes a whole lot to kill someone. Ask any knife murderer. Not that I did personally — I just read it somewhere.

I do a lot of reading. Reading and sleeping. I like Stephen King. You can sort of read and sleep at the same time. People in his books are always nuts. They do one stupid thing and it haunts them for the rest of their lives. Like me, one thing and I get called Cut from then on.

I'm not going to tell you where I get my money because mostly I just bum. But sometimes I sell things that friends give me or they leave lying around and don't really need. Hey, what are friends for? But when winter came, everyone scrambled to get under a roof and it got harder and harder to find places to stay. Now that winter's just about over, I've run out of friends and it's still too cold to sleep outside.

So that's why I'm going to see my folks. I'm broke and I'm hungry and I need a place to stay. I know there won't be any problem. There never is when I go back. They just want me to go to school or get a job. I mean, I understand their point of view, I just don't feel like doing it. I get a buzz in my head when I think about it. But I'll play along. I'll look in the paper. I'll even go out and put some job applications in. Who knows, I might even get a job. But there's not much around, and what can you do with only grade eleven? Like you can pump gas or work in a kitchen doing dishes for five bucks an hour. Big deal. Who needs it?

I do.

My parents' place is on the outskirts of town. I have a sister too, but she's married and has three kids. The only reason I'm telling you this is because I don't want you to think I come from a "broken home," or some stupid thing. I was never abused when I was a kid and the only thing that ever went wrong was my dog died when I was five. Sure, some old guy showed me his dork but I was just amazed at all the hair. Nothing happened. I have no idea why I am the way I am.

Maybe it's those things that do happen to you and you don't even know what they mean. Like this other old guy I knew when I was about twelve.

We used to cross the train bridge and he lived in a shack next to the dump down by the river, just on the other side of the power plant. We would sometimes go and throw rocks at his place to get him to chase us. Of course, he always did.

One day there were four of us skinny-dipping and horsing around in a river shallow between two sand bars, about a half a mile from the old man's shack, when all of a sudden we look up, and there he is, picking our clothes up and stuffing them under his arm. Then he just stands there laughing. He's big, the old guy, and he's wearing a coat even though it's the middle of summer. He's dirty too, like he's been at the dump all day picking garbage. He probably has.

"I got you now," he says. "I got you."

And he does. There isn't anything we can do but try to hide behind our hands and be terrified.

"What should I do with these?" he says, referring to our clothes. "I think I'll trade them."

"No, mister, you can't!" We yell in our shrill twelve-year old voices. We're almost in tears.

"Yeah, that's what I'm going to do. Trade them."

"How're we going to get home?" We're pleading, with visions of ourselves riding our bikes naked through town.

"I'll trade them for a promise," he says.

We listen.

"You promise not to throw rocks at my place, I'll give you your clothes back."

"Yeah, yeah, we promise."

"I don't believe you," he says.

"We *do*, we won't throw rocks, we promise mister!"

"Okay, then come and get them," and he turns and goes, except he's still got our clothes under his arm.

"Wait mister, our clothes!"

But he disappears into the bushes, heading towards his shack, with everything but our shoes. We put on our shoes and follow, half-crouching and yelling. He leaves a trail of shirts and underwear.

When we finally get there, we see four pairs of pants strung out on a clothes line attached to the shack. In front of the shack is an old car seat, and in front of that, a smouldering fire-pit. The old guy appears at the door with a cup of something steaming in his hand.

"Ah, visitors!" he says.

"We want our pants back," I say.

"Help yourself," he says. "Just remember what you traded them for."

We approach like four shy dogs, our tails between our legs.

He sits on the battered car seat. "It's not often I get visitors," he says. "Anybody want some tea?"

"No, just our pants." We are now pulling them down from the line and scrambling into them. My sneakers get caught in the legs. I lose my balance and fall. Sitting on the ground, I yank my pants off again, remove my sneakers and start over.

"Come on, hurry," somebody says.

Suddenly, he holds the cup in the air like he's toasting, except he's looking off into the bush. Then he makes the strangest sound I ever heard. It's like a grunting but there seems to be some meaning attached to it.

That's when the deer walks out of the bush, a beautiful white-tail doe, and right behind her, a little fawn. They walk straight over to the old guy. He takes something out of his pocket and gives it to the doe, then pats her nose. All the while he's doing this, he's murmuring something soft. The doe turns and looks at us, at me really, and just as suddenly as they came, they disappear back into the brush.

I am still sitting on the ground with my pants half-on.

The old guy looks over at us again. "Tea?" he asks.

"Yeah," I hear myself say.

"Yeah," I hear the others.

That was the first of our many visits that summer.

"Everything wants to be round." He said it like it was a rule or a law.

I agree with him. Things break down. They wear out. Crumble smooth. I mean, take sand or a pebbly beach. They started out as mountains. And look how round they're getting. The whole planet's getting round.

If you live in a city, it doesn't look that way. It looks the opposite because we build things — houses, office towers, strip malls. But everything we build makes a hole somewhere else, in a forest, a field or under the ground. Nowhere is there a part untouched by hands. Everything's been measured and marked. And malled.

If you live on the prairies, where I'm from, you might think that everything gets flat. And that's true too, but really it's the same thing. For example, there used to be hundreds of thousands of buffalo on the prairies. There's only a few thousand left. They shot them all. You know why? Not for their tongues, not for the buffalo coats, not for their bones, but for *belts*. Leather belts.

All the big factories were run by steam engines in those days, and the way they turned the machinery was with great long expanses of buffalohide belts sewn together. That's where all the buffalo went. It took two men a whole day to skin a buffalo. And when they had just about run out of buffalo, they discovered rubber, and had rubber tree plantations in the tropics to make the belts out of dead rubber trees instead of dead buffalo.

That's what the old guy said, then he disappeared too.

The next summer when we went back, the place was empty like no one had lived there for a long time. And he was gone. We had no idea where he went, or if he was dead or what.

Sometimes I want to disappear like the old guy.

I get on the bus downtown and flash the bus pass that I found. I won't say where I found it, so don't ask. I sit about half-way down, behind an old lady with lots of bags. I sit next to the aisle, leaving the window seat open. This is so no one will sit next to me. I really don't have to worry because the bus is more than half-empty. It's just about seven, after supper.

It's quickly getting dark. You'd think because of all the snow that light wouldn't die so easy. But it does. The streets are rutted in iron-hard ice and everyone who tries to cross them takes those funny hurried steps that people take in winter. They don't have faces. People in winter never do.

The bus rolls to its stops, picks up people, lets people off. We're getting near my parents' home. The old lady with lots of bags finally gets off. She smiles at me. I'm the only one left, me and the bus driver. We come to a corner where there's a 7 Eleven. The bus stops and the driver gets out. He runs into the 7 Eleven leaving the door open. He's getting a coffee or something.

This is when the wolf gets on. I kid you not. A wolf.

The wolf is big. It's about a meter high. And it's pure white. I know it is a wolf because it has yellow eyes. He pads half-way down the bus till he gets to me. In one slow-motion leap, he sits on the seat across from me.

I just about shit.

I don't know if you've ever had a wolf sit next to you on a bus, but I tell you what, it doesn't make you feel like dancing.

I always liked wolves, or the *idea* of wolves. They're beautiful animals. They're free to come and go as they please. They don't have enemies, except for us — humans, or whatever we are. I'd never seen one up close before. They have these deadly yellow eyes, like they know something you can't even dream about.

Dogs never have yellow eyes, unless they're crossbred with wolves.

So there's these deadly eyes staring at me across the aisle, aimed at me. I don't know what to do. I think maybe I should say something. I say the first thing that comes to mind.

"Good boy," I say.

The wolf doesn't make a sound. He just shows me his teeth. They are surprisingly white, like he brushes and flosses everyday. Except they're really big. "Oh grandma, what big teeth you have." I think about yelling for help. I can see the bus driver chatting at the counter. The wolf licks his lips. I decide to wait.

"Good boy," I say again.

This time the wolf not only shows his teeth, he growls. Not that I can actually hear it, I can feel it. It's like a double resonance in harmony with the bus's diesel.

For the first time in my life, I am truly afraid. I don't know what's going on. This is too weird. Maybe I'm hallucinating or something. I quickly raise my hand to rub my eyes.

This time I hear the growl. Very slowly I remove my hand from my eyes. I lower it to my left sleeve, where I keep my knife. If I can have it out in two seconds, he can have his teeth clamped around my throat in one. The question is, who will do more damage? I leave the knife alone. The growl continues.

It stops when the driver steps on board the bus. He closes the door, puts the bus in gear and we begin again. The driver cannot see the wolf because it's hidden by the seat ahead, lying down.

I look at the bus driver. I look at the wolf. I am wondering what will happen if I yell. I think of the possibilities. One: the bus driver ignores me because he can't see the wolf; two: the bus driver stops and the wolf eats my throat. I quit there. I mean, what's the point?

Then the thought occurs to me.

What is this wolf doing here?

I look at the wolf again. He actually seems relaxed. Smiling. But his two yellow eyes are fixed on me like bayonets. He closes one of them, then opens it. Is that a wink? Do wolves wink? Do wolves get on buses, sit down next to people and wink at them? Not as far as I know. So why is he here? Is it like those whales you hear about crashing into beaches? Or moose wandering into grocery stores? Or like people going to the moon?

We are coming to my stop. Suddenly I don't care any more. I reach up and ring the bell. The wolf watches. He closes his mouth. I've called his bluff. It's his move next.

The bus pulls into the curb. I get up and walk to the rear door. The wolf gets up and follows. I look in that round mirror above the door to see the face of the driver. His mouth is wide open. The wolf and I step off the bus and into the night. The wolf grabs my left arm. He's not going to chew it off. He's taking me somewhere.

When we get far enough out of town, the wolf lets go of my arm. He walks in front of me. He doesn't bother looking back. My leather jacket keeps out the wind, but not the cold. I start wishing I had a coat like a wolf's. My ears and face are numb.

I think of this western movie I saw once. It's about this bad guy chasing a good guy in the middle of a snow storm. And the good guy finds a cave to stay in, leaving the bad guy outside. But the bad guy shoots a buffalo and cuts off his hide to wrap himself in it.

The next morning, the good guy comes out of the cave and finds the bad guy frozen stiff, wrapped in the buffalo skin which is also frozen stiff. The bad guy's gun is still pointing at the cave. The good guy breaks the gun from his frozen hand.

I am wondering what I would look like wrapped in a frozen wolf hide, found dead on some farmer's field next spring, with my knife frozen in my hand.

I suddenly realize the direction we are headed. We are going across the train bridge.

We are heading towards the power plant.

It's like some inner fire instantly heats up and the cold burns off. When we cross the bridge, I jog through the shallow snow and follow the wolf. We pass the dump. We pass where the old man's shack used to be. There's nothing there.

In twenty minutes I can see the orange glow of the plant's lights. The wolf has run to the top of a hill and is outlined against the sky next to a small thicket of woods. He stops. He is waiting for me to catch up. Just before I do, he enters the thicket.

When I get to the hill top, I can see the plant in the valley below, its stacks and buildings spread like a mouthful of broken glass. I go into the thicket where the wolf has disappeared. It is darker and the snow is deeper. I hear the growl, or rather, feel it again. I freeze.

In front of me is a small clearing. In it are four or five dark shapes. They move, quietly. They are animals of some sort. I step closer and crouch. They are deer. Four of them have surrounded a fifth. Two are facing outward and two are facing in. The one in the middle is doing something. There are sounds, the sounds of breathing hard. The one in the middle has spread its hind legs and lowers itself. Suddenly, a black bundle drops to the snowy ground.

The deer has given birth.

The mother turns and immediately starts to sniff her offspring, grabbing at it with her mouth. Suddenly, she backs away. She backs away, and leaves. The other deer sniff the bundle and follow, leaving it alone on the ground. Moving, writhing.

The wolf appears from nowhere, sniffs the writhing mass, then walks a few feet away and sits. The wolf looks at me, its yellow eyes piercing the dark.

It is my turn.

I go to the bundle. Up close I can see that it is a baby deer, struggling to get out of its filmy sack. Another bloody sack lies near the deer. The cord is still attached. I take out my knife and cut the cord. I clean off the film as best I can. I pick up the baby deer. Something is wrong.

It has no legs. There are four little stubs where the legs should be.

Something in me rips and I start crying like I've never cried before. I pick up the little deer and start walking. I know if I leave it, that it will be dead in hours. That the magpies will pick its flesh clean. I carry it back to the train bridge.

When I get to the middle of the bridge, I can feel it is still alive and moving. I hold it close to me and kiss it. Then I throw it into the night. I hear a splash in the dark waters below.

I stand there a long time. I think about jumping. I think of all the stupid things I've done. I think of the old guy. And the wolf.

I hear a train coming. It is approaching from the direction of my parents' house. I head the other way.

— R.P. MacIntyre

Ω

The mole's cry as he sleeps. Velvet death.
We rest in desolation, the mind creeping.

Remember the ridiculous.
The lenient master starves beauty.

Desolate. Desolate. The day and the day and the day.
Remember the heart. Little mole.

Last leaves. First frost.
I am the awaking. Your long cry of love.

— Patrick Lane

When my sister Elsa was a baby she was an angel and my father called her *das Engelein*. At hour house people never spoke in German. My mother would not allow it. Only my father ever did, and we children could hardly understand him. It was the fury of his life having non-German children. One of the furies. He had several. The Brotherhood of Man was another. My father loved the Brotherhood of Man with an ardent and a vocal passion.

He loved his daughters, too, I suppose, but they never knew it. He loved his son, and his daughters knew it. He loved him like Isaac loved his Jacob or like Abraham his Isaac. My father never sacrificed his Floydie on any altar; never even tried to. But he killed his daughters a thousand times over, and this is to be the story of the last time he killed my sister Elsa in her snow-white *Engelein* gown, her wings spread and ready to soar at the church Christmas concert one year in the sandy, dry, hard farming district where we used to live.

It had to be in German. That whole church concert had to be in German. Some of the kids did OK, they had mothers who hardly spoke English. In that community the fathers went out into the world and did the business and learned to speak the language of business. The mothers stayed home and plucked geese, and made quilts and perogies and babies, and crooned them to sleep with Komm' Herr Jesu, and sent them there with a few slaps to the ear if the child went unwilling.

So it was at our house, too. Except for the German and the Jesu. My mother didn't believe in either one. She had had it different at home. Her father was just as German as anybody else in that settlement, but his mind had a different order. His daughter was to go to Normal School to be a teacher, but she chose Papa instead. No wonder, I suppose. Papa was tall and beautiful and imposing and he courted every woman in the district atop his large white stallion, taking them for rides into the hills to show them the wood's violets.

I think the violets stopped when my mother agreed to come into his kitchen, but his passions did not. At least I know we had a violin and lots of talk and booming laughter when the neighbours came, but cold lips and steel blue eyes when they left again.

It was a hard life in a lot of ways: Papa bellering, bellering, from his bed, after Mama died and the third white stallion threw him, for tea and beef broth and pen and paper to write his latest orders.

But this is not that story. I tell it to you in this way, though, because it is very hard, at fifty, to keep it going well. To keep the order. I've had too many other voices inside my head for so long. Too many to keep any kind of order.

Papa was a difficult man. He lived for too many years. I looked after him for twenty-three of them. Mama, I think now sometimes, almost had it easy. She spoke back, you see, and the hate did not gather, black and hard and festering, around her heart as it did mine.

But I want to tell you about Elsa. I think that is what she means me to do when she comes now and stands by my side when I am writing away the blackness and drinking the coffee Papa forbade in this house because it repelled him. She has been dead forty-one years now, I counted it out today, and I suppose she has forgotten how to speak. On account of not knowing the sacred language, ha ha, I never believed it. Papa used to say it was all in German up there, a German pastor once told him.

For all those years I was careful not to care, but now I see that Elsa did not even go there. She couldn't have. The church says no, and they should be right on some things; it is too terrible otherwise to try to live.

Yet all those years I thought it was an accident and I'm sure Papa did, too. I think Mama knew. I do not want to do the thinking sometimes, there is a danger in it. But I think now Mama knew because it raised a real uproar in the way she went to bed and stayed there the day it happened and wouldn't even get up for the funeral.

But that's ahead of it again. I need the order. It is harder than to have it in your head and know it, this setting of it down. Once I wanted to be a writer and I read *King Arthur* over and over until I knew the order of telling things, but now I cannot keep it straight.

It goes like this though. We always went to church. All but our mother. Papa said we had to go to church and learn the glory; it was not safe to live in this world otherwise. And the glory was only good if it came in German. It was the holy way. It was important because it had to do with Christus and the angels and your holy German soul. The words spoke in the old tongue, he said, helped to get you the glory.

That pastor, I knew him, said so and Papa believed him, but our mother didn't. She said it was a peasant's attitude and it was either all true in any language or it was not all true and maybe none of it true and so what, it didn't put bread on the table; but you sure couldn't break it up into German and English and French, it wasn't logical.

And Papa said what was logical was it she would allow his daughters to speak German at the supper table, but the Schroeders seemed to be such English boot-lickers it seemed to be more than a man could expect to have the old tongue spoken around his own fireside. And our mother said, it seemed to her it was Schroeder money brought the coal to keep the fire going in it. And Papa said, "Yes, yes, rub it in," and he took his boxful of blue socialist tracts and saddled his white stallion with her red wild eyes and rode to Elmyra Bitner's to discuss the Brotherhood of Man.

And Mama would scrub hard at the fading red apples on the oilcloth on the kitchen table and make mouths at the way the corners were wearing through and she'd say, "Come on girls, we'll make brown sugar fudge tonight."

And our mother made brown sugar fudge with butter and walnuts most nights he did that. And sometimes when my sister Elsa peered too long into the night from the kitchen window straining to see his white stallion coming back out of the dark night my mother would say, "Don't be silly, girl, do you think a bear will get him or something? He's only gone to get educated; come on and we'll make ourselves some popcorn."

But Elsa wouldn't. She just turned her back on our mother and went and rearranged Papa's pipes neatly beside the family picture taken when there was only Papa and our mother and Elsa and me because our sister Laura already lived just at Grampa Schroeder's. She had to, Papa said she was not his child. I hope that is the order. It seems to fit here. Laura is important; she got lost in a different way. And while Elsa looked at herself being an *Engelein* in the family picture on the sideboard our mother and I would pop popcorn, shelling it first, plink-plank into a pan off the cob, and heating the heavy frying pan on the back of the stove while we did.

Not Floydie, though. Floydie was a boy and anyway he was young and fast asleep by that time of night. But Elsa would only pick away at her bowlful now and again and when Mama said, Come on, eat up, it's just the way you like it, Elsa would get that tight look around her eyes and say, No, I'm saving it for Floydie. And Mama would say, He's spoiled enough, and Elsa would say, You don't like anybody, do you? And she'd go back to the window and look some more for Papa and his stallion and she only left her place when Floydie cried and then she always ran to him before Mama could go.

And yet Floydie was the reason, all the same, why Elsa had to look out into the dark night for Papa with her pink barn-goose eyes that got teary from too much watching. And Floydie was the reason Grampa Schroeder got so mad he kept giving our mother money to buy us girls new dresses for the school picnic and the church concert. Floydie was Papa's Sonny Boy Cereal and Elsa used to be his *Engelein*, but now she was just a girl who had grown a long Schroeder neck and couldn't do arithmetic.

She couldn't learn her German piece, either. For the church Christmas concert you had to learn to speak a piece in German, no matter what. You had to or your folks were shamed forever. Even my mother went to the church Christmas concert. It was call *der Heilige Abend* and nobody missed going. It was holy, and not even the little ones expected to see Santa.

It was as if to say the white light of Jesu shone those nights. The church was lit with candles. Not even the coal oil lamps were lit and certainly not the gas mantle lanterns with their piercing twin eyes. Only candles were holy.

And that year, that last year, Elsa said she wanted to be an angel. An angel in German yet, and with twenty-eight lines to speak. When Pastor asked who would take the part, Elsa's hand shot up and it surprised me. Elsa was not that way. She would rather not speak, even in English, and to anything in German killed her.

Especially speak to Papa. When you have been an *Engelein* and aren't any longer, to stand before Papa and *Ihr Kinderlein kommet, zur Bethlehem Stall* into his pale slough-ice eyes doesn't help to make the wings grow — and if you are one to have had the wings clipped you know this is the right order to say it.

"*Kinderlein,* not *Kidderlein*", Papa told her. "*Baytlah-hem,* not *Bethlehem*; what do you want to put a *thuh* in it for? The people will think you're not raised right. Now start the first verse again from the beginning and stand straight and speak it right. Twenty-eight lines only, a big girl like you, and you can't even learn it."

Hellslänzendem was the word that did it. *Hellzadem,* Elsa said. Who wouldn't? It's hard in German to get all the zeds and enns and urrs in, and lots of times the German don't even care when they speak it. But when it comes to their kids, watch out, they're supposed to all talk like preachers.

I talked German in my head all the time. Nobody knew it. One of the voices in my head was a German man and he told jokes sometimes in German on the pastor when church went on too long. *Hier ist mir ein alter Fart*, he'd say sometimes, and I would try not to smile; to smile was dangerous. And the voice would tell me to go look up Fart in Papa's German dictionary when we got home. Sure, we never touched Papa's books, that was dangerous, too, but I would have if I'd wanted. Only I didn't want to care about it.

Elsa cared too much. It was dangerous. Day by day she sewed on her *Engelein* costume, looking quite often at the picture on the sideboard. She sewed in the parlour where you weren't supposed to use thread because it worked itself into the carpet. Mama told her she could sit there when she caught her sewing at four o'clock in the morning once by the kitchen lamp. Its flame flickered pale and yellow.

Silly goose, Mama told her, it's too hard on the eyes and I could do it on the machine in a minute. But Elsa only turned her back on Mama, pretending she was looking for the scissors, and said, I want to do it. And she'd show Papa after supper how it was coming and he'd say Yes, yes, but you're not gonna spend your life in a dress factory, how's the piece coming? And Elsa would stand there and speak, one angel wing drooping. *Bei des Lichtleins hellzadem* she'd get to, and Papa would look up quick and say *hellslänz, hellslänz*, put the *zed* in it; how come you can't remember? People will think you aren't raised right!

And then he'd call Floydie to him for a game of clap-handies and Mama would say from the parlour door, Come work in the kitchen, the light's better. But Elsa would take her piece out of her apron pocket where she kept it to learn even in the toilet, I saw her once, and her mouth made the words but she did not say them out loud and she watched Papa and Floydie whenever they laughed until Papa said, You could likely learn better in the kitchen. And then she folded her piece up and put it in her pocket and went.

And on concert night she spoke it pretty well, so I don't know why Papa had to do it. The candles were lit in the church and you could almost smell the glory, and people shook hands with everybody they could reach even after they got sitting down in the pews, the fat ones straining hard over their chests to shake with ones sitting behind them.

Grownups even shook hands with two-year-olds, and graced each other *fröhliche Weihnacht* whether they were made at each other or not. And you could smell the Jap oranges from the brown paper bags, each one packed two man's hands full of peanuts and almonds and striped

Christmas candy made into curlicues almost the size and shape of Floydie's new bow tie, and each one with two Jap oranges at the bottom so that you had to dig through all the other good stuff if you wanted to eat them first. One thing, Germans never were stingy when it was nuts and candy and they had the money.

Only we were never allowed to open our bags until we got home. That was Papa's way. You weren't supposed to look anxious, it meant you weren't raised right.

On that night we girls were wearing our new dresses Grampa Schroeder had given the money for, and Floydie looked like a prince, true enough, like Papa said, in his royal blue breeches and snow white shirt with the ruffles. And Mama looked nice and came along to the concert and people graced her, too, and only a few made remarks like, Well at least we see you at Christmas. So it was all good, very good, for once, and Elsa spoke up, spoke right up *Ihr Kinderlein kommet* only with not enough *zeds* and *enns* in it. But she spoke clear and good, her eyes shining and her hands folded and looking up into the candelabra so that her eyes got to be two candles, too. But the trouble was, her one wing drooped because she would not let Mama help her sew.

And Mrs. Elmyra Bitner said afterwards to Papa, Now Floydie, you tell that wife of yours I got time on my hands I could help her next Christmas with the kids' costumes if she wants. And Mama was standing right there, right there beside her, and Mrs. Elmyra Bitner turned to her next and graced her and maybe never even knew her, Mama hardly ever came to church, but Mama said later she did.

And Papa said it didn't matter, why worry about a little thing like that, the point was people thought his kids weren't raised right; how come she let the kid show up with a costume like that? It wasn't the first time, either. We were on the way home and the horses' hooves sounded crisp-crunch on the hard-packed snow of the road and the traces jingled like bells, although Papa wasn't one to put brass bells on the harness like a lot of men did, he said it was frippery. And I tried to think hard about the Jap oranges and how they'd be when we got home and Papa let us open our bags. I had to think hard, hard, about them; to think about Elsa's drooping wing was too dangerous.

So when we got home and Papa had carried Floydie inside, and us girls and Mama had our coats off, Elsa wouldn't even open her bag. Mama was undressing Floydie, fast asleep on the kitchen table, and she had one eye on Elsa sitting silent on a hard chair by the Quebec heater with her piece in her hand, and Mama looked real nice, very nice, she hardly ever dressed up.

And Papa came up behind her, his fur coat and hat still on because he still had to go out and do the horses. And he laid his hand on Mama's shoulder and said, "It's always better after church." And he showed his hard white even teeth under his silky smooth moustache, he was a very good looker always. And Mama just picked Floydie up, and walked out from under his hand and said over her shoulder, "Elmyra Bitner has a lot of time on her hands I hear."

And Papa turned quick to the door and stepped on the paper bag with the costumes in it, I guess I should not have left it there. And he kicked at the bag and it split and the *Engelein* costume got tangled in his church overshoes and he grabbed it and threw it in the corner and didn't even bother putting on his barn boots because he knew he wasn't going to the barn, I guess. And he drove out the yard, the harness traces clanging, no rhythm, no rhythm, because the horses were going too hard, and it was cold for their lungs to go hard. Like Grampa Schroeder said, Papa was not much good with horses.

And Mama came out of the bedroom and picked up the *Engelein* costume and said, "Never mind, Grampa said you looked real pretty." And Elsa grabbed the costume out of her hands and scrunchled it all up tight and held it to her and went to the window to strain her eyes into the night to see Papa going.

And there was no moon.

And that night, before Papa got home from Elmyra Bitner's, Elsa took the key to the box stall and went into the stallion. And Papa found her when he got home.

And afterward he would not even sell the stallion.

And when we moved to town a little later because Grampa Schroeder said so and even bought the house for us, Papa kept it at Elmyra Bitner's and went out from town Sundays to go to German church and ride his snow white stallion.

The words are said. The words of Elsa's dying are now said. They are in order, I think, and it does not seem too dangerous to have them down on paper. And Elsa does not speak yet, but I somehow think, now the words are all in order, if I just sit here and do not rearrange them, and think very hard on Papa, that she will nod and go.

— *Gertrude Story*

WHAT THE DEAD DREAM

The newspaper stories of the end:
white lights, threshold's crossed,
pearly gates, Maker's met.
Told always of course
by those who've come back.

But if I were a medieval gardener
I'd tell you how it starts
from the brow,
the hair that snakes upward.
And that the dead's dreams are green,
rooted in the skull.
Rows of them and on certain nights,
say nearer the full moon,
the ground thrums with their thoughts.
Their bones click and shuffle
on the spot.

What do the dead dream?
I don't know.
Perhaps their dreams are open
taking in all of us.
But I know what I see.
The leaves of those dreams
talking in colours and perfumes.

Maybe they dream forward
not backward.
The problem with memory —
stuck with what's happened
when the dead as the living do
need what's next.
It must be
they're dreaming to meet us.

I know, because over and over
the trees repeat their warning.
Green shout of spring,

winter's one hand bargaining.
Each spring I trowel in the gaudy annuals
a little less hearty
and Thanksgiving, I count my friends.

— *Bruce Hunter*

JEWISH CEMETERY AT LIPTON

They built a village
for their dead
body-long houses of brick or wood
metal grain-bin roofs
headstones crusted with lichen rough
on smooth stone on smooth fingers
marble meant for reading
cut with Hebrew letters
      Moses Raichman
      Grandma Schwartz
or wooden markers
the letters slivered by wind and rain

They planted no trees
but sage   wolf willow   buffalo beans
push through the fence   the mortar,
a star of David rises over grass heads
bent with yellow seeds

In the coffin shed a swallow nest,
a pot-bellied stove for winter warmth

We walk between the prairied dead
touching stone touching wood touching hands
Build for me a wooden house
with one open window

— *Lorna Crozier*

SUICIDES

Not the reasons or the means
or even that it seemed
so often, but how
our parents spoke of it,
their voices afraid,
the way they looked
beyond each other, out
at the dangerous fields, and us
storing it carefully,
as children do,
with the accidents,
burning houses, war,
things that
happen.

— *Leona Gom*

IN THE CEMETERY

The new dead call
Softly to each other
Across the banked fields

But they cannot be heard
Separated by so much
Bitterness and envy

Let them learn
Say the old silent ones
Grinning in the dark

— *Don Summerhayes*

EDICT #4: COWS

If you come across a mystery, don't go looking beyond yourself for answers. Don't head for the library and look it up, don't ask your neighbour or your friends. Mysteries aren't for solving. Think about it. When you head out alone across a field for a walk on a spring day when the air shines and flies hum like summer and you come across a pile of shoes, cone shaped and twelve feet across at the bottom, don't ask anyone else about it. Look at the kinds of shoes, workboots, basketball shoes, sandals, short-heeled Bertinis, hush-puppies: add them up. How many possibilities are there in a shoe? Imagine cowhide, stretched with the patterns of uppers and soles carved out. Imagine revenge and look behind you. There is more than a meadow there. Look for the ruins of a workcamp. Ghost town. Think about piles of clothes at Auschwitz, Dachau. Think Stonehenge. Think Space.

—*Jay Ruzesky*

THE TOWN IS STILL AS THE WIND

The town is still as the wind

Mountains above
are yellow winter light

snow against rock

Trees do not move a muscle

A magpie is playing
the last game
with a golden haired dog

— *Peter Christensen*

TANGANYIKA

After Jim Luster died he went to Tanganyika. He woke up at the wheel of a new car, and the long, black roll of road unravelled into the valley below like a big snake. The landscape was brown, its hills undulating and peppered with stick trees.

He woke up hot and thirsty, his hands on the wheel, his eyes fixed on the nearby trees that were the colour of a deer's hide. The trapped air within the car was suffocating, so he unrolled the window. The heat swept by.

He was tired already.

He noticed the trees on the surrounding hills were twisted — too much wind.

It was an Africa without lions; at least it resembled the Africa he had always dreamed, and Luster was disappointed because there were no lions. If he was going to be dead in Africa, he should have been given lions. But there weren't any animals moving in the valley or the mountains. There wasn't even a bird.

His clothes felt dirty, his mouth dusty, his head full of insect sounds. Yet, he drove on. He wanted to talk, tell himself he was alive, but a squall of crystal-like insect wings drowned out everything, ticking against the windshield and obscuring the route.

He drove for hours down that empty road in the empty valley.

Finally, Luster saw a man gathering hay, and he steered the car onto the dirt shoulder, breaking open a cloud of dust like birds.

The man leaned on a long, wooden rake-thing, waving away the dust from the car with his straw hat as Luster climbed out and slammed the door. The sound of the slamming door echoed in a world that was silent now that the motor was no longer running. It reminded him of when his head hit the rock.

The stranger had dark skin, tanned by years under the sun. A strand of rope held up his baggy trousers. Smiling toothlessly, he resembled a Mexican peasant standing among piles of golden hay.

"Have you died?" the peasant asked, polite, unsure of either the words or perhaps the crazy death they shared in nowhere. He was as solid as stone; big and full of the flesh a man carries in his prime.

"Yes." Luster's ears roared with the sound of the locusts rising from a devoured field. At least something else was alive out there in the empty land. "Where am I?"

"In the valley of Tanganyika."

It sounded logical, and Luster didn't wonder until later if the peasant meant this was a valley in Tanganyika or a valley named Tanganyika. By the time he realized he still didn't know where he was, the man had been left far behind.

Standing lamely in front of him, Luster couldn't think of anything else to say. He wanted to ask the man if he was also dead.

Luster realized the bright hay piled beside the rake wasn't grass. It was the product of huge trees spotted throughout the valley — dead-limbed giants without leaves, burdened by the yellow straw which drifted to the ground at every gust of wind.

"Are you infested?" the peasant asked.

Luster's heart began to pound. His body felt awkward, his thoughts seated above it, as if he were an outsider examining himself. Infested? No, it wasn't disease, unless the disease was too much life. The conclusion was violent and abrupt, but strangely, he didn't regret it. To lie in her arms, his blood leaking onto her, staining the wet stones by the pool, her damp belly cushioning him as the cold seeped from his fingers, up his arms, to the back of his neck. Infested? Is death a disease? Luster looked into the sun. "No." His eyes filled with black spots, so he focused on the peasant, and the spots turned green. The sound of the locusts returned.

The peasant bent to his knees in the straw, searching for something invisible on the ground, ignoring Luster who was still considering infested. There are two kinds of infested. Those who break down, give up, and wait for disease to tag them, and those who fall by chance, get caught by luck and circumstance . . . like him. No, that wasn't a disease. How could he deny the touch of her fingers or that smooth skin on her belly?

The stranger's hand darted forward; he caught something, cupped it in his palm. He stood up and showed it to Luster. It was a silver toad.

"If you're not infested — then you can watch." The man admired and stroked the amphibian his open palm, held it up to the sun and whispered at its head. The toad didn't move. It knew it was in trouble.

He took a small knife from the pocket of his well-used trousers, and with the knife poked out one of the toad's eyes, rolling the tiny ball in his palm as if it were a sacred object. He beckoned for Luster to follow as he walked across the road to a dirt lane while Luster trailed behind like a sick man.

After studying it for a moment, the peasant set the silver toad on the lane and dropped the eye six inches in front of it. The toad sat stupidly in the dirt; then lunged forward and devoured its own eye.

"Let that be a lesson. Never allow anyone to put out your eyes." The peasant shuffled back across the road to his interrupted haying.

Luster couldn't move. The locusts were hungry in the field. It beat at the back of his eyes, that sound like the wind of broken wings, telling him he was going to lose something, and he wanted her arms again, wanted to knead her flesh with his fingers. Alive.

The toad bounced sloppily across the dirt and fell into a pond of clear black water; giant, mossy branches interwove with each other beneath the surface. Green turtles rested on the mud bottom.

One lurched, almost too quick for such a lethargic animal, and its beak engulfed the toad's leg.

Luster turned away, ran to the car, and jumped in, driving off without waving goodbye. He knew he had a long way to go, even if he didn't know where he was going.

And the rock kept rising out of the deep water. Alive. Childhood lovers, they'd come to the same pool and swum naked through the summers for fifteen years, falling more in love each year. The pool. That clear aquamarine water. Cold. The surface rippled around the waterfall. Her naked skin gliding beneath the reflection. It was too beautiful. Why did he jump? Because she had surfaced and cried: "Come in! Come in!" And he had always jumped. Only this time God had moved the rock.

So he drove down that singing, hellish road for what seemed like eternity. His ears were pounding with locusts. His head was looking for all the memories — those that he loved and those he hated, but mostly those that he loved — the cottonwood trees rising above the river where the steelhead ran, the perfect cup of coffee in the morning, the satisfied leap of joy when the right thing falls into the right place. Her long hair spreading around her underwater. And for the first time Luster realized the insufficiency of life. He was grateful for what he had taken, yet he wanted more. He wanted everything.

She killed him. No, he killed himself. He always had to jump. Take that extra step. More love. More height. There wasn't enough life. His fist split the water and the icy world of the pool engulfed him in silence. Down. Down. The boulder rushed towards him. A black iceberg five feet from where it should have been. And he shuddered at the memory of the contact. His hand knocked aside in slow motion, his forehead striking and bending back. It was a dream, the dark bulk filled his vision, the crack that echoed underwater and his back corkscrewing.

He was lying on the stony bottom of the pool, his eyes open, watching her naked body dive towards him, the bubbles streaming behind her, and he wanted to touch her thighs even though he couldn't move.

When she dragged him onto the shore, crying, holding him, her skin clammy against his, he couldn't tell her that God had transplanted the rock the night before. He couldn't embrace her, say good-bye. But he could see. The blood on the stones, on her. She picked up his bathing suit. She didn't want to leave him naked on the beach. She looked so awkward staring at it, wondering what to do in that pained way he'd learned to love over the years. It didn't matter. He wouldn't be alive by the time she found somebody to take him back to town. He'd just be a body beside a pool in a forest. His eyes filled with blood.

The road veered, and at the curve was a large white house. It was square, lined with small, odd windows, something a cubist painter would design. The walls were made of whitewashed stone.

A young girl, perhaps seventeen years old, stood on the roof, leaning against a stone ledge, waiting for someone. When she saw Luster driving towards the house, she waved.

He stopped the car and got out. Not knowing what else to do, he waved at her. It was then he realized he still didn't know where he was, and worse, he had the vague fear that Tanganyika no longer existed. For a moment he wanted to go back and ask the peasant again.

The dark girl clapped her hands over her head and sprang high into the air.

She started to dance, moving slow, banging her open hands against her body and the stone ledge in a manner that told him she knew of locusts and toads and what they meant on this road.

He could only see the upper half of her body behind the ledge. Soon she was joined by another girl who was smaller but also lovely. They danced and hurrahed and threw themselves into the air.

A young man moved alongside them with a mandolin, playing a song that reminded Luster of the insect wings and hay the colour of gold.

The three sang and laughed and danced while the tears burned rivers down Luster's dusty face as he leaned on the car, one hand resting against the hot metal, one hand held to his mouth.

They shouted for him to join them. He was thirsty and tired, and they were so beautiful he found himself sucked towards the door at the side of the house.

The first girl skipped down the stairs and embraced him at the door. He let his hand rest on her waist, and smiled when she kissed his cheek.

Inside the house there were animal noises, the sound of lions at their kill, and he thought: "At last I'm getting somewhere."

The other girl appeared beside him. She ran her hand over his shoulder as if greeting a lover returned from a long journey. Behind her, the young man strummed his mandolin, half-way down the stairs, pretending he was in a trance. Luster could tell he was a fake, and began wondering about the girls. Luster had done his share of dancing — the boy didn't have it. And for a sweet moment, he wanted to show him how to dance.

Then the first girl swung open the oak door, and he peered into the belly of the house. There was a party taking place. The darkened interior was filled with people laughing and dancing and talking. Luster could make out no faces.

She smiled and pulled his ear gently. His hand was still around her waist. "Are you infested?" she asked.

And Luster knew that being infested wasn't a disease, no blistering and corruption of the meat. It didn't have anything to do with the body. It was time and chance. It was life. The rock. "Yes." The locusts drummed under his clothes, all around his body. He knew what was going to happen next.

"Do you want to come in?"

He was tired and thirsty. "Yes."

"You must give us your eyes."

He moved backward, dropping his hand from her waist. He'd been warned; the old peasant had told him what was going to happen when he'd been lucky enough to make the wrong answer. "No, I won't give you my eyes."

"But," she pouted, her hands held tight against her chest, "everyone is here; if you take the road you will never find them again."

"Everyone?" That awful lump was in his throat — the knowledge that he was caught on the hook of his dying. The road, he knew it went on forever, lifeless and lonely. The worst kind of death. Inside the house there was no sun. It was shadowy, yet the party was endless.

"Of course." She pointed to the dim interior. The crowd moved aside and he saw his father seated at a long table, drinking and laughing, pounding his glass on the wood. One by one, he saw them: family, friends — drinking and enjoying themselves, but it was dark and he couldn't see if they had eyes.

"You must go in," the mandolin player insisted. Luster didn't know what to do. He looked at the sun, that huge black wave of locusts moving towards the edge of the valley. Then he contemplated the murky room. She was there.

"Come in. Come in!" she shouted from inside the house. She was naked, as beautiful as ever, covered with blood, holding the silly bathing trunks in her hand. And the rock was behind her.

— *Brian Brett*

He was like a fox
all his life,
gliding into town under cover
of night
and sliding out again,
groceries stashed in a rucksack,
to the safety of
that little farm.
He was hunted by something
all his life,
it always seemed to me.

Today,
there is an open coffin,

affronted by a public funeral,
his little fox face
opens its hunted eyes.
They say,
Verily, verily, I say unto you,
close the lid, if you know
what I mean.

— *Gertrude Story*

GUILLOTINE

Braced for the blade,
the lightning slice of air,
her neck waits

her eyes are closed

She cannot bear
the summer colours,
shifting light, hot wind

An absence of birds
and the stillness of trees
press against her pulse
until her blood
slows, clots into vision

A sudden flurry
of leaves, wings

She opens her eyes,
feels the sun
drop

— *Eva Tihanyi*

THE HANGING

Charles Blessing came from a Boston family with money
but went out after gold to California and was on the way to
Barkerville when he fell in with James Barry a gambler at
Quesnel   Blessing carried this stick pin with a nugget shaped
like a human head upside down on it   and he thought he found
a friend in Barry so they travelled together on the
road to Barkerville and it was the end of the road for Blessing
they found him with a hole in his head lying on the dusty trail
by the pines and in the meantime Barry was strutting around
Barkerville wearing Blessing's stickpin with its horrible head
upside down and before long he had given it to one of the
Hurdy dancers   and when they found Blessing's body they
had to drag Barry back from Yale where he was just boarding the
steamer getting out of the country still wearing his slick new
suit and his pockets full of American coins and they brought
him back to Barkerville where he stood before Judge Begbie
and in the silent courtroom heard the death sentence recited
and they put up a rough scaffold in front of the Richfield
courthouse two miles out of Barkerville and strung him up with
an Indian who had killed a man in Soda Creek and a big crowd
turned out to see the execution

A Hurdy Dancer: I didn't really want to go and see it   he'd
been good to me and after a few dances when he came to the
Fashion that night he gave me this stickpin which was an ugly
sort of thing but worth some money with the nugget for a head
and he had a lot of American money to spend and was buying up
drinks for everyone but I had to tell them about the pin because
everyone in the saloon that night saw him pin it on my bodice
and they were saying things about the pin and where he was putting it
we had lots of fun that night and I wished I hadn't come to
the hanging with flies biting and dogs panting in the heat
and they brought Jimmy up the steps and tied a hood over his head
and the preacher read from his prayer book and then I couldn't
look but I heard a deep sound in the crowd like wind whipping
the trees when I ran crying down the street

A Miner: It was a sight like I'd never seen before in
Barkerville and never saw again   this scaffold they hammered
up in a hurry and the crowd jostling   even some of the ladies you
wouldn't think could stand it at all and then the crowd falling
back when Barry and the Indian were brought down from the jail
at the end of the town   and the Indian looking like he didn't know
what was going on   his face still   not a ripple in his eyes
and Barry was putting on an act to begin with like he wasn't scared
at all   like the good gambler he was   and then starting to shake
when he saw the rope   and the whole thing   the prayers   the hood
the drop   the bodies twisting like fish in a net it was over
and you couldn't really believe that those were dead bodies
hanging there   and the town buzzing in the heat and we went down
and had a few drinks but I couldn't blot out the sight of those
figures like rag dolls now where there was something moving a few
   minutes
before

The Reporter: I went to the hanging because I had to write about it
for the Sentinel but it was painful to watch and it made me
wonder again whether we had a right to take away life like that
even though these two had in their turn taken away life and
it was all unreal   like they were acting in a play in front of a huge
uneasy audience and it seemed a terrible thing to choke to death
in front of men and women who had talked to you a few weeks
before

Bowron the Librarian: I'm sure there were people there for sensation
   only
and perhaps what they tell us about our animal origin is true after all
and later on when I opened up the Reading Room one or two
miners wandered in and nobody said very much   and we all
leafed through magazines and listened to the sounds of
axes and waterwheels and hammering still going on
in the distance

Mrs. Cameron: He'd stayed at my hotel   James Barry   and
I never took to him too much   with his oily hair and drunk half
the time but I wouldn't go to see a hanging and Mrs. Pearson

told me she went and she threw up and was sick all day
and I had to give her a glass of strong rum to calm her down

Judge Begbie: I no more liked this murder trial than I have
ever liked any and yet the Queen's justice must be served
I remember when I pronounced the sentence on Barry after the
jury brought in the guilty verdict and I looked at him and saw
the same desperate look in his eyes that I have seen so many
times before and I went to talk to the Chaplain provided more
for my comfort and support than for the prisoners and I said
Have I done right? Is this God's justice? and felt more
at peace with myself when he reminded me that the Old Testament decreed
an eye for an eye yet there is a dreadful finality in all
of this and I am happier when I can dress down a scoundrel
who has been hoodwinking the public and tell him he is a Dallas horse
thief and like as not to end up hanged when I know there is no
danger he will be

— *Florence McNeil*

UNCLE

All day his name
has reached the satellite, come down,
and clear along the line, my brother says
that he dropped heavy in a room of light,
heart caught on the last beat,
a round stone in the deepest lake
from the dizziest height.

The story tells
of two men working in the fields
of women threshing grain
how does it go? That one will stay —

the grain lie lonely in the palm
and the chaff be blown.

All day long my uncle drops,
the ripples open out.
He has mislaid the place where words wait.
There must be another
alphabet
known wherever there is sun.
I long to speak that simply.

— *Sara Berkeley*

CANCER

The curtain pulling suddenly
    across the open window,
a blotter sucking up
    the white ink of the sun;
it stains a pale circle
    on the cloth.
And we, for the first time
in this darkening room,
can stare unblinded at the light
and see your death interposed.

— *Leona Gom*

PICKING UP MOM

It was just after football practice, I remember that
because my hair was wet from the shower
and my muscles were light but still full of blood
making me walk in an easy, broad way.

Dad's busy at home grouting
around the bathtub so he sends me out
to get my mother at her appointment, pick her up

at the main entrance of the Civic.
His hands liver-spotted with silicone
thumb and forefinger pluck keys from a pocket
toss them at me.
I'm young, enough
to catch without looking, always knowing
where everything is, just able to grab it.

My hair is long and wind
fingers it through the window. I'm not worried
about catching a cold, the day is warm
like mid-July, though September is nearly done.
I drive too fast behind the powerful engine
of my father's car, but I drive
with the road and not against it,
leave the driveway with the first chords
of Supertramp on the radio
arrive at the hospital doors just as Bruce Springsteen
finishes *Born to Run*, perfectly orchestrated.

But she's not waiting, doesn't appear
after a few more minutes, honk of the horn
so I ignore the loading zone signs and park.
It's a new building, all efficiency on the outside
marble inside and white to make it Roman.
When wide sliding doors move aside I can't see her
at first, but there she is behind a clot of white coats
half-behind a pillar and I walk to her
jangling the keys around my finger expecting
her to see me. She sees me
but doesn't spring up, stays leaned against the pillar
and starts to weep, quiet at first, then I hear her. I run
and because I never hold her
this is the first time I understand the way her head meets me
at my chest when we stand toe-to-toe.

I don't want to know so I ask fast,
what's wrong what's wrong but she can't get it out
through shudders so I hold her tighter

till she says it's the *X-rays*.
What X-rays? I answer, she says
to get the X-rays or picture of something
they made her drink orange juice, quarts and quarts
and now she can't stand up without diarrhea.
Diarrhea I say, she nods, sucks tears off her top lip.
I say it again and again to be sure and as I say it I'm already laughing
and her feet are lifted off the ground. We're
walking towards the sliding doors seconds later
and she's yelling at me to put her down
but she's so light,
my heart is so light.

— *Peter Ormshaw*

WEST INTO NIGHT

The late October sun lies west,
a cold slide into the Arctic sea.

Seven miles below the world falls away.
Frozen twilight. Crust of Baffin Island.

Striations: rock and ice, rock and ice.
Cold half-light reaches up and up.

We move always west. There is sun again.
Sunrise that is illusion. Resurrection.

The coldness below is no illusion:
sun can not burn away this ice.

Ice speaks the language of long night.
West, you must always fly to night.

— *Glen Sorestad*

A man leans closer to examine an engraving by Dürer, for at first glance he thinks he sees a screwdriver implanted in the forehead of the diminutive skull at the horses' forehooves; however, on second glance he believes himself to be mistaken. The skull does not seem to be a skull at all, but rather a lump of wood or the figure of a small animal. He shrugs off his first impression and turns to go to the next engraving, but as he turns he notices the skull and screwdriver again, in the periphery of his vision, and he turns abruptly back to examine the engraving again. This time the impression of the skull with the screwdriver implanted in the forehead remains somewhat longer, and then it fades as before, the same way the impression on a television screen will fade once the set has been switched off. Has Dürer managed to leave this impression or has the viewer superimposed it? The viewer cannot determine which; however, now he perceives that he is feeling rather guilty at having taken so much time away from the office in order to indulge his passion for art, and he proceeds to leave the museum.

The city coughs up numerous sounds and smells; he walks along the sidewalk in an absent-minded manner, a condition he understands as having been induced by the impression of the screwdriver driven through the forehead of a skull that might very well have been a lump of wood of the figure of a small animal. He waits in an eddy of pedestrians for a signal light to change, and realizes if he continues along his present route he must pass an enormous pit being dug in the centre of the downtown area and that his senses will be assailed by a myriad of abrasive noises. For a moment he ponders whether to conduct a detour, which will mean a walk of several extra blocks, but suddenly the light changes, the crowd pushes forward and the matter is decided for him.

***

In another part of the city a man sits behind a steering wheel, watching a car in front of him conduct an illegal left-hand turn. He tries to decide whether to pursue the driver. While he is trying to make up his mind, he receives a call on his radio informing him of a mishap some dozen blocks away. He secures the beacon on the car's dash, traverses several lanes of traffic and proceeds to the area of the accident. When he gets there he finds a large crowd milling around, hoping to get a glimpse of the body. Flashing his credentials, he pushes through the crowd to where the victim is stretched out on the sidewalk next to a barrier erected to keep pedestrians from falling into the enormous pit out of which the rusty skeleton of a future office building towers toward the sky. A screwdriver is implanted up to the yellow plastic handle in the man's forehead, somewhat up from the nose; and two tiny rivulets of blood are running down into the eye sockets.

Only two junior officers are on the scene and they are gainfully trying to hold back spectators who surge forward in successive waves in order to see the mess the victim has made on the sidewalk. Certain members of the crowd are engaged in exchanging loud invectives, as well as fists, in their eagerness to see the gore.

***

When I got there only two officers were on the scene, trying to hold back spectators who kept pushing forward to get a glimpse of the victim. I asked the nearest one to give me a description of what had happened and he told me that a screwdriver had fallen from a beam that the crane was swinging into position on the building. Indeed, when I looked up there was a beam swaying back and forth some thirty storeys above me. On seeing it I felt a chill scurry down my spine.

Meanwhile, two paddy wagons had arrived; officers from each of the vehicles began to disperse the spectators, and those who would not leave voluntarily were dragged bodily away, often flailing and screaming, and were disposed of in the paddy wagons. Even then many of them exhibited extraordinary feats of contortion, casting forth arms and legs in final last ditch attempts to link themselves with the gore on the sidewalk.

Half an hour later the scene was finally cleared of onlookers and we were able to examine the victim in relative quiet. I say relative quiet because in this part of the city the traffic never ceases, even for death; and, of course, work continued unabated in the enormous pit beyond the barrier. Indeed, since my arrival, the building had grown by what seemed at least another storey. The growth was independent of the workmen who scaled the numerous beams and girders and was occurring at such an accelerated pace that it left me a little bewildered. But such is the state of modern technology: it overwhelms the senses to such an extent that it leaves one in a dazed, thoughtless state.

***

After several seconds spent contemplating the construction, the Inspector turns his attention back to the victim lying at his feet. It is the look of horror that impresses him: features that would otherwise be quite ordinary have been contorted in such a way as to seem inhuman, an effect that is more than a little enhanced by the screwdriver implanted in the forehead and the two rivulets of blood that flow down into seemingly fathomless eye sockets.

***

I was ready to conclude that the death was accidental. However, when I examined the victim's personal identification I found it to be that of one Geoffrey Milds. That in itself was unimpressive; but when coupled with the fact that the initials G. M. appeared in the butt of the screwdriver, I was given cause to wonder.

I told one of the junior officers to get on the radio to headquarters. "I want a squad from the forensic lab down here on the double. Then I want the owner of that screwdriver found. Meanwhile, make sure no one leaves the construction site."

The questioning lasted all day; and because work on the building could not stop, even for death, we had to scale the girders in order to approach witnesses to the accident. It seems many had seen the screwdriver fall; several, in fact, had tried to net it as it was descending. Those who had tried to net it had gotten relatively close glimpses, so close they could identify the initials in the plastic butt. On each floor there was at least one witness to the descent of the screwdriver so that we were able to establish an uninterrupted path from the thirtieth floor to the first floor and then to the ground level where a passerby, approaching the victim from the opposite direction along the sidewalk, had seen the screwdriver about to strike the victim.

"That was the odd thing," said the witness, "for while I saw the screwdriver about to strike him, I did not actually see it penetrate; because at that moment he jerked up his head — perhaps having heard a shout — and his face changed so horribly I was distracted. The next thing I knew he was lying on the sidewalk at my feet."

"You say his face changed. How?"

"That I can't tell you, Inspector. Not with any accuracy. All I know is it went through these changes, each one a little more horrible than the last, then his eyes rolled back and they seemed to sink out of sight."

***

Although the questioning resulted in many witnesses to the accident, it did not produce the owner of the screwdriver. Several men remembered seeing it on the site. One in particular remembered using it for some purpose he could not recall the exact nature of, but no one remembered leaving it on the beam; in fact, several had distinct impressions of somebody removing it, although they could not remember the face of the person.

"We're always careful not to leave on the beams anything that might fall or hurt anybody," said the superintendent of the site; but nonetheless, the screwdriver had found its way onto the beam; it had been hoisted nearly thirty-one floors and had fallen with pinpoint accuracy on the victim.

When it began to look as if our questions were not going to meet with any success, we suddenly found a man who admitted to having brought the screwdriver onto the site. Although this man admitted to having brought it with him to work, he maintained quite stubbornly that the screwdriver was not his.

"You mean you stole it?"

"No. I picked it up on my way to work. You see, I saw it lying on the ground. I thought someone had lost it."

"Did you lend it to anybody while on the site?"

"Yes, several people. In fact, I remember lending it to the driver of the truck, the one who brought the beams onto the site. But after that I don't know what became of it. I was too busy, and besides I didn't place that much value on it."

Questioning in this manner seemed fruitless, so we asked him to take us to the place where he had found the screwdriver. He took us to an intersection in the east end of the city, only a few blocks from his home.

"You see, I catch a ride with another fellow, and we come to work together. I saw this screwdriver lying in the grass of the boulevard and I simply put it in my pocket."

***

Inspectors, by nature, are thorough, meticulous men, and in this respect I am no different. A man taught to distrust coincidence must by necessity find causality when confronted by seemingly random facts of events. Simply because an event seems accidental is no reason not to suspect something more heinous. Cause and effect underpin all matters seemingly inconsequential and unrelated, and this I felt must be the case with Mr. Geoffrey Milds and the screwdriver.

Ultimately, after much time spent walking sidewalks and knocking on doors, we found that the screwdriver had been in the possession of a man who had used it to install a tail light in his car the night previous to the accident. He had placed the screwdriver on the fender, had forgotten about it after being distracted by a neighbour and had, the next morning, driven off with it lying there, whereupon he had heard a clatter and had glanced in the rear view mirror just in time to see it fly off, and that had been about six blocks from his house. He had not sought to retrieve the screwdriver as he was in a hurry, and anyway he had come by it by accident. Apparently he had found it on his patio where his son and another boy had left it after making repairs to their bicycles. The son, in turn, told us that the screwdriver had belonged to his friend and that his friend had had it in a tool kit he always carried on his bike. On asking the son's friend where he had come by it, we found it had been left at his house by a furnace repairman and that the boy had claimed it for his own. The furnace repairman worked for an outfit downtown and he had accidentally included the screwdriver among his tools while rebuilding a furnace a year or two before. For some reason the furnace repairman had found himself to be without a screwdriver, possibly having left his own somewhere else, and seeing it in the basement of the house where he was rebuilding the furnace he had simply picked it up and started using it and had forgotten to replace it. Each person up to this point had had the screwdriver in his possession several weeks or months, and recalled it instantly on seeing the initials emblazoned in the butt of the plastic handle.

The man who had the furnace rebuilt lived next door to the victim. He told us that one afternoon several years before he had found the screwdriver lying on the lawn between the adjacent properties. He remembered seeing Milds tinkering with the carburetor of his lawn mower earlier in the day and decided to pick up the screwdriver and return it the next time he saw his neighbour.

"I remember putting it on the hall table, and after that I don't know what became of it. One day I noticed it wasn't there and I assumed my wife had given it back to him."

On questioning his wife, we learned that she had grown tired of seeing the screwdriver on the hall table, which was a rather ornamental piece and considered by her to be a show-piece, and had taken the screwdriver downstairs and had put it on her husband's workbench where such items belonged.

At this point we went next door to the victim's house. We found in the basement an array of tools that had been initialled in the same manner, apparently with the red-hot tip of a soldering iron.

"My husband was always very careful with his tools, Inspector. He felt by initialling them they would stand a better chance of getting back to him if ever they were lost."

In the basement, we also discovered a wooden model of Dürer's *Demonstration of Perspective,* a device the victim's wife could not adequately account for, other than he was always tinkering with one project or another.

***

A man sits in an office he suddenly finds uncomfortable and contemplates the enormity of events. He feels perhaps because of some law of causality not yet fully understood that certain things are bound to occur; he ponders the identity of a man found with a screwdriver implanted in his forehead and considers the fact that his initials were found in the plastic butt of the screwdriver's handle, and he feels underlying this is a relationship that is too vast, too ambiguous and too imponderable for his mind to fully grasp or appreciate. He remembers the look of horror on the man's face, for it was not ordinary horror; no, it was the sort of horror that allows one to think a vision has been glimpsed, a vision too frightening to be fully communicated. In looking up and seeing the screwdriver about to impale him, the victim must have glimpsed the horrendous nature of his act when, quite by accident, several years before, he had misplaced this same screwdriver after making repairs to his lawn mower. A man who had desired things to come back to him, he had, by the small exertion of will it took to emblazon his initials in the plastic handle, shaped his own end. No wonder the horror on his face! No wonder his eyes had rolled back into the sockets! For on glimpsing the screwdriver he must have also felt impelled to look inside himself, over the vague terrain of his own interior; and he must have realized the fatal error he had committed: that of exceeding a hitherto unknown law of causality. In recognizing this he had made himself vulnerable, he had allowed a small fissure to develop in his skull, whereupon the screwdriver, finding its way prepared, had slotted itself conveniently into the hole, the tip lodging deep within the manifold tissue of the brain.

***

It is the closing night of the Dürer Exhibition when the crime is detected; apparently a vandal, one exhibiting a great deal of stealth, for there is a guard on duty twenty-four hours a day, has unhung the engraving of *Knight, Death, and Devil* and has driven a screwdriver through the lower left-hand corner and has added certain artistic embellishments of his own: namely a dash of blood and two eye sockets. The police are called in and the Inspector who arrives to assess the crime immediately gives way to laughter. This laughter strikes the curator as rather coarse, for the engraving by Dürer is priceless and this crime has occurred in a museum under his management. He admonishes the Inspector, who in turn tells the curator that he has solved the crime; that he knows who the culprit is, a surrealist living in the neighbourhood. That surrealist is then hauled kicking and screaming from bed and is charged with gross mischief, destruction of property and corruption of the public's sensibilities. At the same time that this occurs, a man half-way around the world finds he has suddenly lost his faith without knowing why, except that he has seen in a dream a man with a screwdriver implanted in his forehead and since then he has found it impossible to believe.

— *Ernest Hekkanen*

GLORY TRAIN

When there's nothing more to give,
a nurse comes in to check your pulse
(but it's been taken). She draws a sheet
across your cavernous wide eyes
still following the rails
where one big headlamp probes
the snow and skims the darkness from the track.

As orderlies remove what's already gone
and wheel it on a gurney to the morgue,
the trainwheels click we're back, we're back,
the firebox swings open, glowing white,
and in the observation car you stand and point
— look, the station that we left so long ago
is still the same, the houses too, and look:
Isaiah and Al Jolson walking arm-in-arm.

— *George Whipple*

Ω

Love again. A dictionary of symbols.
Your body in the night is blue ivory.

A key. A knife. A stone.
Crows. Greed kills when you are young. Go hungry.

Fly me to the ruins. This is love. Runed.
Mockery. Meaning.

Rip out my tongue. My mouth can't mind.
Hold me. Hold me. Inside I am still young.

— Patrick Lane

It was a new voyage — the horizon's endline became clear again, and I saw with new eyes, new blood, new flesh, saw the coruscating body alive. The flowers were blooming — hibiscus, virgin's bower, amaranthus — and they meant a great nothing, a great horror (the huge wave that drowns us when things go wrong). I sat alone in the rocking chair worn smooth by time and movement, knowing I loved you, knowing I was hooked on your body and your beautiful blood, knowing that even then, even as I loved you, another man struggled between your legs.

— *Brian Brett*

NIGHT MUSIC

Mystery
in dusk's undulating shadows
as they give way
to the raw song of the streets,
the unfulfilled motion
of a billion arms and legs
dancing nothing

Mystery too, in the cosmic sieve
through which God's invisible fingers
trickle moons, planets, stars:
in chaos, a symmetry of grace

I will never understand
the process of light-losing suns
as they shrink into black oblivion
or the city hum as it slows into silence

Enough:
the curl of your arm across my breasts
as we lie here in the darkness,
two mortal moments
on a lonely spinning earth

— *Eva Tihanyi*

INTIMACY

I'm sitting at a table in a bar downtown.
My friend Steve is sitting across from me.
He's holding my right hand with both of his and he's
    crying.
He thinks his wife is sleeping with somebody.
People keep looking at us like we're in the wrong kind
    of bar.

My lover tells me I'm afraid of intimacy.
She says intimacy is a beautiful thing.
She says when you're really intimate with somebody you
    can tell everything he thinks and feels just by
    touching him.
She wishes I would learn to trust her.

I wish Steve would stop crying and let go of my hand.
It's not that I'm afraid of intimacy.
It's not that I care what the people in the bar think
    when they look at us touching like that.
Steve's right.
Someone is sleeping with his wife.
I wish he'd let go of my hand.

— *Allan Barr*

NOT YOUR VOICE

The evening is mauve.   My mind
remembers the black things
as green.   That is not your voice
I hear singing,   You were
always the quiet one,

the one who would say,
at most, *I am a good listener*
and you would present your body
as listener.

                  The evening is mauve.
My mind is black.   I cannot
distinguish you from the trees.

— *Garry Radison*

LAST NIGHT

last night we loved
like two bees
all sting and tingling skin

and all day
today I've been humming
at work
in a field of please
a field
magnetic with bees
their sunny buzz and circuitry

I hum to them
my bees
homecoming with pollen
my bees and I
our socks stuffed with gold

— *Chris Collins*

PASSAGE

Wake me gently: in this dream I am
the other woman, creaking your streetlit halls
with my insomnia, misreading the silhouettes
of her possessions. In this dream I am the waning
sharpness your woman fears on her pillow,
the shadow in her bath, the blonde hair
in her sink. I am the last hand
to touch you before she does
I am memory and worse.
                              Wake me
before I jerk from sleep in a bed
which has never held you, before
I stray beyond reach of your voice, tell me again
how it is in your own sleepless nights,
how the lights of your city
throw shadow-bars at your feet
and the cat watches your wakeful orbit
round the woman changing shape in your bed.

— *Rhona McAdam*

A GOD CAN DO IT

What light we know comes
from the winter's edge, the sea shimmering in the
sun's last light falling back on the bay.

Everything that comes together
comes apart too soon.
There's nothing we can call our own.

The things we shouldn't have done we did. I'm afraid of doing
something that always ends. A god can do it,
take the sun and the moon straight out of the sky

and make them one.

Forgive me.

— *Doug Beardsley*

At the bus station in Winnipeg,
buying a ticket for Winkler, Manitoba,
Wayman hears a familiar voice behind him:
"Make that two to Winkler." Wayman turns, and
it's Four Letter Word.
"I told you to stay back at the hotel,"
Wayman says. "I'll only be gone for a day.
It's a high school reading
and they asked me specifically not to bring you."
"Nonsense," Four Letter Word says,
reaching past Wayman to pay his portion of the fares.

"You're not welcome there," Wayman insists,
as he struggles out to the bus
with his suitcase and a big box of books to sell.
"That's not the point," Wayman's companion replies
as they hand their tickets to the driver
and climb up into the vehicle.
"Next you'll be ordered not to read
poems that mention smoking or drinking."

"I don't think you understand," Wayman begins
while the bus threads its way through the five o'clock traffic
and out onto the endless frozen prairie.
"The organizers of this program
asked me not to cause any trouble.
It seems somebody like you was brought into a school last year
and there were complaints all the way to the Minister of Education."

Four Letter Word stares out a window
at the darkening expanse of white snow.
"And you're the guy," he says at last,
"who's always telling people
I'm the one that gives the language it richness and vitality.
Didn't Wordsworth declare
poets should speak in the language of real men and women?"

"But it's a high school," Wayman tries to interject.
"Do you think the kids don't swear?" his friend asks.
"Or their parents? And I didn't want to bring this up,"
he continues, "but you depend on me. You use me for good reasons
and without me your performance will flop."
"No, it won't," Wayman says.
"It will," his companion asserts.
And the two ride through the deep winter night
in an unpleasant silence.

An hour later, they pull into the lights of Winkler
and here's the school librarian
waiting in the cold at the bus stop.
"You must be Wayman," he says
as Wayman steps down. "And is this a friend of yours?"
"I never saw him before in my life," Wayman responds
but his companion is already shaking hands with the librarian.
"So good to be here," he says, picking up Wayman's box of books.
"Now, when do we read?"

— *Tom Wayman*

TELLING FORTUNES

First Madam Sheusov the gypsy
swarthy in a swirl of skirts
with news of your next life
saying look west to know
the weather, east your heart.

Then the tired baba in three shawls,
her pudgy finger on your palm

*Oh yes, oh yes, somewhere soon
you meet two men together.*

And the Cree woman in Kamsack,
with tumbling hair and soft coal
eyes always looking somewhere else,
mumbling the sadness you now wear.

Put your teacup, your tarot cards,
your I Ching aside.
Give me your hand.

I will tell of a night of words,
a dark figure, a voyage, a death,
someone to love, someone to shun.
And kissing your fingers confess
that I could be any of these.

—*Gary Hyland*

ME & MEN & WHISKY

It's a strain waking up in a strange man's bed to the sound of church bells ringing. I didn't think I had any religion left, but the guilt sets in pretty quick with all that solemn clanging in the background.

I never mean for this to happen. It's the whisky — Irish, scotch, bourbon, doesn't matter which. The first few glasses are a warm bath, my face prickles pink, my legs tremble. A couple more and I'm floating in the smoke-blue air. I stop listening to the man I'm talking with and just watch his lips move, the way they curve round his words. I find myself tipping into his open mouth.

This goes directly against my sun sign. Aquarians aren't known as heavy drinkers. We're supposed to be social about it, just a few to keep the conversation flowing. If I were Pisces, it would be a different story. They like to experience the alcohol, that hazy feeling. I guess that's what it means to drink like a fish.

Without an astrological predisposition, booze isn't much of an excuse. Now love, that'd be different. Love can excuse anything. If we're fated to be together, who cares how soon it starts.

I roll over to look at him and he looks good. Thin, tightly muscled arms and legs, long legs, the kind that look great in jeans and boots on CMT videos. Oddly angled cheekbones, but I like a man with a flaw. Dark, curly hair, eyelashes to match. I could fall in love. But then he might not.

He opens his eyes. Blue. I like blue. "Morning, Gina," he says. He remembers me, this is a good sign. He props himself up on one elbow and kisses me. Then he stands all the way up and the sheet falls away. Long legs all right. He says he's going to shower then he'll make me breakfast, do I like scrambled eggs.

Yes, I could fall in love. But I fell into the scotch before I found out under what sign of the Zodiac he was born. I don't like to leave fate to chance, so I grab his jeans off the floor by the bed and rifle in the pockets for his driver's licence. October. Damn, another Libra.

According to Linda Goodman's *Love Signs*, the Aquarius woman and the Libra man aren't a bad match. Comparatively, that is. It's best to steer clear of Libra men altogether. You can't trust them, they vacillate. One minute they could be kissing you and offering you eggs, the next explaining the two of you are just friends. A Libran asked me to marry him once. A day later, while I was still thinking it over, he met someone else. Aquarians aren't all that decisive, but Librans make me that way — decisive about ending relationships.

I get dressed and bolt for the door. I want to be out of there before he's back shaking water at me out of that beautiful hair. I hesitate for a minute in the front hallway: there's the weekend paper, still neatly folded. I flip to Jeane Dixon, quick, just to double check. She's with Linda Goodman: "Don't make any hasty romantic moves; you'll regret it." I hear the shower shut off just as I click the door behind me.

Walking down the street, I start to think, what if that was Sunday's horoscope, not Saturday's. Was it going home with him that was hasty, or disappearing so quick. I didn't even leave anything behind, say a lipstick, or an earring, that I could go back for if I changed my mind.

I fish my monthly star scroll out of my shoulder bag, but it doesn't clarify anything. Not a word about haste. "Friends could help you establish a new understanding with someone important to your happiness," it says. I head to my friend Rosalie's restaurant, The Organic Café. It's the only place open so early on a Sunday. Not many of the clientele are battling hangovers this time of day. Besides me, that is. Rosalie can give me advice, and fruit juice.

"Hey, kid," Rosalie calls across the juice bar. "What are you doing up this early?" I pull up a wooden stool and she gets a closer look. "You haven't been home yet, have you?"

I shake my head, no.

She mixes up something to restore vitamin C and slides it over the counter. It's too yellow and too thick, but I drink it down. Rosalie knows what she's doing. She's a Taurean earth mother, through and through. "You've got a story to tell," she says. "Spill it."

I tell her about my cowboy and ask her if she thinks I should go back there. It's not too late to pretend I just slipped out for some muffins or something. Maybe it could still work out.

"Your men never work out," she says. "Have you ever thought about women?"

She's asked me this before. Not for herself. She says I'm cute but too flaky, not her type. I have thought about women; Aquarians are very open sexually. But so far I haven't met a woman I feel that way about. "I think I prefer men," I say. "Besides, most of the books don't account for the gender variable that way. I need guidance."

"There is a *Gay Love Signs*," she tells me. "I saw it in a shop in Provincetown last year. You work in a bookstore, order it."

I wonder what my boss would think. It could put a damper on my romantic prospects with him. Not that I necessarily have any. He's always getting annoyed at me, the way I mix up the Religion and New Age sections.

"Ah, forget it," she says. "I wouldn't wish you on any woman in your present state."

"So what do you think I should do?"

"Drink less, stop reading newspaper horoscopes and get your chart done by a real astrologer, if you're serious about it."

It sounds as if she's rehearsed this.

"And go home, you look like shit."

I figure Rosalie's right, I'm due for a change, so I show up on time for work Monday morning. My boss does a double take. I've traded in my gypsy skirt for something tailored, and I'm using a chiffon scarf to tie back my hair instead of draping it round my neck in a cloud.

By Wednesday, he's asked me out for dinner. I think about it seriously, it seems like the responsible choice. He's a solid business man, not too old. But I can't really get my mind around the idea of me with a Capricorn. They're supposed to have warm hearts under all that cold ambition but I've never gotten that far with one. Besides, I've got to learn to say no. I say no this time.

Wednesday night, the goody-two-shoes kick has gone so far I even call my parents. It's kind of nice at first, then my mother asks me if there's anyone special in my life yet. She thinks I'm a spinster at 25. I'm relieved when she puts my dad on, he doesn't care much about that stuff. But he wants to know if I've thought about going back to school this September, I don't want to be a clerk in a store all my life, do I.

With life this bleak, I can't resist sneaking a peek at the Thursday morning paper, just to see if there's any hope. "Trust your instincts when it comes to romance," it says. I'm not so sure about my instincts, but at least it points to romance. And sure enough, not much before closing, he walks in. He seems unremarkable at first. Tall and thin. Dirty blond hair cut short. Wire-rimmed glasses and a bulky, grey wool sweater. He browses in the Philosophy section for a while before I catch his eye and then he's got this winsome bewildered expression that draws me over there. His sweater is coming unraveled at his wrists. "Can I help you with anything?" I ask. Anything at all. I mean, it's my job, right. I'm stone cold sober and I want to fall into this man's arms, so there must be something in it.

Soon enough we're in the pub next door. Then in my apartment. I have a book he wants to borrow, he couldn't afford to buy anything at the store. Simone de Beauvoir's *Letters to Sartre*. I haven't read it yet, but some time I will. One of the world's great romances. I figure this is a meeting of Aquarian minds. I'm already thinking of him as the professor, to tell Rosalie.

My apartment is practically empty. Just throw rugs and cushions and one of those hanging wicker chairs. I always think I'm going to go traveling so I don't collect much stuff. Except candle holders, all different kinds. I have a weakness for those. And books I mean to read. But I do have some nice crystal glasses — my mother passed them on when she gave up saving them for my wedding — and a bottle of Glenlivet. He seems like he's worth good scotch.

I pour us each a whisky and he wants to touch my bare feet when I slip off my leather sandals. Before I know it we're half naked. He's got this beautiful scar on his shoulder, so I show him mine, a thin white line that curves under my left breast. He's not impressed. He's already shuffling through his wallet looking for a condom. His mind might be Aquarian but he's pretty business-like when it comes to sex. As quick and casual as a Sagittarian would be. I can't cope with the contradiction, so I send him home before it goes any further. He's not as bad a miscalculation as the guy who wanted cola to mix with his Glenlivet, but somehow worse.

"This can't go on any longer," I whine to Rosalie on the phone.

"No, no longer than another year or two," she answers back. She's losing patience with me, she can't take my love life seriously.

I call in sick to work and spend Friday in bed.

Saturday, I usually go to The Organic Café for lunch. Lettuce and tomato on whole grain bread, hold the sprouts. But I don't want to see Rosalie today. I hate not being taken seriously. There's a poster up on a telephone pole, advertising a psychic fair in the United Church basement, so I go there instead.

The only astrologer is a computer. For five dollars it spits out your chart with a palm reading and a handwriting analysis thrown in free. Somehow, I don't think this was what Rosalie was suggesting last week. I figure I'll get my tarot cards read, at least it's a real person doing that.

He's got black, chin-length hair, a goatee and eyes so grey they're almost purple. Those eyes drag me across the room. He strokes his beard with long, long fingers. I guess he's a Leo with that kind of presence, or no, probably Scorpio, sex appeal running out the door. "It's a dollar a minute," he says. "Are you interested in romance, or a career?"

I choose romance. He gets me to shuffle the cards before he lays them out, then he holds my hand gently while he deciphers them. I think about him touching me other places with those long fingers.

"I see a tall, dark, mysterious stranger," he says. That lets out the professor. It could be my cowboy, but he wasn't so mysterious. Kind of an open book, even if the pages are apt to change day to day. Then it dawns on me this fortune teller could be describing himself.

I file through my mental notes on Scorpions. "Mysterious." Check. "Hypnotic eyes." Check. "Comes closer to knowing the answers to the mysteries of existence than any other sign." Man, I hope so. And Aquarians and Scorpions are usually drawn together by something out of the ordinary, say, psychic phenomenon. We're supposed to be a solid match, if a chaotic one. But Linda Goodman insists that harmony can be attained through astrological wisdom and I bet he's tapped into that.

It's perfect. I wouldn't even have to get out of bed in the morning for the paper. Just roll over and ask, honey, what kind of day is it going to be. Tarot readings over breakfast. No more Jeane Dixon, I'd banish her for this live-in fortune-teller. My future at his fingertips, those beautiful fingers.

He holds my hand a little tighter and winks. Then I get it, just a pick-up line, and the spell of those eyes is broken. He probably doesn't have an ounce of psychic ability, Scorpio or no. I can't be taken in again. I tell him I've run out of money, so he'd better stop. He does, but says maybe he could give me a free consultation if we went for a drink later.

I'm thinking if I wrote my life story, some reviewer would say, "too many men, not enough plot." All of a sudden, I want real direction in my life. I want to figure out myself what happens next.

— *Kate Sutherland*

ON THE HISTORICAL NATURE OF COVETING

I

In the night air I embrace
myself, the only thing I am sure of.
I have wanted too much again,
even from this strange land and the wind
which barely melts my indifference.
You don't have to apologize
for being confused, or too old
to be my lover. It's nothing personal.
I had wanted you to be everything.

II

Let me tell you a story about coveting.
In this story it is 700 B.C.
and a young craftsman works in a mint
in Ionia, making the silver staters
I have read about in books, the coins
that have haunted my dreams.

In this story I am obsessed.
It is not the coins I am obsessed with
but the craftsman. Yet his firm body
holds no real fascination.
I tell him to talk with me.
I want him to tell me everything.

In this story we are in a city named Teos.
I have stayed here long enough
to learn the language. Night and day I am afflicted
by history. This puzzles the coinmaker
but he tells it to me willingly.
He is hoping to win my favour, perhaps a lost eyelash
to pray to at night. He searches my cheeks.
He asks for more stories of snow.

III

In the legend I become impervious;
a collapsed star, infinitely small.
I am alone in this place. I *am* this place,
and there is no-one here to tell me stories.

(And Adam begat Cain . . .)

Only the sound of a new world, moving around me,
the sound of my own waking, a coin
clutched in one hand, and the image
of a boy's handsome face . . .

I am journeying.
Tell me the name of your father.
Tell me the name of your father's village.

— Sherry Johnson

THE HONEYMOON

I didn't ask where we were going, or why. I was content to let the sun cut blades across our path; our raspberry mouths curve into smiles. There were times when even simple words could spoil a perfect moment.

But that day it was good. When I think about it now, anyone who saw us park the van on the shoulder of the highway, then disappear into the trees, might have thought we were just a young couple escaping the heat and monotony of the winding road, too much afternoon sun. Perhaps those with more vivid imaginations took us to a clearing just far enough away from human eyes so we could lie in the cool moss and make love.

"Can't wait 'til tonight, hey, Rand?" I reached for his hand as we crossed the ditch. Our fingers locked.

Randy smiled, his lips thinning over perfect teeth. "Is that all you ever think about?" He gave my fingers a quick squeeze.

I held our hands up and admired the new gold rings.

"I just needed to stretch," he continued. "The drive was tiring me out."

The trees were sparse at the forest's edge. It felt good to walk, to do anything, with this man I'd married just two days before.

"Okay, but if you change your mind ... " I playfully undid the top few buttons of my shirt.

His laughter rolled out. "I'll let you know."

Yes, it was good, walking through the trees with no place to go. Just being. The fresh forest air filled my lungs like a new drug and I couldn't imagine a finer summer day.

This was our honeymoon: four days of camping at a northern lake before we returned to our city jobs. Randy worked in a meat packing plant. I divided the daylight hours between clerking in a confectionary and delivering meals to the elderly. A Caribbean cruise and a honeymoon suite would wait until we were older and financially secure. We were saving, both of us, for university. For the better life I was so sure we would have. Six months earlier, when we met, I was sure Randy wanted that too.

"But what do you know about him?" my mother asked, twisting my long hair into a roll the morning of the wedding. I was the youngest daughter in a family of six children. My siblings had been married, divorced, remarried or not. My wedding was not the ordeal my eldest sister's was: the church, the relatives, the banquet. We made our vows in a city park with just a few friends and my parents wishing us well.

"Enough . . . I know enough." I smoothed my dress, a practical cream knee-length I would wear again and again. We met at a party, became best friends and we've been inseparable ever since. "He's a good man, Mom. A bit of a loner. I know I love him and he loves me back."

A friend's boyfriend worked with Randy at the plant and they introduced us at a barbecue. He was not my first love, but he was the first with whom I felt incomplete when we were apart. He was tall and dark, like the proverbial stranger who is supposed to bring luck. We had a similar sense of humour. We were fantastic together in bed. But what I liked best, though I wouldn't tell this to my mother, is that I enjoyed the mysterious aura that surrounded him. We didn't swap histories like I had with other lovers. With Randy, I didn't need to know about the women he'd made love to, the places he'd been. I knew those things would unfold slowly, like a new leaf, and that would be fine. His mother was in Vancouver and they weren't close. His father was dead, a hunting accident. I didn't press him for details.

"Is his job secure?" My mother, still concerned.

"Yes," I said, thinking not about his job, the apartment we would share, but how I believed he needed me so much because he had never had enough love in his life.

The pines. I had never seen trees so straight, so tall. I wondered how long they'd been growing like that, side by side and still as stars. At the tops of the trees, green branches extended like arms to touch each other. I thought they were like we would be, the way our marriage would surely grow, with Randy and I standing side by side for as long as nature, or the gods, would allow.

I stopped walking to look up and the trees, more abundant now, seemed to sway slightly, although there was no wind. Randy kept walking. I steadied myself before jogging ahead to lessen the distance between us. I was panting when I reached him.

"Oh, there you are," he said, and I wasn't sure if there was relief or disdain in his voice. "I thought I'd lost you."

"No such luck," I said, hoping to make him laugh, or at least smile. I tried to link my arm in his but he shrugged me off.

I didn't like this, not being able to pinpoint his mood. There had been one other time when he'd slipped into this silence, when my brother met him for the first time. Jim was only making conversation. He'd asked Randy about his family, and after, Randy became unsociable. He excused himself shortly after dinner and read a book behind the closed bedroom door. I covered for him, said he had a terrible headache. His sour mood lasted three days, and once it lifted, Randy refused to talk about it. I told him that histrionics of any type were wasted on me and that was the end. He never did it again.

Others had been in the forest before us. There were beer bottles and caps, a small circle of rocks where a fire had been lit. Further into the bush, I saw a man's grey work glove. Further still, a crumpled condom. Somehow, perhaps because I had been paying such close attention to other things, I failed to realize that Randy had wandered far ahead.

"Hey, slow down," I called. He continued, even when I fell still further behind to examine a mushroom.

Sometimes his white T-shirt disappeared behind a tree and then it would pop into sight again in the distance.

"Randy, I'm getting tired," I called, my hands cupped like a megaphone. "Let's turn around." I worried about our van, my van, really, wondered if I'd locked the side door. "I'm afraid of bears."

He called back without stopping. "Come on, I want to see where this path goes."

There was no path. The soft grassy trail that led us into the bush dissolved into higher, sharper grass and bushes I didn't have names for. We'd walked a long time and I was exhausted. "It's late, Rand. We have to get back on the road, get a campsite." I wasn't sure he could hear me any longer; I didn't have the energy to shout.

Yes, I was weary, but it was more than fatigue. Something had changed. The air, our shadows. The trees closed in on me now and the sun was sinking. My bare legs were scraped from fallen branches and from where I'd stumbled over gnarled, protruding roots. At times, in spots where sunlight was a gift, I slid into bog up to my ankles.

Finally, there was a clearing. The trees were much further apart but the sky, the sky was closer.

I was out of breath when I caught him, felt my thin blouse sticking to my back. "This is far enough!" I grabbed his elbow and he yanked violently away from me. In his eyes I saw the red-eyed fox in the ditch, the black and brown bears we'd been warned about.

"You're not my mother." And then he howled, his head thrown back in a guttural wail that came from some dark place deep inside him, and no one was there to hear but the trees and the squirrels and me, the bride. I could have stood there forever and become a part of that scenery, roots growing from my feet to anchor me. I'd come too far to turn around. Randy had taken off again, like an animal across the clearing. It was dusk and everything had a bluish hue to it. I had to rely on my ears as much as my vision, listening for the snap of branches, the crunch of pine cones beneath distant shoes.

What do you know about him? My mother's words whistled through the trees. What did I know about this person? He had no family at the wedding, a few friends from work. He'd lived in Vancouver, Edmonton, making his way east when everyone else was going west. *His mother.* He'd always been kind, gentle, even solemn at times, like there was something going on in his head that he couldn't share. *His mother.*

I knew then that whatever I did know was not nearly as important as what I did not know.

I kept following, although he was far ahead now. And then it stopped. I heard sounds, yes, birds, perhaps rabbits scampering behind trees, but not the sound of another human being in the woods. I was alone.

I yelled until my voice came out only in whispers and then I could take it no longer. There was a hill ahead, a steep incline and a thick tangle of trees. I could not find the strength to climb it, knowing there would be no one waiting for me on the other side.

I found a large dead branch, broke off the twigs and turned around. I swung my walking stick like a blind person through the grass and bushes that slapped my ankles. I thought of every bear attack I'd ever read about, every gruesome movie I'd ever seen.

"Sing." I said it out loud, but my own voice was small comfort. "If you surprise a bear it will attack but if it hears you coming it will usually run away." I was hungry, thirsty and I couldn't think, I couldn't get past *Jack and Jill went up the hill to fetch a pail of water.* Then, many minutes later, *Row, row, row your boat.* I sang to the birds, the white whispers of clouds. *Gently down the stream.*

I doubled back the way I thought I'd come, delighting in every fallen tree, every pile of deer droppings I thought I recognized. When I reached a clearing I'd crossed an hour earlier, I could see the final colours of the sunset and I knew I was headed west, to the highway, the right direction.

It didn't seem to take as long getting back to the trail as it took to leave it and once I was guided by it again, I felt stronger. I made my way, slowly and carefully. There were bears, yes, and surely countless other dangers for a woman walking alone in the woods, but I was no longer concerned with what belonged in the forest. The greater danger, the animal I was even more terrified of, was still out there.

It was dark when I reached the highway. I thanked God for the dime store magnetic key holder under the van's front bumper. I fumbled with the key in the lock and swung the door open. I hardly recognized the woman in my rear view mirror. Sticks tangled in her hair, face scratched and a small spot of dried blood, like a teardrop, under one eye.

I started the van and began driving. There was no one else on the road. The radio crackled and I turned it off, listening to my own breath as proof that I was alive. I was here. I remembered a sign we'd passed at the last junction: services ahead. I would make a call. The police. My parents. Someone.

Then, in the distance, something, an animal leaving the trees. I sped up to get a better look but it was no animal. It was him, running from the ditch, then waving his arms in the middle of the highway. I swerved, but I missed.

— *Shelley A. Leedahl*

A CONVERSATION

I am more than my anger but at this
moment I am possessed by the relief it
offers. Sometime later we will make
love touching as though there were no
danger in these bodies, fresh as first
lovers. We accept the other's embrace
without charge or guilt. Lines

between man and woman we cannot erase.
Our lives belonging to everything we
have touched. Always in trouble, in
each other's hair, saying the wrong
thing, expecting an apology when none
comes. Silent within this room,
our bodies shrivel in rage.
Cold hands, a reminder of heated words
on a frosty evening. Winter begins
inside warm bodies.

— *Robert Hilles*

INFINITE BEASTS

From time to time I watch you closely, with new eyes,
appreciating how much of you I haven't seen

and I'm no longer sure whether it's what I know of you
that attracts me, or what I might find.

When we met, I thought knowledge had limits, that in love
we were finite beasts who shared known boundaries

but watching you touch objects for which I have no desire
I see a measure of longing in your eyes

that forces me to say, I don't know you yet. That forces me
to say, there are places in you I may not wish to know.

In love we are beasts of infinity, crude in our longing
for things that may carry us apart. It's more than biology

or romance, more than drawing thorns from feet
with gentled fangs, more than all we have been told;

it's finding a reason to come together
without killing the wildness we each carry

like a gift we haven't decided to share
and hold inside ourselves with only the edges showing.

— *Rhona McAdam*

Ω

The throttle of pigeons in winter. Eave song.
Now we are anyone. This coming to love.

Our eyes. See. See. The myriad.
Crazed gold like insects. Waiting.

Mad images. Secular despair.
Dreams of pages. It is too cold for night.

When did I look out the window last?
Reproach. Flight in the leaves. First snow.

— *Patrick Lane*

ANIMAL LOVE

Tonight I am of the beasts of the backyard
my face is one of the multitude gazing upwards
at your window, I am one of the rumbling
furred assembly living to twine about your legs
when you step out and among us in the morning

Tonight I am the wild love running
and rampaging through your flower garden
chasing for the pure speed of it
the small competitors for your favour
returning happy, panting to wait for you

Tonight I scratch at your door
behind which you lie sleeping
somewhere in the dark civilized recesses
wherein I would burst in a frenzy of passion
to envelop you in my affection
the nuzzling, love-thrumming love
of beast for beast

— *Rhona McAdam*

HER STORY

I was born in a hospital in a small town
    beside a large shallow lake. My mother
said while she lay there, between the spasms of
    pain, she could hear the hard
flights of mallard and pintail, avocets, bittern
    heron, the ragged v's of Canada geese
come flailing in to the mudflats and reed beds
    around the lake. When I cried they may have
heard me there, the birds gathering on the shore
    before migration.

Once I had appendicitis and there were no birds
    but once, when I was getting my tonsils
out, I lay propped up on the pillows and watched
    the gulls, herring and ring-billed and California
even a glaucous, strut around the incinerator
    pecking at scraps of garbage
generals plotting a coup.

Later, my eldest son being born
    prematurely into the world and the birds
were there then. In fact, we had been out hunting
    and it may have been the squatting in the cold
blind while the mist came off the lake like a wool
    sweater, the steel of the shotgun ice
against my cheek, that brought the birth
    on early. Or it may have been the excitement, the gun
bruising my shoulder, the weight of ducks
    we carried back to the truck, or it may simply
have been the smallness of my body and its inability
    to carry full term. But he was early.
We weren't sure he would live. And the birds
    were there then too. I dreamt them tumbling
shot out of the sky above the hospital.

I live now near the lake I was born beside.
    The kids aren't that interested in birds.
I watch the herons and cranes and storks
    flap over and my husband yells at the gulls
that shit on the fence he's just painted.
    I somtimes think the birds are crazy
to keep coming back to this lake
    tho I love watching them
and I also know
    they can't help it.

— *Monty Reid*

RAVEN WIND

Those ravens now

    somersaulting

on the updraft

above the river

    rising

        dipping

    rolling

playing catch

with a pine cone.

—*Jim Green*

TAKING WING

See how our lives are
bound inside the hollow
bones of birds.

Dove and albatross.

We all would be Icarus.
Some burn with their words,
others reach the heights.

Out here, the stark crow.
Harbinger and omen.

We listen and watch.

We follow their flights
pole to pole. We plumb
the secrets of tiny brains.

Listen to the nighthawk call.
Birdsong blooms in the ear.

Who calls the eagle from its crag?
Who bends the flight of a curlew?

— *Glen Sorestad*

ANIMAL KINGDOM

We are the intruders here
our clumsy camouflage the lodge, its logs
that dwarf the aspen, their suspicion
a muffled sibilance outside our windows.

Wilderness itches to reclaim this spot.
In the morning moths fat as fingers
cling to the window screens
another tree has fallen to the beavers
and the river bank is closer.

The mouse has sprung its trap
eaten the bait and left a single turd
in the frying pan.

Someone saw owls at daybreak
hunched in the middle of the driveway,
fixed on the lodge; owls
we cannot find
in all our books on wildlife.

— *Rhona McAdam*

POEM WRITTEN ON WHITE PAPER

the howling of wolves
and down the road
dogs answer
sharply   the cat
hides between my feet

two deer
slip by the window
quiet as prayer

— *Allan Barr*

The grouse whose head you crush
to stop the wings
elk who runs.

The moose stares dumbly
at the hunter
who has shot eleven times
into his brisket.

He cannot believe
he is about to die.

— *Peter Christensen*

TURTLES

Turtle movements are
infinitely slow, so slow
a line between casual and deliberate
would melt
not quite away.

We cannot tell by
those eyes
whether turtles mean to move
or are moved
by some pull beyond

any history we know
or may project.
Did turtle eyes
survey the first land reaches
without wonder?

Not quite away
is where turtles will go
always. We sometimes have
time on our hands but not
all time like turtles.

— *John V. Hicks*

THE FAMILIAR ANIMAL

1

Note the horny tongue for combing the fur,
the broad whiskers that measure dark openings,
the fine hairs lining the rim of the ear flap
that make it twitch at the lightest intrusion.

No use for the pocket at the base of the ear,
unless you whimsically accept the fond opinion
that imagines a diminutive purse where the cat
hoards all the secrets that you whisper to it.

2

No, the secrets are safe because the holder
lives in another world. Once in a while my cat
walks up to the television and touches a paw
to the glass, wondering, "What's this warm box
purring in the corner." Then she walks away.

And in one of the slides I watched last night,
my daughter smiled in composure for the camera,
but the eyes of the cat she held like a baby
blazed demonic silver when the flash hit, meaning

"I am not in this picture,
I belong in another frame."

— *Bert Almon*

ANNUNCIATION

The children have taken an angel.
They have put the angel in a cage.
See the angel, crouching, impassive,
eyes turned toward heaven, barely room
for the folded wings. See
small girls dancing in a ring,
chanting skipping rhymes,
small boys poking with sticks.

You are very naughty, children. Now
we shall never know what message
the angel came to bring. Whether
a comet on its way to swallow
the earth, and us with it, or whether
a child, a saviour, to have another try
at straightening things up.

Hickory dickory jump him down
Jerry come join the jumping clown
Merry come jump through Bethlehem town

— John V. Hicks

LIKE GOLD TO AIRY THINNESS BEAT
(from *THE SECOND SEASON OF JONAS MACPHERSON*)

West is sunset and west is death. In the cool evenings now I lean into the setting sun, I press my cheeks against the west window and feel as clear as glass. The sun sings through me. It burns red, a dying ember inside my chest and I am happy to say that this has been a life. Each man must say it to himself: it was mine. I lived it, I was nothing other than what I am. And thankful that it was not a life lived alone. Here on this shore where people try to separate themselves from other living things, I was not among the cursed ones who lived alone. I found and I kept and when time came and tore it away from me, I lingered. I fight and grieve and would gladly tear out the heart of any living god who felt he had the right to claim what was mine, but I linger, I do not give in.

Look west and what's there? It's good that death should be west of here. The poets have all found it so. I have read them, God knows why. Even now in my old age they speak to me in my sanctuary of dreams and loneliness and perfect, holy fits of vision and longing. Eleanor and I read Wordsworth together, and Donne ("westward, westward") and even Alfred Lord Tennyson knew my sea from the other side. It was often like staring into a crazy mirror. And later, Kelly gave me Whitman, that crazy Yank, if only they all had been like him, alive, kicking at the throat of all the zealots who wanted to turn democracy into tyranny. If only he was alive today in America, chanting in the streets, cataloguing the vital extravangance of life and vindictive of all the destructive weapons of our imaginations. ("Unscrew the doors from their jambs!") Even Kenzie arrives on a moonless night spilling Robbie Burns into the stars — "That Man to Man thae warld o'er,/ Shall brothers be for a' that."

And west is west and east is east. The twain meet here. Outside my window at sunset. Inland and west, the continent grows heavy with the weight of greed, of progress, of fear and mistrust. I feel it sinking, a lead heart beneath an empty, rotted sky. They came here first, the Europeans, weighted down with God and power and desire. They found this coast first and here in the north it was cold, unforgiving but beautiful. Some stayed and died. Some stayed and killed — the Beothuk, the MicMac, the coastal peoples who knew enough of the ways of the sea to back off when winter came.

And then God swept his hand and the settlers passed on — south and west carrying much of the corruption with them. A few of us stayed in places like this with the cold and the clean and the hard blue line of sea keeping us honest, or called it at least enough — the Highlanders, the Irish, the French, who were not wanted on their own streets. And history did the same to us as it did to all the rest, but after a while it forgot us and soon we were a land of old men staring off into sunsets, wishing again for the sight of canvas knives scoring the horizon.

Thank God someone opened the floodgates here in this dominion and allowed the trade to flow off to Montreal and Toronto like unwanted sediment. If this is poverty, then this is bliss. Yet can a man fight to keep it so? It is not possible.

* * *

Carey arrived without advance notice, last week. He complained of the ruts in the road and his new wife tried to pretend she liked me, but I could see what she saw from behind those cold blue eyes: an old crazy man, a man needing an asylum, a man gone over the hill of life and trapped in a mad valley of demons and spirits. Poor Carey, sad Carey. The love in my heart for the little boy in him was hard enough to find. The boy was still there inside all those adult clothes, behind those frantic eyes. Carey, always searching, always restless as any boy should be, but always so hopeful of immediate salvation that he grabbed from ring to ring until he reached for air and emptiness.

"Things are fine now," he said to me. He meant that he was no longer trying to undo his life with pills or razors.

"Carey and I have a wonderful life," his missus said. I could see that she meant it although the truth was elastic. "We want you to come live near us in Toronto."

"Near?" I heard myself say, sounding like the old grizzly they saw me to be.

"A community of golden agers." The words came from Carey but they were not his.

"What am I, some frigging pedigree dog?"

"You need proper care," the missus insisted. She saw me as an old man who sat around with pee stains on his pants, an unshaven refugee, a victim of age and malnutrition. Who was I to prove her otherwise?

The sun was out, but it began to rain. I have always enjoyed that minor miracle, easy enough to understand, but a miracle all the same. The wind was blowing water miles perhaps from clouds too distant to see, that's all. Each drop fell like warm diamonds on my face.

"We should go inside before we catch pneumonia," Carey said, a man now of responsibility. I remembered when Eleanor and I had nursed *him* through pneumonia. He had not caught it from a sunshine shower but from the hospital where he had gone to have his tonsils out. His mother and I sat up through many nights just listening to our boy breathe, warding off anything else the hospital was offering up to kill him.

"Dad, we want to see that you have proper care and that you're near us. Now that . . . she . . . is gone, you need someone."

"I need, yes, but not what you think." They were looking around the old house now, just standing there, staring like they had been dropped into some medieval chamber of horrors.

"I need to use the bathroom," the woman said. We had not yet even been properly introduced. I didn't know her name. God what a terrible son Carey had become! What an awful, senile old goat of a father I must have seemed to him! Here we were, staring down each other in purgatory.

"It's outside. Go left, you can't miss it." Poor girl turned white, held her kidneys, I guess, rather pee inside the grimy walls of some gas station restroom, just as long as the toilet pulls a flush. "But you can just go anywhere in the woods, it's okay with me," I added. Instead she sat down at the table.

"We were thinking we could sell the land. I already talked to a developer in Halifax and he believes in this property."

"Goddamn, son. *Believes* in it?"

"He can subdivide, make mini-estates. Sell them to the oil people, the West Germans, the Americans maybe." Honest ambition and hope in his voice, the voice of my own sin. The voice that thinks of land as a piece of real estate. So it can be undone. You can be born here, raised here, feel the veins in your blood fill up with salt from the sea and minerals from this very plot, then drive off to an inland city and learn that it was nothing more than real estate. All this in the blink of an eye. I said none of it.

"Americans, West Germans?"

"With the money, Carey and I can take care of you, have you properly taken care of. You shouldn't live here like this."

"Like what?"

Her truthful answer was slow to come out and, in the end, she lied . . . "Alone."

It amazes me to think that what I felt for them both was pure, unmitigated hate. Had I spoken too quickly, they might have sent off for men and strait-jackets. I might have been lost forever. I understand that here in Canada, you only need a doctor, maybe it's two, to say that you are incompetent. Then it's all over, you lose your freedom. I turned away from them, though. I fired all that hate into the wall. It stood well, lost nothing. This is a good house. I've given it lots of anger and hate before and it's never come back on me. Those upright walls of wood placed lovingly together by Eleanor and me could absorb it all. So much love went into this place that it would withstand anything. Go ahead, drop that righteous bomb on me instead of Halifax, see if the structure would hold.

If Carey's wife had seen my eyes then, she would have run for the rented car, locked the doors, turned on the radio and closed her own eyes. But when I turned around, I had swallowed it all up. I had wrapped it carefully back into my life, into my memory of who this younger man was and who he had been. And I knew as well that he was the product of Eleanor and me and the world and one of the three of us had not fully done our work. And maybe I was to blame or maybe not. It mattered little.

"I'll make some tea," I said and smiled. "Then I'll make us some food." I said nothing more about the proposals. Two fighter jets flew over then, red wingtips carving away at the sky. The sound crashed inside the room and was gone. When I got up to look out the window, I saw the raindow there in the north and the sun leaning almost as far south as west. Before the light was gone from the sky, Carey remembered who he had once been and relocated the land that was still inside him and I could even see that his wife understood. We climbed down to the base of the cliff and sat in the sunset and I told them about saving the whale, about my pigeons, about the summer that never happened and more. When it was time for them to leave, it was Carey's wife, her name I had learned was Annie, who said to me, "We understand now and we both love you very much." Carey had already started up the car, but I knew it was him talking to me as well as Annie. It was probably my fault I had never taught him to express his emotions. Men, in my day, were lousy teachers. They could teach a boy to hoe, to mend nets, to build barns or fix engines, but they couldn't teach a boy to say what he felt. I had really botched that one.

Carey did roll down the window of the car as I walked over to say a last goodbye to him, and I knew it would be the final one. We shook hands. Men could do that, I looked deep in his eyes and saw me in him. The uncertainty of the younger man, the fears, the inabilities, but a will to get on with it. He nearly cracked the bones in an old man's wrist.

When their tail-lights had faded from the driveway, and the east was given back to green and black, I went back to the window and watched the last soft glow of red that ringed the land beyond Halifax — Sambro Light ticked a white flash every minute — as I gathered the fading sun inside my chest and felt it warm against my ribs as it dreamed me back into myself.

* * *

I gave up on the fasting for a while, worried that Death was out there to trick me after all, to trip me up in my own madness and steal in through the window without my knowing it. I could still eat but had lost a great deal of the will to want to do it. Desire. When you're young, you never believe you will lose the hunger for food, the demand for sex, or the thirst for booze. Maybe some don't. Maybe some are glad to lose the drive for it. To me, it's just a surprise, that's all.

Summer sometimes doesn't really make itself comfortable in Nova Scotia until September and this year, September was summer's favoured month. I went out to my garden and saw how I had neglected it, let the weeds tower over the beans, let the lettuce go to seed. It didn't seem to matter to me before, but now it was a demand. I picked up my hoe and planned to bring order back to the wilderness. There was a strong ache inside me, something that wanted to ignore all this and get back to the things I could do with my mind. As I began to hoe out the pigweed, I thought about what I had been up to. Was it just the learned ability to hallucinate, or something more than that? It wasn't just a clever, inexpensive way to entertain myself without a television set. I wasn't convinced that it was all made up, that it was the conjuring of a senile old fart. Sure as the devil, the younger world would not tell me it was a sane thing to do, or that I was making contact with other levels of existence. I wouldn't try to convince anyone of that anyway. But it was the power that gave me back my life, the past and the present, and I was free to move around within a realm more satisfying than what this other, mundane world had left me. And I would leave it at that.

A faint morning was now lifting, leaving a damp, warm land to dry out beneath the late summer sun. I could feel it pulling the sweat up through my skin and it felt very good. Even the sourness of my own unwashed self smelled good to me, for smell is a strong drug that also retrieves the past and it reminded me of the afternoons Eleanor and I had worked here on this plot of soil, removing the rocks, wondering at how they grew back like hard potatoes, almost day by day, throughout the summer.

The rocks had grown back this year with abandon. I had not been around to play their games and the garden was theirs, shared with the pigweed, the chickweed, the miner's lettuce, couch-grass and wild camomile. I'd be hard-pressed to find the beets and parsnips, the turnips and cabbage for winter storage. If I had to, I'd live out of cans this winter.

I unbent my back, feeling the years gathering revenge in my spine. Nothing like a hoe to make a man feel old and crooked. Then I turned around and saw that I was nearly face to face with a heron. It had landed behind me in absolute silence and stood there, not four feet away, among the broken weeds and brown peas. It did not move, nor did I. This blue heron, like all others I had ever seen, possessed grace, power and beauty unlike any other bird or creature alive. I had watched them for years in the shallows by the inlet and at the marshes of Lawrencetown and Chezzetcook, but I had never seen one up on land, in a man's garden like this. I wondered if my visionary quest had reached beyond the fast, if the bird was here as a manifestation of something still wandering in my mind.

That bold spear of a head, the needle-like orange bill and a neck like a powerful weapon, cocked and ready to fire. I had seen her, or others like her, stand in infinite patience on a foggy pond, legs invisible, hanging like a wraith in mid-air, motionless for hours at a take, then darting the neck into the glassy water and pulling out an eel as long as its own length, before swallowing it whole. And when it flew, you could see that the wings carried it with such ease that perhaps the body had no weight at all. On a grey day, it could make itself invisible in the wink of an eye, that silver-grey frame dissolving in the air, or pulling itself up into the clouds with one incandescent flap of wings, then landing again in the shallows like a gentle kite pulled in by a gossamer thread from beneath the eelgrass.

She walked around, not toward me. I flashed again on what I had seen as a child, fresh out of Halifax, sitting in Margaret's hot kitchen reading a book about dinosaurs to get my mind off the loss of my mother, the confusion of my father. I remember going out to the inlet and watching one land before me — a pterodactyl, alive and living on the Eastern shore. How Margaret had laughed at me for that. When I later told my father, he asked first what a pterodactyl was and when I explained, he looked at me hard and sad, no humour in his face, then he pulled me to him again and scraped his rough chin across my face until I thought I would bleed.

Joe Allen Joe had explained the Great Blue Heron to me as well. He had no trouble convincing me that they were his dead relatives. "They return, you know," he said, "I have never lost a relative who does not return. Some come back as snakes. This does not surprise me. But the ones I loved always return as Greywings." I let him lead me inland to the little ponds set in the notches of the coastal hills, places where gulls and ducks gathered and herons as well. He had names for the birds in each landlocked lake. "You can talk to them from along the shore. They hear you and remember who you are, but you should not go too close. They have already travelled a great distance to come back to your land and you should give them plenty of room." But Joe enjoyed being in their company, to be again with great-uncles and cousins. He would never let us get too close or try to feed them. Once or twice he tried to teach me to speak their language, and I was frightened by the curious sound that he could make in his throat. The herons would answer him and once it so frightened me that I ran off through the forest, almost losing myself once more in a thick wilderness of stunted spruce and fog until I reached the edge of the headland where the broken trees fell off the banks of the drumlin down the dirt cliffs to the sea. Then I followed the coast home as I had often done. I couldn't count the number of times I had become lost as a child growing up here. Always I had found some mechanism to lead me to the coastline, then my way home would be clear. A man is never lost if he knows where the land ends and the sea begins.

So, at first, I left the garden heron alone and continued hoeing, believing it would remain if I didn't try too hard to make contact. She walked a close arc around me and I watched her as I worked. When she had almost completed the circumference I saw her other side and realized she was having trouble keeping one wing up. It drooped as she tried to draw it up on her back until finally it fell and trailed on the ground. There was dried blood upon the lavender grey and I felt cheated out of my small miracle. I knew why the heron was here in this unlikely place. It had settled here with me because she too was about to die. Damn!

I walked over to my shed and, still pretending to ignore the bird who stood like an ornament now among the broke weeds, I found a section of fishing net that had washed in. Returning to the garden, I found her standing on one foot, an eye half-closed, but quick to regain her footing and grow fully awake as I approached. I closed my own eyes, centred on where she was, then without opening them, heaved the polypropylene net out and over her in one quick move. She let out a shriek and nearly escaped but I gathered the edges of the net and held her still.

Fearful of choking her or doing more damage to the wing, I quickly untangled the bird, wishing I had worn heavy leather gloves and a helmet for I was certain it was ready to spear out my eyes. I had to brace the neck like someone holding back a snake and I also had to arrest the flapping wing. She weighed almost nothing. All feathers and spirit, as Joe Allen had said, nothing more. But the power in her neck and feet was tremendous and when she finally grabbed onto my hand with her beak, I thought she would cut clean through. I let her hold on though, and as her feet dug deep into my thighs and the beak clamped down on my hand like a rattlesnake, I eased her out of the net and into the house. For the world, as I had always known, was often in need of repair and usually against its own will.

— *Lesley Choyce*

SNAILS HAVE MOVED INTO MY BATHTUB

snails have moved into my bathtub
I've been here a long time
there's a backlog of work for them to do

yesterday the phone stopped ringing
today no one came to the door
to pound   pound
a mouse whimpered by
bewailing lack of food in the house

the snails are playing in the hairs of my legs
jumping from fibre to fibre
their slow motions warm me like blood
as they move up to nest in the forest

mould grows   clouds my nose   mouth
I try to breathe less often   like a fish
keep my eyes open
I expected webs
instead the skin of my hands and feet has crinkled
shrunk close to bones
I have learned to crack shells
suck the cool jelly

at first I was afraid to sleep
last night   my eyes glassy in the dim
reflection from tiles
I dreamt of a tank in my past life
where hammerhead sharks froth   a frantic pacing
back and forth against the light
their snouts pounding pounding
frayed and bleeding against the glass
flesh falling to the sea grass below
where the snails feed

— *Brenda Niskala*

MIGRAINE

Through sleep she senses the flower
opening in her head; its petals
and thorns push against awareness, break
into light, a blinded presence
springing through cracks in her skull.

She would unroot this dark garden
if she could, but it lives deep.
It climbs from her spine
and shoulders; her neck is the stem
of a black uneven blossom.

She dreams a pale releasing haze
but the doctors must be certain;
not knowing the symptoms they are after
she cannot lie still, and they find her
nodding against concrete, held by the lattice
of this pain and her fingers
bent white against her own walled garden.

— *Rhona McAdam*

PENSEROSO

It is a cat, crying in the lane.
All my winter afternoon I have wondered
where sorrow was hiding. It insisted
itself on my trivial reminiscences,
my hearth's dolour, my indoor
reconstructions of summer. Light
your lamps, put your kettles on
to boil, call friends in,
make merry in the soft light,
ring little tea bells, drown
my lingering sadness, the cry
out beyond the gate, in the creeping
of my darkness, a retreat for sorrow,
there in the lane, crying.

— *John V. Hicks*

Ω

Pleasure. Success. Order.
Wisdom is laughter at the end.

The hardest to forgive is a friend.
Trust. Honour. As you go.

Don't be sorry. Art is short. Life is long.
Here. You pull the wagon.

Go. Move your mountain. Turn around.
Behind you is a mountain. Move it again.

— Patrick Lane

THE EXQUISITE BEAST

At the casual hover of a hand
your skin converts to camouflage
and reflexively you arm yourself.

But the exquisite beast, the animal you fear
is dead, died years ago, wasted
from running, something bursting in his brain,
flesh and fur gone from his carcass, white bones
sinking in the ground-drift of time.

Your eyes have been lying all these years.
And the terrified others, the game safe
and love forfeit, have all been lying.

You stay on the plains away from trees
and ledges where he might pounce. All
through the night your cabin lights blaze.

But he is dead. He is dead. There is a path
you never take along the coulee's brow.
Follow it and find his ordinary bones.
Spend a night in conquest of them.
Then ride out of your badlands. Home.

—Gary Hyland

THE MAZE GAME

Paquette stood at his living room window and watched the snow. It came down steadily at a stubborn, unhurried pace. It had all day. And all night. And all day. No relief in sight, according to the radio.

Paquette was torn. As janitor of this place, sooner or later he would have to go out and shovel the snow. No one would blame him if he waited until the snow stopped. That's what most people did. Still, in some ways it would make the job easier in the long run if he did some shovelling now, if he got one layer off at least.

Or got one on. Depending on how you looked at it. Which was the problem. There was nowhere to put it. Already, along the streets of the city, snow plows had furled snow into ice fortresses. Citizens, shovelling themselves out, had turned sidewalks into walled corridors, front yards into roofless igloos.

Another layer of plaster on the wall, thought Paquette. What a job snow shovelling was getting to be! Bend and lift. Bend and lift. Already he could feel the soreness of his muscles.

Behind his back a clock ticked the rhythm of the snow. Otherwise, the house was silent. Paquette lived alone now, since Marie and Rick bought that new house in that snazzy suburb. "Don't worry, Grampa," Marie had said when she left with the truck one Saturday afternoon in October. "You can come and see us anytime you feel like it."

And they came back often, on Sundays, for supper. Today, they would be here in a while. In the kitchen, in a big black pot on the back burner of the stove, goulash bubbled. The air was thick with garlic. Marie did not like to smell up her new house with garlic. But she loved it, the smell and the taste. He knew that.

Around him Paquette felt the presence of the other tenants of the house. At least he was not alone. Still, it was not the same as having Marie. Borrowing parts of people for an hour here, an afternoon there, was not the same.

Marie used to tell him how you can't own other people.

"No one said anything about owning," he said. "Some people belong to each other, that's all. People in families, husbands and wives.

"Don't lay that trip on me, Grampa," Marie would answer. This was during those years when she was growing up and after her grandmother died. "If you belong to other people, how can you belong to yourself?"

"That's dumb," he used to say. Maybe he had even shouted. Remembering it now, he could hear himself shout. "You gotta belong to somebody! Otherwise, you're nobody!" Paquette took a breath in and thought how life is one long good-bye. His mother and father, his wife, his daughter who went to the Coast. Now Marie. And saying good-bye doesn't get any easier. He knew that now; that was one thing he had learned.

Constance had warned him. On her deathbed. "Be careful, Romeo," she had said. "With just the two of you now, you'll break each other's hearts. Be careful." As it turned out, those were her last words.

Paquette considered putting on his coat, his boots. Snow demanded a lot of effort, one way or another. Still, he did not hate it. What would be the use of that? He simply accepted snow as inevitable. That's life, he thought. Whether he liked it or not.

Now, even the clock was silent, as though time itself was drawing breath for another onslaught. Where is everybody? wondered Paquette.

Across the hall at the back, the Corset Lady stood at her window looking into a white cave. Her old eyes hung down in triangles of worry. Willie should be back by now. It was not like him to stay out this long in the cold.

This morning when she opened the window, he did not want to leave. He put one paw out into the snow and brought it, stiffly, back. He sat and looked at the snow with his good eye. Finally, she had to give him a shove. His dark shape arched a moment against white before bounding into the blank space.

Narrowing her eyes, the Corset Lady could make out faint shapes of garage, trees, lane, houses across the lane, white against white. Or she thought she could. She had been looking out this window for so long, she no longer knew what she was seeing or what she was imagining. Maybe it's all the same, she thought.

Upstairs, above the Corset Lady, Popi sat at his kitchen table holding his chin up with his thumb, a cigarette dangling between index and middle finger. He, too, was looking out the window. From up here, down there fences were walls, two feet thick. Back walks leading to garbages and garages were narrow as secret passages.

His mind was full of white silence, when just then it was broken by something dark moving in from the edge. Toque, scarf, the shoulders of a winter coat, a travelling coat rack passed Popi's vision as the top half of Mrs. Easterbee floated down the lane. And another movement —Wong next door running his back yard maze with a bag of garbage, his short legs mincing the snow. When Wong reached his back gate, the two solitary players in Popi's game were within a few feet of each other.

Popi's eyes flared.

Just as Wong entered the lane, Mrs. Easterbee turned in at the further gate and headed for port.

Popi took a long pull on his cigarette and let the smoke out slowly.

In the next room Rita sat on a bed sorting pictures into an album. She stopped with a photo in her hand. She brought the photo closer to her face and looked in. She saw two children standing beneath a tree. The boy had a scowl and a bandaged knee. The girl had a smile and a straight hairbow. The girl had never been any trouble.

"Was I born?" the boy in the picture says. His eyes even then burning darkly with all he saw.

"Yes, you were born," Rita says, her face young again and smiling. "You came out of mommy's tummy."

"Like a kangaroo?"

"No, you were inside mommy. When you started you were very small like my teeny fingernail and you grew and grew and I loved you even when you were teeny like my fingernail."

Outside, the snow fell and stuck to the window and to the white walls of the house.

Across the hall, the Widow Tree looked out at the front. Surely, Lilah would be home soon. She had left in such a huff. It didn't seem to take anything to get her going these days. She had come into the kitchen looking for a snack as per usual. Tree heard her own voice speaking, the way she would tell it to Rita later when Rita dropped in for a cup of tea.

"I was getting breakfast, I hadn't had a thing to eat yet, when in she comes. Like she had her breakfast an hour before, and now she wants to eat again already! And I said to her in just the same voice I'm using now, calm as calm, I'm making myself a piece of toast and I'm very tired this morning. I was, too, because I'd been up sewing half the night on her new dress and I didn't get it finished, I might add, and she wants it for next week, so I says to her, I'm very tired and I don't want any hassle at least until after I've had my coffee and why you have to eat nonstop from one end of the weekend to the other is more than I'll ever know. Well! you should've heard her. That's all you ever do is yell at me and why did you ever have me anyway if you don't want your lousy kitchen messed up and I can hardly wait to leave this dump, and on and on and on, and I hadn't even raised my voice!"

But where is she? wondered Tree. What is there to do out there on a Sunday afternoon in winter? With all this snow. Out on the streets. Inside, thought Tree. The only place to be on a day like this.

Beneath her, Paquette thought how he would not be able to see the car stop at the curb. Because of the snow and the high walls. And he had to go out and make them even higher. But that was his job. To keep the walks clear. He stirred. No sense waiting for it to stop. Maybe it would never stop. That's what it looked like. Snow forever. Outside, he had a better chance. He might see them sooner that way, maybe spot their car coming down the street. The least he could do was clear a path so they could get into the house.

Paquette turned. Somewhere a door clicked.

Is that her? thought Tree, holding her breath.

Is that him? thought Rita, raising her head.

Is that him? thought the Corset Lady, trying to see.

Is that them? thought Paquette, pausing.

Popi, the poet, heard only his thoughts spinning white.

— *Cecelia Frey*

CITY EVENING

Ocean darkens. Night flows in.
Planes howl overhead eighteen times each hour.
Roofs call vigilance; brass birds gleam in the city.
The small snow has come; exiled footprints appear.
Early autumn, white dew on the road.
Early evening, north wind soaks my sleeves.
Owls peel darkness from the moon's face.
My friend, you are far away, your letters
                do not reach me here.

— Helen Hawley

THE WARNER BROS./SHAKESPEARE HOUR

"Will you walk out of the air, my lord?"

The fine tuning won't prevent
channel 4 from drifting into 3
as a faint background
so that *Hamlet* is haunted
by ghostly figures
of the Coyote and the Roadrunner

As Hamlet says *"To be or not to be"*
I can make out the Coyote climbing
a ladder suspended in mid-air
Convention says he won't fall
until he tops the ladder and looks down
He'll smash on the desert floor
and come back renewed in another frame

Hamlet finishes his soliloquy
and greets the fair Ophelia
The Coyote has built a bomb

and lights the fuse
He has no trouble taking arms
while Hamlet is the man who looks down
and knows that resurrection
is not a convention of his play
We share his terror
rung by rung

— *Bert Almon*

COMING HOME

I am the absence I see, or
    feel in you

it is myself I am missing

the empty place   I want
is my silence

the absence of sound
    ringing

— *Anne Campbell*

Before he opened his paper, he glanced down the row of faces opposite. He was not looking for anything. His mind was on an incident at the office that is lost to him now if he tried to recall. It amused him how the English scrutinised each other in the Underground, planted in their rows like beans. He liked to catch two people watching one another without their eyes ever meeting. Yet when he was caught looking someone full in the face, he quickly averted his eyes. If it was a woman, even a plain woman, he was aware he often blushed. Frequently when the carriage was empty he played the game with himself in the window opposite. On good days he risked a wink or a wry smile. In general, he was troubled by his weight and thinning hair, and looked quickly away.

He liked to see a pretty face on the tube. He liked to know without looking that a slender leg was three feet from his own; the hollow of an ankle could arouse in him a peculiar melancholy that was pleasant. Sooner or later he always became engrossed in his paper. Sometimes he thought of his wife for a little: not in clear pictures, but in words and abstractions. She was a gentle woman.

He had a theory: on days when a lovely woman sat across from him, there would invariably be three or four more in the carriage. On these days he did not notice the twelve stations go by. Even the men seemed exemplary specimens. He would smile to himself, thinking what a flaw in the design he was. The lower buttons on his shirt gaped, his trouser leg rode up. He didn't mind. If, on the other hand, an ugly woman sat opposite, her companions were likely to be drab. Everyone's hair looked greasy. Dandruff prevailed.

The train was full but not crowded, and he got a seat at once: his favourite, at the end. With pleasure he folded his paper and patted it down in his lap. In his first, cursory glance he saw her, but the tiny sound he made involuntarily in his throat was swallowed easily by the train's hum. Suddenly, he had no desire to scan the rest of the faces opposite, nor to make out the reflections of his neighbours in the windows. He looked quickly at his paper. He had read the first paragraph twice. He felt a strong desire to look at her again. She might be getting off at the next station; like hundreds before her, she would disappear in the crowd. Beauty was made to be gratefully admired. He raised his eyes. She was staring an inch to the left of him. She looked transfixed, the word came to him, clear as a bell. Hurriedly he looked away, annoyed with himself, but at the same time acutely troubled. He felt a sensation at the back of his neck and knew it must be the beginning of a blush. Her look! He stared at a point on the door, struggling to think why her look troubled him so greatly. Certainly she was striking. She had the bone structure of a very lovely woman, her hair was silky and escaped from her black felt hat in the kind of tangled curls he particularly liked. Who did she resemble? No one. He realised he had never seen another woman like her. But it was not her face that kept him in this suddenly heightened state — it was her expression. She had stared a little to one side of him with a look of wildness, there was no other way to describe it.

Stiffly, he returned to his paper and read the same paragraph. His eyes fixed on the last word, unseeingly, as he realised that the train was slowing at a station. Once again, she might get off. She might leave. In ten seconds he could be staring at an empty seat, unable to believe she was no longer there. He had to look at the face one more time. His sense of foolishness was uncomfortable, but as the train stopped and she did not move, he let relief embolden him and glanced across. Her eyes were closed.

He did not hear the babble of alighting and movement in the train around him. For a moment he held his breath. He felt a brief, unidentifiable ache in his abdomen. She sat very still, almost stiffly, with her hands loose on her lap. Her clothes were dark — he took them in confusedly, tensely aware that at any second she might open her eyes and look at him. An infinitesimal scene tripped through his head: she saw him, she was angry, she shouted something, reached across and slapped his face. He felt a hot blush spreading from the roots of his hair, he could feel the tingling on his cheek that followed the sharp impact of her hand.

On her lap, the fingers of one hand clenched suddenly into a fist, then relaxed. She wore no rings. Her eyes were still closed: he allowed himself three agonisingly long seconds taking in the lashes, the cheekbones, the perfect skin, then looked dazedly back down at the paper in his lap. He brought one hand out from under it and studied his nails with care. Details like the white of his cuticles brought him slowly back to rational thought. My god she's lovely. He though the words once, loudly, then felt a delicious, tantalising power. If he read his paper for a little longer, before they reached the next station, he could turn the page and take the natural opportunity to glance idly round the carriage. It bothered him that someone might have seen him staring at her, seen the incriminating blush. He wanted to look around defensively, aggressively even, to subdue any knowing looks he might receive. But I am ridiculous, he thought, and again the words came loud and clear. Ridiculous. An old ass. He thought with a smile of his son's latest phrase: a spa. You're a spa daddy. He had rebuked him for using it just the other day.

The train slowed and all thoughts were wiped from his mind. He turned the page of his paper with difficulty. Despite years of practice the paper refused to fold. It rucked in the middle, the inside pages slipped sideways; it was a mess, and the train had stopped. Still, she did not move and he felt absurdly like laughing. One more, then, one more indulgence. At last he got the paper straight. She was staring down now, directly at his feet. He felt his toes stiffen. Briefly he tried to picture his shoes: which ones was he wearing? What colour socks? Her hands were moving in her lap now, a vague fumbling movement — but her eyes . . . did she never blink? Abruptly she lifted her head, but in the moment before he turned his away, he saw that she was looking distractedly to one side, listening to an announcement from the platform. The train would take one of two branches at the next station. Sometimes they changed their minds, you had to listen. The doors closed and he hadn't heard. Let it be! If she alighted at the next station, well, he could too! It didn't matter which line he took. They joined up later and he rode on for several stops.

On the second page of the paper his eye was caught by pictures of the war; tanks, explosions, soldiers, the waste sickened him. His eyes felt irritated and smarted as though stung by the desert sand. The whole world gone mad, and for what? Life went on. Take the woman: it was plain to him she was caught up in some close drama of her own — what might it be? By the cut of her clothes she was a well-bred woman. He winced as two lines of thought crossed his head: here he was, calmly wondering what sort of calamity might have befallen her that she could look so stricken; at the same time, his thoughts were a hotbed of fantasies. He pictured her crossing a bridge in the wind, her dark coat billowing, her hair blowing across her face. For a moment, as his mind focussed sharply on this scene, it seemed unbearable that his woman should be someone he had casually sat opposite not ten minutes ago on a train. How had he worked himself to such a fever pitch in that time? How had the few glimpses of her face worked so powerfully, and stirred such agitation, such peculiar excitement as he was now feeling?

In a moment he had decided: if she left the train at the next station he would follow. He would casually cross to the other branch, as though it was something he naturally had to do. If she crossed too, perhaps they could continue their journey together in harmless, onesided companionship, in a sort of secret union; it was, after all, harmless and so . . . harmless . . . her calves were crossed and elegant in dark stockings, the skirt long, the knees shapely through the light fabric; the train was slowing, he frowned and clutched his paper. Should she move, he must be ready to follow quickly; so easy for a figure to be swallowed in the crowd, the teeming carnival of the underground . . .

She was not getting off. She was looking above him, her mouth a little open, and he imagined in the brief glimpse he allowed himself that her breath was coming in short gasps. Perhaps she was ill! Again he felt his scalp prickle as he stared intently at the newsprint. He hated illness in public places. But she did not look ill. He was sure she wasn't ill. It was something else. A matter of love, surely, a matter of the heart. In spite of himself, he felt like smiling; a middle-aged gent on his way home from the office, making up stories about a pretty face. Strangers on a train. The doors closed. He really had intended to get off the train if she had! What would be do, follow her? She would have left the station, and then where would be be? Stranded, on the platform, the picture of foolishness. It was not like him to risk looking foolish. In this way, he tried to swallow it down, the rise of his feelings, the lightness that took hold. The next stop was Waterloo: he though of that picture of the bridge in purple smoke and dusk. She would get off at Waterloo. She would cross the bridge in the evening with the sky and the water turning just those lurid colours: a dark, threatening cumulus of blues and purples.

Far underground, where seven tunnels met in a wide passage, seven streams of people merged and massed at the foot of the escalator. She took the right hand side. She was a swift and accurate mover in the crowd. He trod on toes and elbowed people out of the way, distantly amazed at his own rudeness. He almost lost her on the steps behind a group of boys. He almost lost her again passing through the ticket barrier. Caught behind an old man, his impatience turned to panic. There was only one reason he was emerging from Waterloo station at five on a Tuesday and it was itself so elusive he had difficulty keeping it in his grasp. She was slipping away from him. Gritting his teeth, he pushed through the crowd, muttering excuses, his eyes fixed on the black hat thirty yards away. "Alright, alright," the ticket collector said, and an old lady nearby clucked reprovingly.

The black hat was still visible beyond the people walking the long corridor at the back of the concourse. Red railings. White tiles. It was a long time since he had been in Waterloo station. A beautiful building, with its latticework and gables. He remembered it well and knew if he glanced to his right, past the telephones, he would glimpse the lofty iron trelliswork of the roof. She was now turning towards the York Road exit.

His shoes sounded smartly on the tiles and for the length of the corridor he allowed himself to feel as full of purpose as he sounded. In fact, he was in a strange state. He rational side was sitting back, far back in the shadow of this thing, whatever it was, that was driving him forward in her pursuit. Having left the train he knew there was no turning around. The balance tipped, his excitement tampered with the valves of his heart, he was passing through fire. He could just see the tails of her coat billow as she turned the corner. He racked his brains to recall the geography of the place: another flight of stairs and then a confusion of turnings and exits — the red iron gates folded back from the main exit ahead. He would surely lose her there. The humiliation of turning back now! He broke into a heavy run.

It had begun to rain, an unsteady drizzle, and commuters were pouring into the station. By the taxi rank, he stood a moment, out of breath already, searching for her. She had broken free from the crowd and was heading for Waterloo Bridge. Years before, he had worked for a while with the homeless on the Embankment. He and a group of others had brought them food, sat around the fires when they were welcome, listened to the stories. Memories of that time flooded him as he descended to the riddle of subways and emerged on the great bowl, wet now and bleak as ever. She was entering the far tunnel, the one that led up to the bridge itself. To follow her, he would have to pass them, the shambling figures round their fires, huddled in their blankets. Suddenly, he felt his face begin to burn with shame. Once he had come here with time and food to offer the hopeless. Now he hurried blindly across the concrete, his thoughts in uproar. Follow her! Follow her you fool! Soon she will be gone. Soon you will walk by the river, by the Queen Mary and Cleopatra's Needle, to Embankment station to catch the next train; for that is what you are going to do, you sad old man. No more of this. You are a plain man. No more of this madness then. It does not belong in the vessel of your life. It was not meant.

Ahead, he saw them, overcoated men, hanging around by the bottom of the ramp. They watched her pass by, hands in their pockets, and he imagined their eyes, dull and hooded. They let her go by, no one made a move. His face was still burning, though he knew they could not see, and his hands hung stiffly by his side. No time, he muttered to himself as he approached. One of the men moved his hand, scarcely bothering to make a supplicatory gesture. He shook his head quickly. No time now to fumble in pockets for a coin and shrug off the response in a welter of discomfort and shame. She was on the bridge. Let me go now, her pleaded silently to the hunched figures, let me go.

The crowd moved from North to South. She walked by the rails and people stepped aside to make way for her. It was difficult to see distinctly, but he thought that people turned as she passed and he understood this. Like him, they could not help taking a second look. He imagined the whole flow of city workers coming to a halt, piling into one another, trying to turn back and follow her. It seemed as though only he was going in the right direction. I am walking to Embankment station, he told himself, but he knew it was not so. He was following this woman. Something in a stranger's face had made it impossible to remain on the train he travelled on every evening to his home in Woodside Park. He had done something unaccountable; now he felt as though the gesture had launched him into an uninterruptable state. With the wind hitting him hard downriver and the rain blowing on his face, he knew now he could make no mistake. He was carried forward, against the crowd, his eyes continually seeking and finding the woman ahead. He was filled with a sense of irony, but it had no object.

It was simple on the bridge. He even gained on her, making up for the gap that had widened in the station. She was now ten yards ahead, no more. He could see her ankles, the dark heels of her shoes on the wet pavement. Her hat sat crookedly and the wind blew her hair exactly, yes exactly as he had imagined. He laughed aloud, and the sound was carried away on the wind. Now he had a chance to look around him — the vast panorama of the Thames, Westminster to Blackfriars, the proud riverbanks. It was years since he had walked here. He felt tiny. They were all specks, hurrying across this great structure, pendulously draped across the expanse of roiling water. Even the river was tiny, a blue streak on a map, dividing the grey stain that was London. Only she was something, this woman. By her very rejection of everything around her, she became something herself. He was nothing, he knew that, and he did not mind. She was something and he had understood. Now he was allowed to follow her; for a brief span of both their lives he would bind them together. It was irrelevant that only one of them knew. One was enough. And besides, he thought, I'm glad it is me. After all, what if she were following *me* across Waterloo bridge towards the rich promise of the city beyond? I would never have seen those eyes. I would be less than I am.

It remained with him, this inexplicable feeling of wellbeing, all the way across the bridge. Rain was damping his hair down. There were dark streaks on his coat, his briefcase was bubbled with tiny drops. He was able to keep up without effort. As they neared the city side, his thoughts began to roam around the hub of streets leading to Covent Garden and the West End. Still, he did not allow himself to speculate where she was going. His thoughts were dreamlike, everything unpleasant was submerged.

It came as a shock when she made a rapid turn and began to descend to Victoria Embankment. A quick decision was needed: on the bridge, where there were hundreds of people, it was easy to follow her without being noticed. On the Embankment there were few people; he would be conspicuous keeping ten, even twenty yards behind a lone woman. He stopped by the parapet where it curved out to the steps down. She had already disappeared but she would emerge below; he could see then where she went. Once again, he told himself that he was going to walk to Embankment station. His eyes on the dirty blue and white of the Queen Mary, he waited until she would have emerged below. Yes, she was there, heading upriver towards Cleopatra's Needle. The stairs were wet and the passage smelt dank.

He could hear the cars passing outside, but for a few seconds he was alone on the staircase, clattering down, his hand out in case he slipped — and she was out of sight. Now, he thought, imagine she is gone. When you emerge, she is nowhere to be seen, the bond is severed and you carry on . . . as though . . . nothing . . . In the moment he reached the street, his eyes sought her avidly. She was still there, crossing at the lights, walking straight in the rain. He followed, grateful, absurdly relieved; happy again.

The gap was wider than ever. He could scarcely make out the details her hair made against hat and collar. Her hands were pale marks against her coat. The lights had changed again and he could have done a dance of impatience as he waited for a break in the traffic to dash across. But there she was, familiar now, he held her warmly with his eyes. He wished to speak to her, silently in his head, but could find no words. I am here, they sounded like the words of a foolish middle-aged man in a mac, and he was no such man. He was nothing.

She was approaching Cleopatra's Needle now, they were rounding the river together, and for the first time her steps faltered. So used to the pace now, he faltered momentarily too. What to do? It was raining: he couldn't sit on a bench, he couldn't stop, it was out of the question. Such an interruption now would lift the lid on a scene of great emptiness. She was walking quite slowly now, with none of the purpose that had carried them across the bridge. Her hands hung limply by her sides. Rain drove in gusts against their faces. He was blinded and he felt at risk. Great peril, somewhere, just behind him, breathing on his neck. Instinctively, he raised a hand to the back of his neck as though to swat a fly and at the same moment she stopped. She had reached the sphinx, the first of the two that flanked Cleopatra's Needle. She put a hand out as though to touch the stone, but it touched nothing. As he watched in disbelief, walking as slowly as he dared now, she turned and descended the few steps to the parapet overlooking the river. Standing there, she put her hands flat on the broad wall. The wind chose that moment for a vicious squall that lifted her hat and carried it in a trice up, somersaulting once, and then swiftly out over the river and down until it was lost from view. She did not seem to notice. He could see one side of her face, close enough now to make out that her eyes were open and staring across the river, wild as they had seemed on the train, staring at his own feet.

There was no alternative. He must pass her by, leave her behind. It never entered his head to do otherwise. But his eyes were fixed on her. If he had to tear himself away, he would see her until the last possible moment. She looked tragic now, standing like that, with her hands spread out, flat on the stone, and her hair blowing unchecked across her face. As he reached the sphinx, once again as close to her as he had ever been since leaving the train, able to make out the curve of cheek and neck, she tipped back her head and shouted. The words were blown to him, fouled by the same wind that carried them. He made out sounds, sounds only, they made no sense. For a blind moment, it occurred to him to stop, approach her, touch her shoulder. As soon as it was conceived, the idea of intruding on her distress revolted him. Turning his collar up, he began to walk quickly, past Cleopatra's Needle, past the second sphinx, up the bank of the Thames River towards Embankment station.

Before the bridge he crossed and entered the station in a crowd of others. Through the ticket barrier and down, mechanically following the black arrows. All at once, he was on another train platform, waiting in the close air for another train. On the surface, his thoughts were childishly simple. He observed several things: on the opposite platform, a man shook out his umbrella with a grimace. A child skipped close to the platform edge. He felt the need to urinate. Deep in his brain, the sounds he had heard were being swapped and juggled, echoing in patterns that veered close to sense, then back to unintelligible sounds. But before the train reached the station, while it was still rumbling through the dark, something clicked and he could clearly understand what she had said. The headlights were visible now and a grubby wind blew. They were suddenly obvious, the words, and he felt momentarily exalted. Turning a little, catching the last moment of quiet before the air filled, he began to say them over and over, softly, to no-one in particular.

— *Sara Berkeley*

FULL LUNAR ECLIPSE

For a moment
the sky holds a perfect yin-yang,
the moon coupling with the earth's shadow

and me embracing a memory
by the cold, still river.
Through the moon the earth

darkens my face.
Suddenly I am a veiled woman
with no-one to mourn for.

November 28/93

— *Sherry Johnson*

LOOK MISTER

look   look mister
the sun is yellow

the sky is blue and yes
i'm wearing a cinnamon hat

and there   can you see it
a tree in my back yard

three little birds
busy being birds

o   and look   mister
your eyes

brilliant and brown and small
getting smaller

— *Greg Button*

STEALING GEORGE

Cindy's my friend got worse troubles than me. She finally gets this baby George but something goes wrong. He's up at the hospital and Cindy feels so bad she calls me up. "Long time no see," she says. She wants to talk, mother to mother. Cindy's twenty-one been trying to get a baby since she was fourteen at Alderwood Treatment Centre so I know she's happy at having George. Only something's not right, she says. George's not breathing too good. And then she starts to bawl right over the phone.

Some people think it's funny for Cindy and me to be friends. She's this short, fat Indian and me, I'm this skinny white chick got dyed yellow hair. But I say, fuck'em all in the tits. Cindy and me, we once shared the girl's dorm at Alderwood and that makes us friends for life. She was in for B & E's. Me, for having a drunken Mom. They said I was acting unruly.

So Cindy comes for a visit, eh? and she's not looking too hot. Fact is, she looks like shit. Looks like she's been run over a couple of times by a fast truck going backwards. She's all crumpled up, got this wrecked plaid coat on looks like she slept in it. Turns out she did. In the Goodwill Box at Safeway.

"Sybilla, I feel so bad," she says, getting herself comfortable on one of my kitchen chairs. "They doing all sorts of stuff to George, got wires and tubes sticking out of his chest, won't let me get near. I'm afraid he's gonna die." And then she starts to bawl some more.

I mix up a fresh batch of Kool-Aid, try to cheer her up.

"Remember that time at Alderwood when you bit through that worker's coat?" I says.

"Yeah," she says, grinning like the old Cindy, "that dumb broad grabbed me when I wouldn't vacuum the rug."

You had to see Cindy back then. Five feet tall, about 200 pounds. And mad all the time. That shrimpy worker didn't have a chance. Getting sat on served her right. Had to go to the Hospital for shots Cindy bit her so bad. And all those workers did to Cindy was haul her off to the Therapy Room for some all-night talk about her feelings. That's all we did back then at Alderwood. Yak about feeling hostile and keep the place clean.

"Hey, Cindy," I say now, "you still feeling hostile?"

"Damned right," she says, and we laugh so hard Christian my kid comes running out from his Spiderman cartoons to see what's going on.

We remember other stuff, too. That time at Hallowe'en when she shook the ketchup bottle so hard and the lid came off and went over that worker Carlos's head. The times we snuck down to the pantry after the sleepover worker went to bed and got boxes of cookies and cans of pop if we could find where they was hid. And that crazy Alan Kamouroski finally burned down the doctor's office, used to talk in a secret language to his G.I. Joes. And Ben, the old crippled-up janitor, used to give us cigarettes if we'd show him what was in our pants.

We laugh so hard that day we have a great time.

So after that, Cindy moves in with us, eh? 'cause she's got nowheres else to go. She wants to be around in case something happens to George. But we got to be careful, got to keep our noses clean. Ever since Miss Hope, the Public Health Nurse, got the SPCA to raid this welfare dump on account of all the stray cats I keep, I'm being watched. Welfare's watching me. Miss Hope is watching me. The cops are watching me. And I know what they want but ain't ever gonna get. My kids. Christian who's nearly three and the baby, she's just turned one. They ain't ever gonna get my kids.

Last summer when they dragged away most of my cats — that Miss Hopeless said I was acting like an unfit mother. Unfit mother! What does she know? Never had a kid herself. Just this scrunched-up old broad, got wrinkles and a big fat nose, it's no wonder she's still single, no wonder at all. Not that there's much to be said for guys that knock you up then bugger off, the assholes, like them two guys did to me. Like some Indian did to Cindy, leaving her with a three-week-old baby got some kind of trouble with his lungs. Makes me figure, Cindy and me, we got to stick together, got to help each other out when we can.

It's only three months since they raided my cats, only left me with Gimp — but I'm getting more cats all the time. About four strays now and Gimp, she's about to have more babies so any day things will be back to normal.

And it turns out Cindy likes animals too. Before I know it, she's found this dog only got one eye. She was down at the dumpster at the Safeway Mall looking for extra food and this poor old thing just followed her back. We gave him a bath and he didn't look too bad but he smelled. Boy did he smell. From some kind of sores on his back. I wanted to take him to the vet but, as usual, my welfare money had run out and I couldn't borrow from Cindy, she'd just about used up all the money she brought from the reserve and the special money she got from welfare. So we just gave the dog a bath every day and fed him warm milk and crunchies.

One thing I wish is I was smart enough to have a lot of money so's I could have a clinic like that nun had looking after all the stray, sick things. I don't know why but all the animals come to me like somehow they know Sybilla's here to care. They just show up at my kitchen door needing help and I take them in. Now if only these busybody social workers and nurses would get off my back, I could get on with my important work.

But anywho, back to Cindy. Every day she hitches a ride to the hospital and every night she comes back and cries. They tell her George is still being sick and Cindy's sure he might not make it. When she tells me this I start to bawl too and grab for Christian and the baby and hold them tight. After a few days of this, things get pretty gloomy. Not only that, but things get pretty hungry, too. I hate to say this about my best friend, but Cindy eats like a horse. Ate all of Christian's Froot Loops in only one day. Eats bread and jam all the time and is always opening up cans of soup. I have to start to hide stuff when she's out so's me and the kids can get something to eat.

So one morning I finally says to her, "Jesus, Cindy, we got to do something," 'cause I'm thinking next she'll be eating the cat's crunchies and I'm beginning to feel more pissed off at her about the food than sorry for her about George.

But Cindy thinks I mean only about George and she says, "Yeah, Sybilla, maybe we should steal him right outa the hospital, bring him here for you to work on."

At first I think she's fooling but she's getting this kind of light all over her face and she's acting all happy and excited for the first time in days so I know she's really serious.

Then I'm thinking, Jesus, what am I gonna do now? I ain't ever worked on a baby sick like George before. I mean, I know what I'm doing with my cats and my dogs but a baby like George? Shit, I mean, what if we bring him here and he croaks? What would Miss Hopeless and the rest of them do to me then? And my kids. They'd be grabbing my kids for sure then.

So now I figure I got a problem and that problem is Cindy. But no way can you change Cindy's mind when she's got it made up. She'll just scream at you and call you a useless fuck and maybe even punch you in the head. I've seen her do it hundreds of times at Alderwood. She's strong and can really hurt when she wants to. Hard to believe her real name is Cinderella when she acts like that.

So I go along with her and we make up this plan, eh? about how we're gonna steal George, 'cause I figure somewheres along the way I can make things turn out different. I don't want to let on I'm scared shitless so I get all dressed up like I mean business. Got these black high-heel boots I found at the Sally Ann and this short jean skirt. Got this man's big red sweater and wear all my necklaces. It's a crime the stuff people throw away. Like all my beautiful necklaces. You have to pay five bucks at Shoppers Drug Mart just for one of them. Me, I can pick them up for 25 cents each down at the Sally Ann or St. Vincent de Paul's. I just about can't believe that they're even for sale. I mean, how could anyone throw them out? I mean, they're practically diamonds and people throw them out like they was junk!

But anywho, back to the trip. I dress my kids up, too. Christian's got on his blue suit and bow tie, what I got him for his Sears Portrait. The baby's in her pink, frilly dress. Only thing she's needing is shoes 'cause it's raining out. So I put two extra pairs of socks on her and hope she don't get cold.

I fix up Cindy, too. Try to spike her hair but it's too heavy and don't spike too good. So we settle on a pony tail and eye makeup and pink lipstick. She looks pretty good when I'm through. I can't do nothing with her clothes, though. She's too fat to fit into mine. So she just wears her jeans and the same old plaid coat.

So then we head out the door, eh? and I get scared all over again. We're walking down the street and I'm going, Jesus, I'll bet all these neighbours around here are probably staring at us like we was some crazy parade. I'll bet they're almost knowing what we're up to. We even got the one-eyed dog following us. And then I'm thinking, this is all these jerks around here is needing, another big deal to get excited about like when the SPCA raided my cats.

So we keep walking down the street out of this subdivision and heading for the highway and I'm looking around at the ticky-boo yards and all the cars and boats and trailers parked in the driveways. Me, I got to hitch a ride everywheres, there's no buses out here. But these people,

I'm thinking, they got everything and yet they're always complaining about my cats, giving me all this trouble. They got all their stuff and their nice houses, you'd think that'd be enough for them, but oh no, they can't leave Sybilla alone, got to have her ass, too.

So anywho, we head out to the highway. Cindy's not saying too much and I'm still hoping she'll change her mind about stealing George. Christian, he's skipping beside us having a great time like it was Christmas. The baby, she's hanging off my hip. As usual.

Once we get to the highway it takes a while to get a ride and we start to get frozen but finally a muscle car stops. Got this one guy inside with a moustache and grinning like a loonie thinking he's shit-hot. Cindy and Christian get in the back. Me and the baby, in the front.

So this guy goes, "Where you ladies heading?" And then he revs his engine, makes it sound like it's gonna explode, makes the baby scream.

"Just give us a ride to the hospital, will ya?" I go and he looks at us strange and says like he's worried, "What's the matter?"

This makes me feel okay, like maybe here's a guy thinks of other stuff besides that thing between his legs.

So I says, "Naw, everything's all right. We're just gonna visit Cindy's baby, got sick, he's staying up the hospital."

Then he revs his engine again and we take off. And I'm thinking, I hope Cindy got that part about us visiting George. I didn't say "stealing" him, I said *visiting*. Next thing I know this guy's passing out cigarettes, Menthol Light, and now I'm thinking, what kind of a guy smokes Menthol Light? Maybe he's weird or something, maybe he's a case.

So then this guy says to me, "Your kids?" meaning Christian and the baby.

"Yeah," I says and can't think of nothing else to say so keep quiet. But this guy's looking at my crossed legs every chance he gets, doesn't think I'm noticing but Sybilla notices just about everything. I know pretty soon he's gonna put the make on me and he's not half-bad looking either. What I'm not sure of is, do I want him to?

Nice car though. Must have cost a mint. Pretty soon he's put in a tape, some heavy metal rock, and this makes Christian jump up and down in the back seat. Me, I'm smiling to myself, suddenly having a good time — never mind the Menthol Lights — and turn around to look at Christian and then I look at Cindy and remember what it is we're gonna do. What a downer. Now I'm feeling all twisted again.

So I says to this guy, "Would you turn down the music?" 'cause I'm feeling all edgy now and he does and I'm like Thank-you, and next thing I know we're at the hospital driveway. We all get out and he drives off in a big hurry leaving rocks flying everywheres. So much for the big romance. One rock hits me in the knee and it starts to bleed like anything.

Oh great, I'm going, now we'll have to go to Emergency for a band-aid and then I go, yeah, maybe that is great. I mean, now, maybe I can stall for time.

So there we are, all heading up the hospital driveway and me, I'm limping like I was crippled, try to give the baby to Cindy to carry but she won't go. And I'm sure hoping that Emergency Room is full when we get there and have to wait for hours to get me fixed. Then maybe Cindy will forget all about stealing George and we can just have a nice visit and then go home.

But no such luck. The Emergency Room is empty. Cindy decides to go on up to the second floor to see George and wait for us there.

So Christian, the baby and me, we go into Emergency and this nurse takes the gravel junk out of my knee and puts on a band-aid. And all the while she's asking us questions like how old are the kids and what are their names. She's being so nice to us, I just about can't believe it. And everything's so white and clean and safe in there I suddenly feel like I could lie down and go to sleep and have this nurse look after me and the kids forever.

But natch, it don't go like that and we gotta say goodbye and try to find the elevator to George and Cindy. We find it all right but the problem is there's this Gift Shop right next to it and Christian, he wants to go in, have a look around. They got all kinds of neat stuff in there like little dolls with knitted dresses, I'd love one of them. And chocolate bars and magazines and two old ladies with grey hair and pink blouses making a big fuss over the baby. And I'm thinking, this Hospital sure is nice. I could stay here forever. But what I'm really thinking is, I don't want to go up and steal George and so I'm stalling anyways I can. But finally, the only thing I can figure to do, eh, is to tell Cindy what I'm thinking, like how they taught us at Alderwood, and hope she don't get too twisted. Leastways I'm figuring she won't try to bite me or something right in broad daylight, there in the Hospital.

So we get in the elevator and go up to the second floor. Soon as the door opens we see Cindy standing in front of this big glass window and she don't say nothing when we get to her but grin at us and then point to George in one of them plastic baby beds.

Finally she says, "They took the wires offa George. We don't have to steal him now. They gonna let me feed him."

And then she starts to bawl and me, I start bawling, too, not only for being happy about George, not only that. I'm bawling because now I don't have to do nothing about making him better. Now I don't have to do all the worrying about is he gonna die.

So we leave Cindy, eh? She's gonna hang around till two when she can give George his bottle. Christian and me and the baby, we go down to the Gift Shop, get three chocolate bars to celebrate. George is gonna be okay and me and Cindy, we can go back to being best friends like before.

We head out of the hospital and into the rain, happier than three pigs in shit, and we're hardly out of the building when all of a sudden that muscle car pulls up, got the same guy inside. He hangs his head out the window and says, "Wanna ride?" and me, I'm getting a big thrill now thinking this guy's been waiting for us, thinking why not?, ain't this something? Maybe finally here's a guy who ain't an asshole, maybe here's a guy who'll care.

So we get in, eh? and I'm like "Thank you, you can give us a lift" and I slam the door and he says, smiling really nice, "Where to?" and hands me a Menthol Light and then me and Christian and the baby, we take off with him down the highway, rocks flying everywheres, like nobody's business.

— M.A.C. Farrant

WAKE-UP

    to hide in the abstract
    or step out swinging
    a freeway under each arm

    it's one or the other

    or somewhere between head and heart
    like this morning
    the old woman slowly
    picking and eating crabapples
    at a bus stop

    — *Chris Collins*

THE POET AND FRIENDS (2)

With a mop of wild hair, pants tucked into socks
bookbag balanced on his made-from-scratch bike
you wouldn't take him for a Romantic — for a
sensuous soul. But he is — beneath a ton
of glib learning, his heart's like a marvelous
nude, all covered with hats and yellow
raincoats. And every once in a while he'll
fall off his wheels:
words combing the mud for a real presence,
nude blinking back tears in the common light.

    —*J. Livingstone Clark*

THE CAT CAME BACK

Miller met Carpenter, a cat under his arm, on the landing.

"Been to the vet," Carpenter said, apologetically.

"Sick?"

"Had him neutered."

"Shame," Miller said.

"Yeah, but, you know, the spraying."

Miller nodded and went on downstairs and out the door. Carpenter turned the key.

He had forgotten to open the blinds and the room was dark. He put the cat down and it limped to a corner of the rug. It was still woozy. Carpenter put the mail on the table and went to the window. The cat curled up and went to sleep in the shaft of sun that streamed in. Carpenter turned on the flame under the coffee pot. He heard water running.

The phone was ringing as Carpenter came out of the bathroom.

He had left the tap running in the tub and the floor was awash. His shoes sloshed as he walked across the kitchen.

"Hullo."

It was Potter. "I'm breaking it off," she said. She sounded angry, annoyed.

"What?" Carpenter asked. He was frowning at the bathroom door.

"Us. You and me. It's over, finished, through, *kaput.*"

"I don't understand, Carol. Yesterday . . . " There was a trail of soggy footprints leading across the parquet floor.

"Yesterday, of course, *yesterday* is exactly what I'm talking about. *Last night.* Maybe you don't remember."

"Uh . . ."

"*Jesus.*"

"Oh, that. I said I was sorry about that."

"*Sorry?* Christ, why were *you* sorry? *You* got to come all over me. I'm the one who was left high and dry. Dry, hah. High and wet, I should say."

"You know I do everything I can to satisfy you," Carpenter said. He reached for the chair but it was just half a hand further than the cord would stretch. On the table, the rhododendron was listing, its underleaves a delicate, chalky green. The asparagus vine on the refrigerator had died.

"Bull-fucking-shit you do. You crawl all over me, leave black and blue marks all over my breasts, bite my lips, give me goddamn hickies that embarrass the hell out of me the next day, cream all over my belly. . . shit. Would you dream of lowering yourself to putting your sunshine pure tongue anywhere near my goddamn clit?"

"Carol," Carpenter said. His ear was beginning to hurt.

"I'm sick and tired of your using me like your fucking fist, you pimply, smelly-assed . . . impotent creep."

"Carol, wait a minute . . . "

"So don't come around any more. I can't stand the thought of you touching me, it makes me want to puke."

"Wait a minute, Carol, I'm not no goddamn impotent." Carpenter was shouting.

"Oh, yeah, that's right. Ha. That's something I never could understand, anyway, why you pull it out right before . . ."

"I AM GODDAMN NOT," Carpenter shouted. He hung up and slumped into the chair, his elbow knocking over the vase. It smashed with a bell-like crystal tone.

"Oh, shit," Carpenter said.

The coffee pot was boiling over, spewing black liquid and gritty grounds over the stove, down onto the floor. He burned his hand picking it up and dropped it on his foot. Coffee spilled on his trousers, searing his shin, and puddled down into his shoe.

"Jesus, what a day."

He went into the bathroom to get the mop. The pond on the floor had acquired a bluish sheen and glistened up at him like a reproach.

Carpenter retreated into the kitchen. There was a little bitter coffee left in the pot and he poured it into his mug, the one Potter gave him for his birthday. He sat in the sunlight browsing through the mail, a stale cigarette burning between his fingers. He kicked off his soggy shoe.

Bills. Electric, gas, telephone. He looked up at the calendar on the wall beside the refrigerator. It's the 11th. There are also two letters and a telegram which he weighs in his hand, distrustful. He puts the yellow envelope at the bottom of the pile.

The electric bill is higher than usual, the telephone bill astronomic. He studies the list of long-distance calls carefully. Only a few look familiar. The gas will be turned off tomorrow if the bill isn't paid.

"Holy shit."

He puts his face in his hands and the smoke from the cigarette curls into his eyes, making them tear. He can just imagine the vet bill when it comes.

Carpenter sighs.

He takes a sip of coffee and burns his lip. "Shit." The mug slips from his hand, lands squarely on the edge of the table, teeters tauntingly as his hand darts for it, tumbles over. His hand slams against the sharp edge of the table top. The mug shatters. The puddle beneath his feet hardly seems to grow wider. The bright parquet floor, smeared with sunshine like a slice of toast dripping with butter, is pocked with muddy footprints, craters in a minefield.

Carpenter examines the letters suspiciously. The envelopes are typed, with no return addresses. He peers at the postmarks. One is familiar. He slices the envelope open with a fingernail. It will be from his father or his sister. He recognizes Louisa's slanted hand. Just a short note:

"Father very ill. Come at once. This may be the end. Lou."

Carpenter went rigid. "Oh, no." He read the words a second time, then a third, but there was no more. He turned the page over but it was blank. There was nothing more in the envelope. He looked around him, like a threatened man searching for a weapon. On the rug, the cat slept peacefully, curled and slick.

He tore open the yellow envelope and unfolded the telegram with trembling hands.

"Carpenter: your truantism has gone too far. In adherence to article four, paragraph B(2), of the current contract, ISUBA, with this firm, your employment has been terminated. Wainright, foreman."

Carpenter's hands jerked. He read the telegram over.

"What? Truantism? The son of a bitch. He can't . . . the son of a bitch." He gritted his teeth. "Wainright, you son of a bitch, you fucking, cocksucking, asshole-licking son of a . . . you, you motherfucking son of a *bitch.*"

The telegram drifted out of his fingers and floated onto the pool of coffee on the table. Carpenter put his elbow on it and propped his forehead against his fist. His gaze came to rest on the letter from his sister. "My God," he said softly.

He got up suddenly, putting his shoeless foot down hard on a shard of the splintered mug. "JESUS FUCKING CHRIST."

He hopped to the bathroom, blood spilling in blotches from his coffee-stained sock. He sat on the rim of the bathtub and pulled off the sock, inspected the gash in his heel. It looked deep. He stood up to reach for the bottle of alcohol on the shelf and slipped on the slick tile floor, falling backwards into the tub. "AH, AH." His head hit with a sharp crack, like a schoolboy farting in a closet.

He lay stunned, body in the tub, limbs draped over the rim. Blood dripped from his heel. Water dripping from the tap struck his eyelid. He opened his eye and a drop plopped in.

"Jesus." He banged his head against the tap scrambling up.

He shook his head, sending the blood racing through his temples, pounding like a landlord's fist.

He pulled himself out of the tub. "Father," he said.

Carpenter bathed his foot and swathed it in bandages, then limped to the phone. The receiver was silent in his hand, hollow.

"Hey, what is this?" The words seemed to echo back through the earpiece. He flicked down the receiver button, fanned at it. Nothing. He banged the receiver down, knocking the phone from its table. It clattered to the floor, where he took a kick at it with his bandaged foot. "Shit. JESUS!"

He padded down the hall and knocked on Mason's door. It swung open on a moon face. The eyes in it slinked down and up over Carpenter's body.

"I'm sorry to bother you."

"Then why do it?"

"I beg your pardon?"

"And well you should."

"I'm sorry, I'm confused. I've just had a bad shock."

"It knocked one of your shoes off, that's for sure," Mason said. He had a nasty whine, like that of a jigsaw, somewhere deep in his voice.

Carpenter looked down. Blood was starting to seep through the bandage. "Yes, I cut my foot."

"I can see that," Mason said.

There was an uncomfortable silence.

"I'm, uh, I'm sorry to disturb you . . . " He raised a hand to cut off any interruption. "But, I'd, uh, like to use your phone. It's . . . an emergency."

Mason looked at him with pity. His tiny eyes were like raisins in a round loaf of whole-wheat dough.

"You've cut your foot and you want to use my phone."

"For God's sake," Carpenter said, "my father may be dying. *Please*."

Mason moved aside, snorting through his round nose. "Why didn't you say so?" The whine deepened.

"It's long-distance but I'll make it collect," Carpenter said.

Mason didn't reply but Carpenter could hear his breathing behind him. He gave instructions to the operator. "It's sort of personal," he said, hopefully, glancing up. Mason dropped heavily into the soft chair beside the phone and averted his eyes.

At first, Louisa wouldn't accept the call.

"Louisa, it's me."

"Now you call, you bastard."

"I just got your letter today . . . "

"If you're going to talk, you'll have to accept the charges," the operator said. Her voice was metallic.

"I'll accept a call from him over my dead body."

"Louisa, how's father?"

"How's father? *How's father?*"

"I'm sorry," the operator said sharply, "but you must . . . "

"Did you hear that?" Louisa asked her. "Now he asks me, how's father? Here I sit in black, the earth from the cemetery still on the bottom of my shoes, and he asks me, how's father? Did you ever . . ."

"*Father.*" Carpenter said the word like a cry of pain.

"You'll have to accept the charge or you can't talk, miss."

"Louisa, listen to me, please, I just got your letter today, what . . ."

The phone went dead in his hand. It radiated an empty silence, as if it, and he along with it, had been thrust into an endless hole. Beside him, he could hear Mason's breathing.

"I . . . I . . . I . . . " He stared at the receiver helplessly.

"Not bad news, I hope," Mason said sweetly.

"My father . . . died."

"Oh, that's too bad. Nothing serious, I hope."

Carpenter stared at him blankly.

"I should have gone," he said weakly.

"Yes, you certainly should have."

Carpenter moved toward the door. Behind him, he heard Mason dialling. "Time and charges, please," the jigsaw said.

He slumped into his chair. His foot throbbed. He went to the bathroom but hesitated at the door. He went to his bedroom and stared at the photograph of Potter on the dresser. She was smiling and the edges of her teeth were sharp. The plant had died. He opened the blinds. The window was broken. Sunlight streamed in like a slick of caramel, blinding him for a moment. There was a noise behind him.

Miller heard a scream and a clatter as he laboured up the stairs, his arms filled with groceries. He stopped on the landing and listened. Cautiously, he pressed at Carpenter's door. It swung open. Carpenter was lying on the kitchen floor, doubled up, hands between his legs, moaning. The cat was standing in the doorway between the kitchen and the bedroom, a knife in his hand.

"*The sonuvabitch,*" the cat said.

— Dave Margoshes

Driven from the house by the mindless joy of
someone else's kids,   I escape to the garden:
the little patch of green I call Paradise.
Hasn't my wife done a nice job?   I hear
myself cooing to the pigeons next door:
daisies, portulaca, daffodils and glads.
It's nice enough,   if you don't mind the
wires overhead: Presenting *The Garden*,
by Sask Power and Piet Mondrian.

But the dogs in the alley are barking boors
and the trucks and lawnmowers never stop.
Only in the shed is there quiet enough,
for Pissarro's *Garden With Trees in Blossom,
Spring, Pontoise* — where stillness
endows on its new white petals   a clear
light breaking free from the ground.

— *J. Livingstone Clark*

ARTIST IN THE STREET

Baudelaire, friend of a friend of mine
the one who sought the night
and the lines that preserve it from ruin
he too savoured the fractured stars
broke the cold of winter with women
decked in the colours of the avenue

he watched the city lights
while the ice fog gripped
the delicate throats of trees
with the prehistoric fire of diamonds
tonight buildings loom tragic
like headless shoulders of great men
authentic his voice
touches the moment
his heart lies bare

— *Bruce Hunter*

AFTER THE STORY BROKE

After the story broke
he sat in the window
watching the skinny girls hugging themselves
and the sleek cars at the curb.
He picked up his pen.
'I miss my favourite girl,' he wrote;
he put the pen down. It was there
the story broke.

It was dark
in the narrow alley of his life,
she had been light,
he was silhouetted in her light,
a man with his hopes
all riding the same high wire.
As long as she was there
he held to the burning train of his dreams
as though there were time
for every hope to bloom
among the cobblestones.

After the story borrowed and blown
he walked with this head down,
he stood in the dim-lit alley
listening for trains,
trying for the face of his girl
but he could only recall
how she struck light
and his shadow was thrown
long, like one
who stoops to a heavy load
and looks suddenly old.

— *Sara Berkeley*

Ω

再见

ZAI JIAN

Despite the triumph of spring
the spectre of death appears.
It has persisted through winter,
can no longer be exorcised.
The Expert's wife goes to Hong Kong
for a cancer examination.
Descent into Hong Kong
is a shock to the system,
though China's Experts dream
all year of "going out" —
to ride a subway,
see the latest Neil Simon,
smoke cigars, gorge
on cheese and Armagnac.
An Anglo-Yankee halfbreed
clinging to the belly of China,
all neon and vulgarity,
decompression chamber
between East and West,
Hong Kong's wealth
glitters and stinks.

The final corruption
or a universal future?

The sentence is passed —
immediate return to Canada,
a shuddering halt to the journey.

Back in Nanjing, classes proceed,
substitutes are trained,

crates of books given away,
then the Shakespeare tapes.
Face is steadily earned.

There are official leavetakings,
and private rituals of separation.
The Little Expert's class
gives him the most touching
festival of farewells.
In their innocent goodbyes
future reconciliations glow.

Lao Fan plays a final sonnet
on his still resounding *er-hu*.

— *Ken Mitchell*

We were friends immediately and for the next five nights it was impossible not to get drunk with them. It was my first day in the Yungas, I was battered and gasping from the crazy plunge down the mountain from La Paz: four hours in the back of a truck, waterfalls spilling liquid ice on our spines from cliffs overhanging the single-lane track wrapped against the mountain-face; there was a woman who shrieked and curled herself around her baby like a snail's shell each time we rattled towards a waterfall. The one moment I dared to look down, the dark green void below was unmarred except for a gouged path that stopped short at the scarred skeleton of a truck.

"How did you travel down here?" they asked me. I told them. They wrinkled their brows and shook their heads. Roberto said: "Twenty-six trucks crash this year, four buses. The bus is better."

I could scarcely believe this was Bolivia: the bright colours, the heat, the view from this hilltop town. The long vertebrae of the mountains, their dense green lofting white mist above them, stretched towards me from the distant wall of the valley. After weeks of denuded altiplano, thin air and chill drizzle, I had descended into paradise. I sat in a chair on the balcony of the hotel, looking out over the broken, drooping leaves of the coffee plants, wafts of polyglot conversation settling on me from the balcony above, where travellers of various nationalities were chewing coca leaves and discussing the effects as their gums and jaws turned numb. Out on the street that evening I met the musicians.

They were playing in an open doorway off the central plaza. I joined the crowd that had gathered to listen to them. The group consisted of five young men: none looked more than eighteen. They played the Andean flute, the guitar, two *rondadores,* or sets of pan-pipes, and a *charango* — a small guitar whose armadillo-shell body was ruffled into glossy, liver-coloured scales. Their music was keening, monotonous, compelling; but perhaps because I was no longer in the highlands, the tunes they played sounded less morose than other Andean music I had heard. The flautist and the two youths who puffed on the *rondadores* were dead serious, but the guitarist cavorted for the crowd and the *charango* player, the group's leader, a strong-faced, sleek-haired youth named Roberto, would interrupt his playing to tap his fingers on the pleated belly of his *charango*.

We started to talk during one of the breaks in their performance and by the end of the evening I was their devoted follower. Three or four nights a week they would trail around the town, stopping into hotels and restaurants, their brave, haunted music piping fiercely. If the owner requested it, they would stay for the evening to entertain the customers. The price they charged for their labour was a generous and unbroken supply of hard liquor. The instant the restaurant owner or hotel manager nodded his approval of their music they would lower their instruments and erupt into a spate of bargaining. What was there to drink? Rum? Aguardiente? Vodka? Offers and reactions would volley back and forth. When the musicians received an offer they considered acceptable they would all look at Roberto and Roberto would nod. The waiter would scurry into the back of the restaurant and return carrying a pitcher of potent spirits. The musicians would seat themselves around a table, the waiter would pour the first round of drinks and the music would begin.

They could play for hours. The hollow pumping of the *rondadores*, the almost metallic plucking of Roberto's *charango*, the silkier chord-changes of the wooden guitar and thin trill of the flute would weave together, the flowing give-and-take among them almost imperceptible. Whenever the music seemed to be on the verge of sinking into monotony one of the musicians would strike out on his own, and the others would respond to the changed course, following it, resisting it or mocking it with bursts of sound and sidelong glances. Drink took no observable toll on their playing. As I had become their friend, I was supplied with a glass at the beginning of the evening and was offered a fill-up at every round. At the rate of one glass of aguardiente or vodka to every two or three of theirs, I was reeling by the end of the performance. Muddled recollections come to me of dragging myself arm over arm up the wooden outdoor staircase of my hotel, weaving across the balcony to my room, laughing giddily at the twitching tropical night, and waking to the morning glare with a head scoured as clear as crystal. I never got a hangover from those nights. Perhaps I was spared because I did not usually drink; or perhaps it was the influence of the sad, supple, resilient music.

The musicians asked me what I did in my country. I began to list some of the jobs I had held. Roberto interrupted me. "Are you an artist?" he asked.

"Yes," I replied, on the strength of a few adolescent poems. "Of course." Well, why not? Wasn't I as much an artist as they were?

Roberto strummed a chord on his *charango* and the piping symphony died away. "The goal of any artist," Roberto said, without pretension or anxiety, "is to be heard among the people, to make himself known among the people."

"Like Víctor Jara," said the guitarist. "Compañero Víctor, playing to keep up the people's spirits in the stadiums in Chile, until the military cut off his hands."

As if moved by Jara's ghost, the musicians slipped as one man into a sombre rendering of half a dozen of Jara's songs. It was two o'clock in the morning and the restaurant was nearly empty. The customers had left and the waiters and kitchen staff, sipping aguardiente at the back of the dining room, constituted the musicians' only audience. They leaned back in their chairs, watching and listening. A sea of empty tables stood between us and them. The sea swayed in time with the music. I was very drunk.

It was my last night in the Yungas. We had spent the evening in a restaurant on the outskirts of town, down the hill from the centre, where the streets were deep trenches of loose dust and the stone sidewalks flanked the trenches like knee-high causeways. When the musicians had completed their rendition of Jara's songs we drained our glasses and careered into the street. I toiled uphill. At the edge of the central plaza the streets turned to tightly locked cobbles, the sidewalks sank. The walls of the plaza were plastered with faded beige posters proclaiming the virtues of General Torrelio, Bolivia's current dictator. The photograph in the centre of each poster showed a heavy mustache, a peaked military cap, braided epaulettes.

The plaza was deserted; the streetlights cast a wan light. Roberto danced to the wall of the plaza, insinuating the neck of his *charango* under the dog-eared fringe of a poster of Torrelio. He dragged the end of the instrument across the rough stucco, ripping the general's face from ear to ear on three identical posters plastered side by side. The tattered posters gaped in the night shadow. Roberto examined the neck of his *charango*, caressing with his palm the tip that had scraped across the stucco. "No damage," he announced, and smiled. He looked at the shredded posters and said: "The artist makes himself known among the people."

I felt myself breaking into laughter. I laughed and laughed. The musicians howled. Their laughter fed mine and I said goodbye to them with an effusiveness they seemed not to have expected from a gringo. They embraced me firmly. *"Artista!"* cried Roberto.

Before catching the bus to La Paz the next morning I steeled myself for the terrifying mountain trail with a hot breakfast in the small restaurant beneath the hotel. A teenage boy was taking orders; he stood behind a counter, listening to music from a tapedeck. As I sipped coffee and ate a warm bun it came to me through the haze (for the first time my drinking had made me groggy) that I had heard the song before. I caught the boy's attention, pointed at the tapedeck and said: "A song by Víctor Jara, no?"

The boy's brow wrinkled.

"The music," I said. "It's Víctor Jara, right?"

"I know of no such person, *señor.*"

I apologized, embarrassed that either my Spanish or my tin ear for music had failed me. A tall German who had been staying in the room beside mine entered the restaurant, sat down at my table and ordered breakfast. The boy disappeared into the kitchen. The music continued to flow from the tapedeck. The cassette cover lay face-down on the edge of the counter. Curious, I bent forward, closed my fingers around the plastic cover and turned it over. The cassette had been bought blank and used to tape a record. An unformed hand had scrawled a single word across the cardboard liner: *Víctor.*

"Do you understand this music?" the German said.

Jara's voice broke into *Recuerdo Amanda,* a song I recognized from the night before. " 'I remember Amanda'," I translated, returning to my seat. "It's about remembering someone."

That afternoon, during the long climb, waterfalls beat a sombre tune on the roof of the bus. The musicians' notes poured through me all the way back up to the chill, bleak altiplano.

— *Stephen Henighan*

RUTH

The slow-footed gait of the trees.

Green is heavy on their bones, bends
their backs into the road.

In an open motorcar we move
between thair ranks likes delegations
through Spanish refugees.

All of us are on the move, down
to the water. As if it's the border
of some better ideology.
We're all thirsty for it, whatever it is.

    Even hills of the Golan on the other side
    fall to their knees
    to take from the sea.

Close, in the shadow of the water
trees break ranks and run. They run
in anxious thickets with outstretched arms.

Ruth stops the tires on the gravel.
Doors catch their latches behind us.
Rolling up one trouser cuff
she keeps moving forward, enters the water
twisted into its ripples.

Feet wide as on ice, or snow,
I look for potholes of her feet, a warning
that I will also fall
through a thin crust to beneath.

No matter how unobtrusively we walk
the water takes us deeper.
But we are returned another half, reflections

of air borne bodies — the purer halves
now cut away from their sex.

The poplars stand on the water
like naive believers. Ruth in this reflected grove
reaches to me. She wants me
deep as her.

Uncertain with the bottom
my arms spread like a wire walker's
and I go to her

through aching gestures of the trees.
In water their arms seem to shudder
under the weight of colour and wind.

— *Peter Ormshaw*

Ω

WORDS CONTAIN SLEEP

Our words contain more than sleep. They
pass between things. Language seeing
itself reborn. The windows contain the
light. It does not pass through but
lives in the glass, shining out in both
directions. Sleep has a structure outside of
words. And we are too close to our own
sleep, waking at night hallucinating.
Sleep pulls us out. It is a costume we
dress our terror in. It is the unseen
existing in light. Nothing remains when
we wake but a few random names or images
Sleep has no fragrance. When we dream
our bodies are suddenly immune to meaning.
We remember only certain things upon waking
Our bodies petrified by the reality there.

— *Robert Hilles*

THESE ARE THE HOUSES

these are the houses
I live in
only in dream.

this one overlooks
a lake, another
has a private orchard
    a riding stable.

in each house
I am somehow
different.

my cars & children
vary, unsure of
details I slip
    out of character

am held in suspicion
by even my closest
associates.

there is something
of me, of these
places missing:

each house
an unfinished world
I wander by twilight

calling your name
to the darkness
like a child.

— *Ken Cathers*

SUMMER MORNING

Three-thirty, and the dark begins to bleed.
A bird cries terror and twists it into song.
All the still night the key has clicked in my heart,
Winding the spirit to its accustomed pitch.
And now the rods grate on their rusty bearings,
The gears jerk into motion, the jangled tune
Brays at my window — Mortal! Mortal! Mortal! —
As the great wheel swings into the morning light,
Its prancing steeds impaled on glistening bone,
And I round the gaudy spindle of my fear.

— *H.C. Dillow*

CROW IN THE RAIN

crow in the rain
in the razor-
      sharp
           stillness
calling
         calling
like blood
to a murder

— *Greg Button*

DRAWING BY A SCHIZOPHRENIC

The head is a house. There are many little rooms. Each one has a door that leads to the other.

The first is quiet, a table where a woman kneads soft dough while a mouse sleeps at her feet, all curled and quiet.

In the next is a maniac hammering at walls like an exploding star, or it could be an exploding star like a maniac in the universe. Yes, it's a self portrait.

There's a room with a rose uncurling, a room with the darkness becoming light, and another with the day becoming dark.

A series of circles, each one inside the other.

Every colour of the rainbow.

Something hard.

Something like a river.

The doctor is examining the dead skin of a patient.

In another, there is a war where everyone fights with burning spears and runs away.

A naked lover.

A room full of toys.

The secret spark that breeds more places to hide.

There are many little rooms. Each one has a door that leads to the other. Yes, you are inside me now.

— *Brian Brett*

YOU ARE AMAZED

From the shadows
of your drifting town
lovers emerge. You try
to feel outraged. Why
have they stolen your body
to perform in the streets?

Your discreet acts of love
hindered your vision. Now
sunlight displays
their tanned flesh. Now
you are amazed at
the pornographic beauty
you possess.

— *Garry Radison*

DREAM

what is it
that draws me
to you

the memory
of your death
only a blur

an image   of
a man, drunk — falling
from the dark

pier, his face
part of the white
flash   dwindling

in the calm
water. is it
the sound, the

stir of the sea
against this shore,
the warm wind

that could be
a breath, a whisper?
I stand on

the same landing, a
gull cries in the far
night. this too

happened   as you died,
faded through   the
closing retina of
water: you looked up
& there was
someone   standing

against the sky.
that night   I
was too young

to know you
though I woke
found myself

in a dark
house   calling
your name.

— *Ken Cathers*

THE PARABOLIC PLAIN

Over the plains they come,
>the denizens of the first order.

Walking tall, stooping once or twice for water and herbs.
These are the magicians of dawn. Stopping each hour for
prayers and cigarettes, lying down with their children
on the spring green grass.

>Over the plains they come, down
the small river valleys to bathe at the weirs. And no one sees
them anymore. No one measures their solemn beauty against the
crippled children of time.

>Duration has become everything in
this place. And over the plains swing the sojourners of a
timeless dawn. And no one sees them anymore, working their
intricate silver in the soft lilac light. Small hammers
beating like the heart of a poem.

>For only poems travel
with them, embroidering the prairie with infinite design.

>The children are fine,   saith the plain
>saith the earth.

>The children are fine,   saith the sky
>saith the dream.

The children are doing fine, so don't worry. The children
of the denizens of the first order.

>Their beauty is matchless
and the inflictions of time will never enter the realms of
their solemn inclination.

>And over the plains we follow, walking
quietly, unsure of true north or any other proposition. And
where the sun marks its absence on the lip of the earth,
there we mark our terminus. The realm of those children
and the timeless inclination.

—*J. Livingstone Clark*

THE TULPA
(From *DANCE OF THE SNOW DRAGON*)

Sangay watched his treasures disappearing one by one into the robber-lord's saddle-bags.

And then an odd sensation — a kind of shiver down his spine, as though someone had touched cold fingers to the nape of his neck — made him turn his head far enough to glimpse Jatsang from the corner of his eye. She was standing to one side of the path, wearing a curiously blank expression. It was almost as if she had fallen asleep on her feet.

"And the dagger," prompted the bandit, when Sangay had handed over the last cake of tea.

With that, Sangay's long habit of obedience, of docility, vanished. He could not give up the sacred dagger. The Guru had hidden it in the summer valley, intending that one day Sangay should seek it out. He knew, as surely as if someone had whispered it in his ear, that he alone was meant to guard it.

"No," said Sangay. He spoke softly — after years in the Dzong, one always spoke softly — but no one hearing him could have doubted his determination.

"Give me the knife," said the robber. The point of his sword rested a scant inch from Sangay's breast.

Sangay's heart fluttered in his throat like a trapped bird, but he did not move. Thoughtfully the robber shifted his sword-point upward, till it came to rest just under Sangay's chin. The dagger is precious, thought Sangay, as he felt the cold pressure of the blade against his throat — but is it worth dying for?

Slowly he drew the dagger from its sheath, and offered it to the bandit. With a wolfish smile the man closed his fingers on the beautiful dragon-hilt.

Then the robber's eyes widened, his mouth fell open, and he looked down in horrified bewilderment. The dagger had begun to twist and writhe in his hand as though it possessed a life of its own. Suddenly the blade whipped around, and with tremendous force wrenched the robber's wrist back upon itself. As Sangay stared in astonishment, the dagger blade drove deep into the man's left shoulder, piercing tigerskin robe, silk vest, skin, and flesh.

The bandit shrieked. Blood welled between his fingers as he pulled in vain at the dagger. Slowly he slid from his saddle and fell to the ground. There he lay curled on his side, panting with shock and pain.

But now the other horsemen were moving in on them. Sangay cursed his unpreparedness. There was no time, now, to unfold his travel-bow, much less to string it. Still, Jatsang seemed calm enough. She stood spraddle-legged, feet firmly planted, knife in hand, defying the nearest bandit to make his move. The bandits eyed her uncertainly. They too had seen the way the *phurba* had sprung to life and buried itself in the flesh of the man who wielded it. And the woman wore the white skirt and five-tailed hat of a magician.

One bandit, more nervous than the other, said, "Put Duggur on his horse, and let us be off."

"No, no," said his fellow. "We must first avenge Duggur's injury. It could be a mortal one." And he raised his sword in the air, and rode down upon the sorceress. In the midst of his horror and dismay, Sangay marvelled at Jatsang's serenity. Not so much as the twitch of a lip, the blink of an eye betrayed her as the sword came up.

And then there was something — a huge, unexpected, inexplicable something — towering up behind the bandit. One moment it was nothing more than the hint of a shape, a swirl of mist, a vague thickening of the thin grey air. And the next moment, it was real, and immense, and unequivocally flesh and blood — a knight, tall as two ordinary men, as handsome as a god, looking down on the bandits with an expression not so much threatening as curious and eager.

He wore the rings of knighthood on his head, and a long pleated robe the colour of the evening sky. In his belt was a sword of antique design, and on his left arm was a shield covered with rhinoceros skin. He reached out and with one deft movement twitched the bandit's sword in mid-stroke from his hand and threw it clattering down the mountainside. Leaning down from his great height he seized the two robber-lords by their silken scruffs, lifted them from their mounts and tossed them casually to the ground. Then he stood gazing at Jatsang, looking for all the world like an enormous, good-natured, obedient dog.

From somewhere behind Sangay came muffled moans, and the nervous stamping of a horse.

"Give back what Duggur has taken," he heard one man say, "else this sorceress will send her curses after us." With a series of small thuds the food, the scroll, the bag of zi-stones, the silver-hilted dagger, all landed at Sangay's feet. Then hooves pounded across the dusty earth, as the robbers rode off with their wounded comrade.

Finally Sangay managed to sputter, "How can this be, Lady? One minute there was no one there, and the very next . . . "

"Have you never seen a *tulpa*, a mind-phantom, made? No, I suppose not — in the Dzong, they only teach you to make tea and butter-images."

"I have heard of such things," said Sangay, tilting back his head to admire the phantom knight.

"He *is* a fine fellow, is he not?" said Jatsang. "I have not managed anything so impressive since the night I drove off a pack of wolves with thirty fire-demons. But now I suppose I'd better send him away."

"Must you?" asked Sangay, mindful of the long journey ahead.

The *tulpa* looked hopefully at Jatsang. Had he been the noble dog he so much resembled, thought Sangay, his ears would have stood up, and his tail would have wagged.

"Well, perhaps not," said Jatsang, wavering. "Maybe for a day or so . . . We'll see. After all, it was no small task, inventing him."

Sangay gathered up his treasures, and they went on through the bleak dead land; the tulpa plodding cheerfully behind them, a vast, benign and strangely comforting presence.

***

That night the *tulpa* crept close to Jatsang's small fire, spreading his great hands over the flames as if to warm them, as the others did. He neither ate, nor drank, nor spoke. As Jatsang nodded in the fire's warmth, Sangay saw the *tulpa*'s form grow vague and insubstantial, translucent almost, so that the dim outlines of bushes and rocks showed through his flesh. For a long time Sangay watched and waited, curious to see what would happen when the sorceress slept; but finally he fell asleep himself.

They set out again at dawn, plunging down a series of steep hillsides into lowland jungle. Here the ground was wet and yielding underfoot, the air sharp with the swamp-smell of decay. From either side of the path high walls of flowering shrubs pressed in upon them. Like so much else in this strange land, the colour and scent of the blossoms seemed subtly wrong. Plum-coloured, magenta, mauve, viridian, livid as bruises against the dark-green, waxen leaves, they filled the air with a sickly perfume. Sangay's feet made a squelching sound as he trod upon the spongy track. His throat was clogged with the marsh-reek and the smell of rotting flowers.

Presently, as the ground rose again, they reached the edge of a forest full of copper-coloured trees. It had a kind of marvellous artifice about it, like a painted forest in a *manip*'s box. The bright, metallic leaves were veined with black, as delicately as silk embroidery, and spotted here and there with verdigris. As the wind rose, the wood was filled with soft clattering, clashing sounds like temple-chimes. Truly, thought Sangay, this was a forest where holy saints might walk, or gods.

Leaves, like thin flakes of copper-foil, brushed against their faces. As they went farther into the wood, a glimmering red-gold carpet covered the path. But now the light was fading, and among the trees were shifting, whispering shadows, dark as fire-blackened bronze.

Sangay could hear the soft clashing of the leaves; the faint sighing of the wind through the branches; the occasional snap of a twig under Jatsang's feet. And then, gradually, a new and unfamiliar sound crept into the stillness: a slithering, a seething, a rasping, that lifted the hair on the back of his neck.

Something was raising itself up, uncoiling itself with a slow terrible purpose out of the clotted shadows of the wood. Suddenly, all around them, the mountainous shapes of serpents loomed black as charred wood against the bronze gleam of the trees. Their tongues spat flame, venom dripped and hissed from their jaws. Where their breath struck the air a dense bile-green vapour churned and swirled.

Sangay drew his sleeve across his face, an instant too late; a tendril of the green mist, curling down from the upper air, had wrapped itself like a scarf around his head. He felt the sharp sting of it in his nostrils and the roof of his mouth, burning its way down his throat. As his lungs spasmed, he heard the tight, agonized whistling of his breath.

Sangay sank to his knees, choking, retching; his chest was on fire. And then Jatsang was kneeling beside him, pressing to his face a scrap of cloth soaked in an oily liquid smelling pungently of herbs. As he sucked air through the wet cloth, Sangay felt his chest loosen a little, and the terrible burning eased.

Jatsang's hand gripped his arm and he heard her voice, low and fierce, in his ear. "They are creatures of your mind, Sangay. I cannot help you — you must save yourself. If you have no fear they cannot harm you." With those same words, as softly spoken, had Wanjur once vanquished Sangay's demons, but this time Sangay could take no comfort in them. He was sick with terror, rooted where he stood. He was aware of nothing in the world but a black glitter of scales, a restless swaying of wedge-shaped heads, a darting of forked tongues, a writhing of mist, a vast, undulating, inescapable movement.

His heart was a hollow drum in his chest, his blood was dust in his veins.

"I cannot . . . " he managed to gasp out. And then huge hands were grasping him by the waist, swinging him high into the air. Tossed unceremoniously across the *tulpa*'s shoulder, Sangay was not so much carried as wafted aloft, a feather suspended on a pillar of cloud. The *tulpa* was tall as a mountain now, but with as little substance as the rank green gases that billowed around them.

Gently, almost tenderly, the *tulpa* set Sangay down. The copper forest lay behind them, a black wall half-hidden in drifting clouds of serpent's breath. Green meadows stretched before them, bright with gentian and summer lilies. In the farthest distance, the sun glittered on ice-crowned peaks.

***

For three days they had been travelling along a windswept ridge. Above lay cold grey slabs of rock; below, a narrow alpine lake skinned over with ice. At these heights there was neither shelter nor wood for a fire. Sangay dozed uneasily, his bones aching from the cold. Curled up in her skin cloak, Jatsang slept on undisturbed. Beside her, the *tulpa* snored faintly. In sleep he did not vanish, but grew pale and nebulous, like clotted mist. There was no more human warmth in that great billowy shape than in a bank of summer clouds, but still Sangay took comfort from his presence.

On the third night they came to the end of the ridge and descended into fir woods. Sangay gathered armloads of dead branches for fuel, and broke off some of the lower limbs to make a bed. His spirits lifted, thinking how comfortably he would sleep that night.

At dawn, while Jatsang still slept, he rose and gathered a fresh stack of firewood.

"What are you planning to do with that?" asked Jatsang, mildly curious and half asleep, as she watched him bundle it up with a cord.

"Carry it on my back," said Sangay. "There's high ground ahead, and I mean to be warm for another night at least."

Jatsang made a noise somewhere between a groan and a yak's grunt, indicating her disgust. "It will weigh you down like a stone," she pointed out, "and you have trouble enough to keep up as it is."

"Think how much faster I will walk after a good night's sleep," said Sangay stubbornly.

Jatsang shrugged. "Give it to the *tulpa* to carry, then."

"But he is a knight," said Sangay, shocked.

Jatsang looked at him with amused contempt. "He is a *tulpa*," she said.

But Sangay shook his head. Phantom shape though he might be, the *tulpa* had the true look and bearing of a Hero-Knight. To treat such a being as a mere servant, a bearer of firewood, would be a disrespectful and unseemly act. And so Sangay shouldered his burden himself, though — just as Jatsang had predicted — the weight of it slowed his steps on the steep parts of the path.

As for Jatsang, uphill, downhill, were all the same to her; and perversely, it seemed, she had stepped up the pace. For all that he was mountain-born, Sangay found his chest growing tight in the thin air. Finally, as he began to lose ground, Jatsang turned and snarled at him, "In the name of all the vulture-headed ones, Sangay, you try my patience too much. Either throw that wood in the gorge, or let the *tulpa* carry it."

And so he surrendered his burden to the *tulpa*, who gave him a cheerful grin and tossed the bundle onto his shoulder as though it had no weight at all.

Sangay marched on with lightened steps, still thinking about the hot meal and the warm bed he would enjoy that night.

Towards evening they came to a gorge spanned by a narrow, swaying bridge of bamboo poles. The farther side was hidden in mist, and white water raged below. Jatsang stepped out cautiously, with Sangay close behind, setting his feet down slowly and carefully on the ice-slick surface. He stepped off the far side of the bridge with a small sigh of relief; then realized that the *tulpa*, whom he had thought was close behind him, was nowhere to be seen. What could have become of him? Sangay peered anxiously through the mist. Surely this huge, brave warrior was not afraid of heights?

Then, as a gust of wind parted the fog-curtain, Sangay saw the *tulpa*. He was standing in the centre of the bridge, with his back turned to Sangay. He had unfastened the rope on Sangay's precious bundle of firewood, and slowly, deliberately, like a child absorbed in a favourite game, he was dropping the sticks one by one into the river below.

"*Tulpa*," shouted Sangay, in bafflement and helpless rage. Hearing his cry, Jatsang whirled round. The *tulpa* turned too, gazing at Sangay with malicious glee as he tossed the last piece of firewood into the abyss.

***

They had been travelling for many days, and as the country grew ever wilder and more strange, so too did the behaviour of the *tulpa*-knight. Where once he had followed them with a dog's docile obedience, now he slunk at their heels like a great stalking cat, so that they were forever watching their backs. At times he fell so far behind they thought they had lost him; and yet in the narrowest places he seemed to take a malign delight in crowding them to the edge. In appearance, too, he had altered. Sangay saw with dismay how lean and scraggy he had become. The great broad face, once so placid and sweet-natured, had a haggard look, and into the eyes there had crept a hint of something sly and manipulative.

"Jatsang," said Sangay, in grief and bewilderment, "what is happening to the *tulpa*?"

Jatsang glanced over her shoulder to make sure their troublesome companion was safely out of earshot. "Alas, it's as my teacher warned me," she replied. "I did not heed him, for I imagined I was too strong, too clever. But as you see, little monk, the *tulpa* is no longer my creature. He has become a thing apart from me, possessed of his own will."

"But what will you do, Lady?"

"Do? Why, I suppose I will have to destroy him."

Sangay's heart sank. Do you destroy a faithful guard dog because he digs up your garden or eats your shoes? Sangay would have answered no — but he was not Jatsang.

"Please, Lady," said Sangay, "do not kill the *tulpa*. He acts out of thoughtlessness, like a child — maybe if we are patient, he will mend his ways."

"How long shall I wait?" asked Jatsang. "Shall I wait until he drops *me* over the cliff instead of the firewood? If he is set loose in the world he'll be a danger to anyone who crosses his path."

It was as though the *tulpa* had heard, or sensed, those words, so quietly spoken. When they halted, high up on the mountainside on a rocky ledge, to eat their evening meal, the *tulpa* hovered over them, an irritating and unsettling presence. His expression was wheedling, cajoling, sly as a monkey's. He reached out a hand to grasp the hem of Jatsang's robe; roughly, she slapped it away.

"Where is the tea?" Jatsang wanted to know. She upturned her pouch, shaking out bits of dried-up cheese, crumbs of buckwheat cake, a few grimy grains of rice. Scowling, she peered into its empty depths. "Sangay?" she said accusingly.

"I have not touched your pack," he said. His voice, in his own ears, sounded shrill and defensive; the *tulpa* had set his nerves on edge. Jatsang looked at the *tulpa*, who returned her gaze with cheerful insolence. Mimicking her, he pretended to hold an imaginary pouch, and fumbled through the invisible contents with his great, splay-fingered hands.

"Accursed one," said Jatsang, in a voice so soft that Sangay could barely make out the words, "What have you done with our tea?"

The *tulpa* rose and strolled to the edge of the precipice. Gleefully, he pointed into the yawning gulf below.

An awful silence followed. Sangay held his breath, waiting to see what would happen next. Jatsang's face was white with fury, but all she said to the *tulpa*, in a curiously flat, indifferent voice, was "I am sick of the sight of you, *tulpa*. Go sleep behind those rocks, where we do not have to look at you."

Instead of obeying, the *tulpa* moved deliberately closer to the fire. Jatsang ignored him, and Sangay knew that the decision had been made. From now on, she would simply bide her time. After a while, like a bored child the *tulpa* began to scoop up handfuls of small stones and toss them into the air. Tiring of that game, he threw one at Jatsang, hard enough to sting, and barely missed her head.

Clearly, the time had come. "Go," said Jatsang to the *tulpa*, her voice low and furious. "You are banished from this world. I have no more need of you."

The *tulpa* got heavily to its feet. What a clumsy, shambling creature it had become, thought Sangay — when once it had been a thing of grace and dignity. Where now was the noble friend, the brave protector who had snatched him from the serpents' jaws? Heartsick and without hope, Sangay offered up one final plea. "Maybe we do not need him now, Lady, but think of the journey that lies ahead . . ."

"For what will we need him?" Jatsang snapped. "To tramp through the fire, and wreck our belongings, and ruin our firewood, and split our heads with rocks? We can manage well enough without him, little monk. This is a demon I have called up, and I will be rid of him."

The *tulpa* stared sullenly at Jatsang, defying her. And then slowly he began to walk towards her — stiff-jointed, swaying, like a wooden temple-image imbued with unholy life.

"Back, back," Jatsang hissed. Her jaw was clenched so hard that all the cords in her neck stood out. She began to curse the *tulpa*, a furious gust of words streaming from her lips. She leaped and whirled, stamping her feet hard on the ground at every turn as though she were crushing the *tulpa*'s head beneath her heels. She hurled more curses, spells of banishment, mystic syllables, exorcisms. All the while the *tulpa* — insolent, unmoved, immovable — went on staring at her with cold inhuman eyes. Finally, in her fury, Jatsang raised her hands and in a low, terrible voice she spoke a last dreadful incantation. Sangay felt a blast of icy wind howl down across the plateau. So suddenly did it descend, and with such unexpected force, that Sangay was nearly blown off his feet. Staggering to regain his balance and pressing himself against the cliff-face, Sangay saw that the wind had caught the *tulpa* and lifted him up like a great air-filled bladder. Now it was sweeping him irresistibly towards the edge of the precipice. Over he went at last, tossing and swaying like a monstrous kite, drifting and turning in that vast grey gulf of air.

The wind buffeted the *tulpa*, tore at his hair and garments, rasped at him with sand and grit scoured up from the empty mountain-tops. And finally, in its frenzy, it ripped head from shoulders, limbs from body, flesh from bone. Tattered scraps of the *tulpa*, whipped and tossed like prayer-flags, hung for an instant in the icy air; and then they dissipated.

Jatsang sighed, shivered a little, and with the slow stiff movements of exhaustion, turned back to the fire.

"We are rid of him at last," she said. "He will not return."

In her voice there was neither relief nor satisfaction — only a sorrowing acceptance. Moved by comradeship, and his own grief, and a sudden unexpected pity, Sangay crept closer to her side.

"May you be happy," he whispered. "May you be peaceful. May you be free from pain." They were the words he would have spoken to a fellow monk — the only words of comfort he could find.

Jatsang gazed down at him. Her face seemed gentler, younger, in that flickering light. "Tell me, Little Monk," she said, "he *was* a fine *tulpa*, was he not? Better even than the thirty fire-demons . . ."

"Yes," said Sangay, sadly. "Surely better even than those."

Jatsang gave him a wry smile. Then she yawned, and stretched until all her joints cracked, and threw another juniper-branch onto the flames.

— *Eileen Kernaghan*

FISH MAGIC

The delicate white bones of a fish
gleam underwater among rushes and shells.
She takes them home in her pocket,
sets them above the stove to dry
like wishbones.

        When they are ready,
she casts them on a red-and-black silk scarf
to read her future. The jawbones
mate in a horrible fish grin. She tries
to grind them to powder but the stone pestle
splits in her hand, reveals
the fossilized traces
of a sharp-toothed fish.

        That night
translucent red fish rise as from a great depth
to her bed, glow above her
in the silky black of her sleep.

— *Allan Barr*

THE MASS IS OVER

The mass is over, they have gone in
but wind flays the church's sides
I fear my frail cover will be blown
Despite the sunlight on confessional doors,
Desultory coins,
The urgent reaching of the women's prayers.

I have taken refuge from a bitter shower
And find myself at Christ's fire
Yearning for things I've had
And won't have again
Because I have done wrong.
He passes — and a shudder of sparks
Ignites the recognition,
A dark object in a field of light
Where I have come for shelter
In the warm eye of the wind.

— *Sara Berekeley*

A HYMN TO GOD THE FATHER

O God invisible as music, let me know
Thee in the least reflection of Thy much,
in termite, tick and earwig, in the glow-
worm striking matches on the dark, the house-
fly scratching his humungous-huge orbed head;
in all the creepy, crawly, earthbound things,
the bandy ant in black fatigues, the slow
gelatinous, fat snail.

                And when I climb
to Thee in prayers that fall as if unsaid,
O Alpha and Omega, Logos, great I AM,
I know Thee in the nit, mosquito, flea;
in pollywog, boll weevil, gnat and louse
— and with the praying mantis, worship Thee.

— *George Whipple*

DROUGHT

words
do not come
through me now

there is
just this silence
I live in

under
the wild child
in the locked attic

this house
a dead end
street   where words

do not come
turn back
like birds

refusing to land.
myself   empty rooms
lights left on

— *Ken Cathers*

Ω

COMPLINE

There were many reasons, unspoken, why
progress was no more than satisfactory; why
purpose, measuring first ventures against
outcomes, settled for the partial success.
We look now to the beneficence
of a quiet night. Rest is never earned.
Fading light offers a final inkling
of the drained glass, grain by grain
the mounting cone of time spent.
It is enough; hope is in the ritual
reversal, the upending; peace
takes now the night's measure. Amen.

—*John V. Hicks*

There are no last lines.
The trout in winter consumes himself. No waste.

The answer is not an answer. It refuses faith.
How we search for what is already known. Leaf. Stone.

Blood on my tongue.
But to rise with the wind. That ecstasy.

As the line moves. The leap!
Thrashing there.

— Patrick Lane

NOTES ON CONTRIBUTORS

Bert Almon grew up in Texas. He lives in Edmonton where he teaches English at the University of Alberta.

Allan Barr was born and raised in Saskatchewan and now lives in British Columbia.

Mary Bazylevich was born near Goodeve, Saskatchewan. She lives and writes in Saskatoon.

Doug Beardsley was born and grew up in Montreal. He lives in Victoria, B.C., where he is a writer and editor.

Sara Berkeley was born and raised in Dublin, Ireland. She currently lives in Inverness, California.

Brian Brett was born in Vancouver. He lives and writes on his farm on Salt Spring Island, B.C.

Tillen Bruce was born and grew up in Edmonton. In 1980 he moved to Saskatoon and writes full-time.

Catherine Buckaway was born in North Battleford and has lived most of her life in Saskatchewan. She is acknowledged as one of North America's leading exponents of Japanese miniature poetry.

Greg Button lives and writes in Moose Jaw, Saskatchewan.

Anne Campbell was born in northern Saskatchewan and now lives and writes in Regina. She is the head of public relations at the Regina Public Library.

Ken Cathers lives in Ladysmith, B.C., where he writes poetry and works in the forest industry.

Marilyn Cay was born in Prince Albert and lives near Tisdale, where she farms and writes.

Lesley Choyce was born in New Jersey and settled in Nova Scotia in the 1970s. He teaches at Dalhousie University and runs Pottersfield Press. He is the author of over thirty-five books of poetry, fiction and nonfiction.

Peter Christensen grew up in Alberta and now lives near Radium Hot Springs, B.C., where he works and writes.

J. Livingstone Clark is from British Columbia and has lived in Saskatoon since 1984. He teaches English at the University of Saskatchewan.

Chris Collins was born in Ottawa and raised in Saskatoon where he currently lives.

Dennis Cooley was born in Estevan, Saskatchewan. He is a professor of English at St. John's College in Winnipeg.

Lorna Crozier was born in Swift Current, Saskatchewan. She lives in Victoria, B.C., and teaches Creative Writing at the University of Victoria. She was the 1992 recipient of the Governor General's Award for poetry.

Mel Dagg was born in Vancouver and currently lives near Parksville on Vancouver Island. He has taught at many colleges and universities across Canada.

H.C. Dillow was born in New York City. He lives in Regina and is a retired professor of English.

NOTES ON CONTRIBUTORS

Paulette Dubé was born in Alberta and lives in Jasper where she is a French immersion teacher.

M.A.C. Farrant was born in Australia and now lives and works in Sidney, B.C.

Cecelia Frey was born in Padstow, Alberta. She lives in Calgary where she writes and teaches Creative Writing.

Leona Gom lived for twenty years on a farm near Hines Creek, Alberta. Since 1972 she has lived in White Rock, B.C., where she writes and teaches.

Jim Green was born in High River, Alberta. He works as a resource development officer at Fort Smith, Northwest Territories.

Helen Hawley was born in Swift Current and grew up in Saskatoon and Regina. She lives in England where she works as an artist and writer.

Ernest Hekkanen was born in Seattle, Washington. In 1969 he moved to Canada and now lives and works in the Vancouver area.

Stephen Henighan was born in Hamburg, Germany, and immigrated to Canada as a child. He lives in North Gower, Ontario.

John V. Hicks was born in London, England, and came to Canada as a child. He has been a long-time resident of Prince Albert, Saskatchewan, and is the city's Poet Laureate.

Robert Hilles was born in Kenora, Ontario, and lives in Calgary where he teaches computer programming. He won the 1994 Governor General's Award for poetry.

Bruce Hunter was born in Calgary and currently lives in Keswick, Ontario. He teaches English at Seneca College in Toronto.

Gary Hyland was born and lives in Moose Jaw, Saskatchewan, where he now writes full-time after a distinguished teaching career.

Sherry Johnson was raised in Eastend, Saskatchewan, and currently lives in Saskatoon where she is studying English at the University of Saskatchewan.

Terry Jordan was born in Central Butte, Saskatchewan. He currently lives and writes full-time in Allan, Saskatchewan.

Eileen Kernaghan was born in Enderby, B.C. She lives in New Westminster, B.C., where she writes, teaches part-time, and co-owns a bookstore.

William Klebeck was born in Foam Lake, Saskatchewan. He lives in Wynyard, Saskatchewan, where he writes and practises law.

Patrick Lane was born in Nelson, B.C., and currently lives and writes in Victoria, B.C. He is a Governor General's Award winner (1978) and author of over twenty books of poetry.

Shelley A. Leedahl was born in Kyle, Saskatchewan. She lives and writes in Saskatoon.

John Lent was born in Nova Scotia and grew up in Edmonton. He currently lives in Vernon, B.C., where he teaches English at Okanagan College.

R.P. MacIntyre was born and lives in Saskatoon where he is full-time writer.

Kim Maltman was born in Medicine Hat, Alberta. He lives in Toronto where he teaches Mathematics at York University.

Dave Margoshes was born in New Jersey and grew up in the U.S. He moved to Canada in 1972 and currently lives and writes in Regina.

Rhona McAdam was born in Duncan, B.C. She now lives in London, England, where she works and writes.

NOTES ON CONTRIBUTORS

Florence McNeil was born and lives in the greater Vancouver area where she is a full-time writer.

Ken Mitchell was born in Moose Jaw, Saskatchewan. He teaches English at the University of Regina and is the author of many books of fiction and poetry.

Brenda Niskala was born in Outlook, Saskatchewan. She lives in Regina where she works and writes.

Charles Noble was born in Lethbridge, Alberta, and currently divides his time between Banff and Nobleford, Alberta, where he farms.

Peter Ormshaw was born in Regina and currently lives in Mayerthorpe, Alberta, where he is an RCMP officer.

Garry Radison was born in Kamsack, Saskatchewan, and lives in Yorkton, Saskatchewan.

Monty Reid was born in Spalding, Saskatchewan, and lives in Drumheller, Alberta, where he works at the Tyrell Dinosaur Museum.

Jay Ruzesky was born in Edmonton and now lives in Victoria, B.C. He teaches at the Malaspina University College in Duncan.

Nancy Senior was born in Roseboro, North Carolina. She lives in Saskatoon where she teaches French at the University of Saskatchewan.

Glen Sorestad was born in Vancouver and lives and writes in Saskatoon. He co-founded Thistledown Press in 1975.

Gertrude Story was born in rural Saskatchewan. She lives and writes near Saskatoon and is one of Saskatchewan's favourite storytellers.

Andrew Suknaski was born and raised near Wood Mountain, Saskatchewan. He lives in Moose Jaw.

Don Summerhayes was born in Hamilton, Ontario. He lives in Toronto and teaches at York University.

Kate Sutherland was born in Dundee, Scotland. She teaches law at the University of Saskatchewan and is currently attending Harvard Law School.

Eva Tihanyi was born in Budapest. She lives in Welland, Ontario, where she writes and teaches part-time at Niagara College.

Tom Wayman was born in Hawkesbury, Ontario. He lives near Nelson, B.C., and is a champion of the poetry of work.

George Whipple was born in St. John, New Brunswick. He lives and writes in Burnaby, B.C.

Andrew Wreggitt was born in Sudbury, Ontario. He lived much of his life in B.C. before moving in 1985 to Calgary where he writes full-time.

Seán Virgo is a respected writer, editor, and teacher who is well known in literary circles across Canada. He has published both poetry and fiction to critical acclaim. His editorial work reflects not only his scholarly aesthetic but also his insight and generosity. He has taught English literature and creative writing at several Canadian Universities and has held the position of Writer-in-Residence in a number of cities.

Seán Virgo has an intimate knowledge of the geographical and cultural landscapes of Canada, having lived in many places from the Queen Charlotte islands to the outposts of Newfoundland. He resides in rural Ontario.

CONTRIBUTORS

Bert Almon, *27, 55, 127, 202, 221*
Allan Barr, *175, 200, 277*
Mary Bazylevich, *114*
Doug Beardsley, *65, 177*
Sara Berkeley, *55, 87, 88, 160, 223, 249, 278*
Brian Brett, *126, 151, 174, 264*
Tillen Bruce, *69*
Catherine Buckaway, *53*
Greg Button, *232, 263*
Anne Campbell, 58, 222
Ken Cathers, *262, 265, 279*
Marilyn Cay, *28*
Lesley Choyce, *204*
Peter Christensen, *30, 150, 201*
J. Livingstone Clark, *123, 240, 247, 267*
Chris Collins, *176, 240*
Dennis Cooley, *125*
Lorna Crozier, *76, 148*
Mel Dagg, *41*
H.C. Dillow, *263*
Paulette Dubé, *121*
M.A.C. Farrant, *233*
Cecelia Frey, *217*
Leona Gom, *26, 112, 149, 161*
Jim Green, *198*
Helen Hawley, *23, 221*
Ernest Hekkanen, *164*
Stephen Henighan, *254*
John V. Hicks, *60, 201, 203, 213, 280*
Robert Hilles, *37, 78, 94, 192, 261*
Bruce Hunter, *66, 147, 248*

Gary Hyland, *179, 216*
Sherry Johnson, *59, 122, 128, 186, 232*
Terry Jordan, *97*
Eileen Kernaghan, *268*
William Klebeck, *27, 89, 126*
Patrick Lane, *25, 39, 57, 75, 111, 139, 173, 195, 215, 281*
Shelley A. Leedahl, *188*
John Lent, *73, 80*
R.P. MacIntyre, *129*
Kim Maltman, *31, 36*
Dave Margoshes, *241*
Rhona McAdam, *77, 177, 193, 196, 200, 213*
Florence McNeil, *158*
Ken Mitchell, *252*
Brenda Niskala, *65, 76, 212*
Charles Noble, *32*
Peter Ormshaw, *161, 258*
Garry Radison, *176, 265*
Monty Reid, *35, 196*
Jay Ruzesky, *150*
Nancy Senior, *158*
Glen Sorestad, *40, 90, 163, 199*
Gertrude Story, *140, 156*
Andrew Suknaski, *53, 63*
Don Summerhayes, *28, 149*
Kate Sutherland, *181*
Eva Tihanyi, *60, 157, 174*
Tom Wayman, *67, 123, 178*
George Whipple, *171, 278*
Andrew Wreggitt, *92, 94*

PUBLISHING CHRONOLOGY

1975	*Wind Songs*	Glen Sorestad
1976	*Dark Honey*	Ron Marken
	Inside is the Sky	Lorna Crozier
	Octomi	Andrew Suknaski
	Prairie Pub Poems	Glen Sorestad
	Summer's Bright Blood	William Latta
1977	*Between the Lines*	Stephen Scriver
	Hail Storm	Peter Christensen
	Portraits	Lala Koehn
1978	*Gathering Fire*	Helen Hawley
	Now is a Far Country	John V. Hicks
	Old Wives' Lake	J.D. Fry
	Towards a New Compass	Lorne Daniel
1979	*Ancestral Dances*	Glen Sorestad
	Curried Chicken Apocalypse	Michael Cullen
	East of Myloona	Andrew Suknaski
1980	*Blue Sunrise*	Bert Almon
	Dirt Hills Mirage	Barbara Sapergia
	Land of the Peace	Leona Gom
	The Mushroom Jar	Nancy Senior
	Winter Your Sleep	John V. Hicks
1981	*The Book of Thirteen*	Gertrude Story
	Disturbances	Greg Simison
	In Transit	Colin Morton
	The Life of Ryley	Monty Reid
	The Nobel Prize Acceptance Speech	Tom Wayman
	Rig Talk	Peter Christensen
1982	*Benchmark*	Bruce Hunter
	Branch Lines	Kim Maltman
	The Gardens of the Wind	Alden Nowlan
	Just Off Main	Gary Hyland
	The Overlanders	Florence McNeil

	Seventh Day	Lewis Horne
	White Noise	Garry Radison
1983	*Ambergris Moon*	Brenda Niskala
	Beyond Here	Jim Green
	Fielding	Dennis Cooley
	Kiss Me Down to Size	Ken Rivard
	Silence Like the Sun	John V. Hicks
	The Way to Always Dance (F)	Gertrude Story
1984	*Afternoon Starlight*	Charles Noble
	Barkerville	Florence McNeil
	Deep North	Bert Almon
	Frieze	John Lent
	It Never Pays to Laugh Too Much (F)	Gertrude Story
	Moving Through Deep Snow	Don Polson
	Northbound	Leona Gom
	Orts and Scantlings	H.C. Dillow
	Prophecies Near the Speed of Light	Eva Tihanyi
1985	*A Linen Crow, A Caftan Magpie*	Patrick Lane
	Dancing Visions	Anthology
	Heartwood	Gerald Hill
	Man at Stellaco River	Andrew Wreggitt
	The Need of Wanting Always (F)	Gertrude Story
	No Feather, No Ink	Anthology
	The Prismatic Eye	Doris Hillis
	Rootless Tree	John V. Hicks
1986	*The Beekeeper's Daughter*	Bruce Hunter
	Black Swan (F)	Gertrude Story
	Death is an Anxious Mother	Anne Campbell
	Falling Together	Lorne Daniel
	Out of the Willow Trees	Peter Stevens
	Small Regrets (F)	Dave Margoshes
	Through the Nan Da Gate	Ken Mitchell
	The Top of the Heart	Lesley Choyce
1987	*Evolution in Every Direction*	Brian Brett
	Forgetting How to Fly	Mark Lowey
	Heavy Horse Judging	Don Summerhayes
	Hour of the Pearl	Rhona McAdam
	Medieval Hour in the Author's Mind (F)	Ernest Hekkanen
	The Nefertiti Look (F)	Cecelia Frey

	Side Glances: Notes on the Writer's Craft (NF)	John V. Hicks
	Southeasterly	Andrew Wreggitt
1988	*A Dancing Star*	Doug Beardsley
	Dedications	Dennis Cooley
	Forms of Captivity and Escape (F)	J.J. Steinfeld
	The Fungus Garden (F)	Brian Brett
	The Last House on Main Street (NF)	Gertrude Story
	Paradise Café & Other Stories (YA)	Martha Brooks
	Sticks and Strings	John V. Hicks
	To Die Ascending	Peter Christensen
	The Violent Lavender Beast (F)	Ernest Hekkanen
	Walking at Brighton	Dave Margoshes
1989	*Creating the Country*	Rhona McAdam
	Home Movie Nights	Sara Berkeley
	Island (F)	Alistair MacLeod
	The Last Map is the Heart (F)	Forrie, O'Rourke, Sorestad eds.
	Making Movies	Andrew Wreggitt
	Outlasting the Landscape	Robert Hilles
	Penn	Sara Berkeley
	Red Earth, Yellow Stone	Anne Campbell
	Riding into Morning	Catherine Buckaway
	The Second Season of Jonas MacPherson (F)	Lesley Choyce
	The Selected Paul Durcan	Paul Durcan
1990	*A Few Words for January*	Shelley A. Leedahl
	Calling Texas	Bert Almon
	Daddy, Daddy	Paul Durcan
	Earthworks	Chris Collins
	The Eleventh Commandment (F)	J. Thiessen/A. Schroeder
	The Face in the Garden (F)	John Lent
	Fire Beneath the Cauldron (F)	Geoff Hancock, ed.
	In Light of Chaos (F)	Béla Szabados
	Let's Hear It For Them	Charles Noble
	The Love Song of Romeo Paquette (F)	Cecelia Frey
	The Mystery of the Turtle Lake Monster (YA)	Jeni Mayer
	Spin Cycle & Other Stories (F)	Judy Berlyne McCrosky
	Where the Rain Ends	William Klebeck
1991	*After Atlantis*	Gary Hyland
	After Sixty: Going Home (F)	Gertrude Story
	Nine Lives (F)	Dave Margoshes

		Passing Through Eden	George Whipple
		Sanctuary	Ken Cathers
		Sick Pigeon (F)	M.A.C. Farrant
		Tanganyika (F)	Brian Brett
		West into Night	Glen Sorestad
		Yuletide Blues (YA)	R.P. MacIntyre
	1992	Am I Glad to See You	Jay Ruzesky
		The Blue Jean Collection (YA)	Peter Carver, ed.
		Fish House Secrets (YA)	Kathy Stinson
		How to Saw Wood with an Angel (F)	Gertrude Story
		The Mill Under His Skin	Lyle Weis
		Month's Mind	John V. Hicks
		The Mystery of the Missing Will (YA)	Jeni Mayer
		Nights in the Yungas (F)	Stephen Henighan
		The Swimmer in the Deep Blue Dream (F)	Sara Berkeley
		The Chambered Nautilus	Allan Barr
		The House Weighs Heavy	Paulette Dubé
		The Women on the Bridge (F)	Mel Dagg
	1993	Adventures with Miss Flint (YA)	Don Sawyer
		Counting Two (Child)	Gertrude Story
		Farm	Marilyn Cay
		Inside of Midnight	Greg Button
		Inside Passage	Doug Beardsley
		It's a Hard Cow (F)	Terry Jordan
		Laws of Emotion (YA)	Alison Lohans
		Old Habits	Rhona McAdam
		The Purity of Arms	Peter Ormshaw
		Site Dreams (F)	S.M. Longbottom
		Soldier Boys (YA)	David Richards
		Suspicion Island (YA)	Jeni Mayer
	1994	Angel Wings All Over	Anne Campbell
		The Blue Camaro (YA)	R.P. MacIntyre
		Breakfast of the Magi	J. Livingstone Clark
		Facts about Water	Sara Berkeley
		Sky Kickers (F)	Shelley A. Leedahl
		Why Were All the Werewolves Men? (Child)	Richard Stevenson
	1995	Big Burn (YA)	Lesley Choyce
		Blow the Moon Out (F)	Judy Berlyne McCrosky
		Dance of the Snow Dragon (YA)	Eileen Kernaghan
		Horse Sense (F)	Tillen Bruce

The Lie That Had to Be (YA)	Sharon Gibson Palermo	
Notes Across the Aisle (YA)	Peter Carver, ed.	
Pale Grace	Sherry Johnson	
Saved By the Telling	Eva Tihanyi	
The Seasons are Horses (YA)	Bernice Friesen	
Steppe: A Novel	John Weier	
Summer Reading (F)	Kate Sutherland	
Wheelings	Doris Hillis	
Wind Shifter (YA)	Linda Smith	
The Winter of the Leechman (F)	Mary Bazylevich	
What Is Already Known	Seán Virgo, ed.	

Note: (F): fiction; (YA): young adult fiction; (Child): children's; (NF): non-fiction. All other titles are poetry.